liquid GOLD

liquid GOLD

BY OWEN CLOUGH

weka
ficton

www.owencloughbooks.com

Cover design: Tania Hassounia of www.Drawer Full of Giants.com

National Library of New Zealand Cataloging-in-Publication Data

ISBN Paperback 978-1-99-116070-6

Published in New Zealand

A catalogue record for this book is available from the National Library of New Zealand.

Kei te pâtengi raraunga o Te Puna Mâtauranga o Aotearoa te whakarâfangi o tênei pukapuka

This book is dedicated to

My wife Kaye for her support, my daughter Tania, my son Brent and my granddaughter Sofia.

Acknowledgements

Once again there are always so many people to thank, for their help and support.

My family have always been supportive and have encouraged me to keep going when the brick wall starts to surround you.

My daughter Tania and her business drawfullofgiants.com for the design of the book including the set up ready to print. I cannot thank her enough.

To all those people in the New Zealand defence force who gave me suggestions and advice.

My sincere thanks.

Author's Note

This book is a work of fiction. All persons, places and events in this story are a product of the author's imagination, and any similarity to real people, places, events and organisation is coincidental. The book is not intended to be fact, or to describe or portray any real world persons, tactics, beliefs, policies or future events.

"The future belongs to those who prepare for it today"

-

Malcolm X

CHAPTER ONE

Australia, 100 Years In The Future

Australia was dying with the breaking down of law and order as the tenth year of drought sucked the moisture out of the country. The monsoons in the far north never arrived; therefore, sugarcane crops and farm stock all died. Grass turned to dust as the major rivers around Australia, including one of the largest, the Murray, dried up. Furthermore, the country was up the old proverbial without a paddle, and no one had the faintest idea how to escape their predicament.

Back in 2020, meteorologists warned the politicians of the day that this was going to happen, even advised they work with their specialists to find a remedy and to not stick their collective heads in the sand. By rights, they should have kept large reservoirs in the far north of the country as security to catch the monsoons, when they had monsoons, and then to pipe the water down to the dry states when required. They suggested looking at the Middle East as an inspiration and build saltwater-reticulated processors to convert saltwater to fresh. Oh, the government had a few already. Though too little and too late. Now they had a country where they had to ration the water each day to ten litres per person, and that was a strain on both the population and the country. There was just not enough water to go around.

Western Australia, Victoria, South Australia, and the Northern Territory had succumbed to the drought, with no water at all. The dust storms to the west were huge. Hundreds of kilometres wide. They swooped down from the north, blanketing towns and cities in their wake. Australia was forced to move millions of people, which created a disaster never-before-seen in the country's history.

They evacuated most of the population eastward to a spread of two hundred and fifty kilometres inland from the Eastern Seaboard. To encompass Albury on the Victoria border to Cairns in Northern Queensland, the government then ordered Tasmania to take a million people: the island state was overwhelmed.

The water riots hit the country in the fourth year of the drought and never relented. Martial law became the norm as men and women were recruited into the newly combined police force of New South

Wales and Queensland. By then they had abolished the remaining states. However, Australia wasn't broke, far from it. They had their mineral resources to sustain the country. They still received adequate rain in the East to top up the dams, and for the crops and small farming blocks. The dairy industry didn't cope well, so dairy imports from New Zealand were increased at a fast rate to keep up with the demand.

Along with the lack of water, there were not any sufficient jobs, which left 25 percent unemployed. These problems caused massive unrest. At the helm was a right-wing coalition government that was fast becoming a dictatorship, as elections had gone out the door. Australia had pulled away from the monarchy years before and had become a republic with its own president. However, the government perceived their president to be weak and easily dictated to.

With the warnings of global warming over the years, and the seas making inroads into the swanky suburbs of Sydney, extending up the East Coast of the country, Australia wrung its hands as if this was just in the too-hard basket.

Throughout the world, the sea level had risen two metres in some places, though a lot less in Australia and New Zealand, with enough height for dykes to become the only way to protect major cities close to the sea. Holland's expertise in dyke construction was in demand. Some rivers closer to the coast were tidal, and overflowed into suburbs upcountry. It forced the government into action, but once again, too little, too late.

With the population blowout of sixteen million people arriving in the East from the Western states, the government decided in their wisdom that it was time for drastic measures. Their idea was to deport some of the population back to the country whence they came. Depopulation was the catchword and the first people who had New Zealand connections were the ones for the chop.

There were two million Kiwis living in Australia. A lot were citizens, but the majority weren't. Back in 2000, Australia changed its immigration laws pertaining to New Zealanders. Before 2000, Kiwis and Australians could travel between the countries freely. After a year, they'd become citizens of that country with full rights to all welfare, hospitalisation, doctors, pensions, and all government departments. The Australians were classified as Kiwis in New Zealand, and New Zealanders classified as Australian in Aussie. This changed in 2000 and kept changing until, by 2020, New Zealanders who could afford to pay for their naturalisation papers had to pay fifty thousand dollars each. Also, have a job that earned at least one hundred thousand dollars a year. Those who didn't or couldn't afford the fees or had lower-paying jobs were temporary citizens. Even if they owned property and paid their taxes, they could not vote in the local or state elections: they were not entitled to any government subsidy at all. In 2025, they had to pay for medical expenses and then education and become non-citizens even though they held good jobs. Most had an excellent education, which meant nothing. They were second-class citizens.

Scapegoats had to be found. Additionally, as the government of Australia pointed out, it would not compensate any deportees sent back to their country of origin. The New Zealand government, in a show of solidarity, told the government of Australia that they would not allow people to step foot on New Zealand soil, destitute. They petitioned the United Nations and demanded that Australia show proper humanisation and compensate those people who had for all their lives been Australian. Australia capitulated, but not the full compensation. There was a method in the Aussie madness. Not only were they going to deport unnaturalised and naturalised Kiwis, anyone who had grandparents born in New Zealand were for the chop.

This caused genuine anger, as now they were not only deporting New Zealanders, they were deporting second and third-generation Australians. With the water riots taking the headlines, the Kiwi affair slipped under the radar.

The first of the millions of deportees were about to cause a headache for the New Zealand government. New Zealand was between a rock and a hard place. Kiwis were saying to send all Aussies home from New Zealand. Saner people were claiming they were New Zealanders, so do we want to be like the sods across the Tasman; the rational thinking won. There was no tit for tat. The New Zealand Aussies were safe. However, the problem for New Zealand was about to multiply. How does a country of eight million integrate a couple of million people? The majority had never travelled to New Zealand or had any family in the country. Even if they had close family, there was one hell of a lot who only had distant relatives. The Australians who had close family could not just turn up and say, 'Hi, Cuzzie, got room for us?' The government was working on this scenario until they could generate some long-term plans. This was the start of the depopulation of Australia.

It wasn't just New Zealanders who took the hit. Once the Kiwi deportation swung into action, the Aussie government thought since they got away with the New Zealander problem, let's hit the Muslims, then the Pacific Islanders, Middle Easterners, and finally the Asian nations. Millions of Australians ended up homeless with no country. Only a few countries around the world bothered to stand up and be counted. New Zealand tried but had so much on its plate, working out a strategy on how to house, feed, clothe, and where to settle its own people. It was overwhelming.

When the first deportees arrived in Auckland on the liner Emerald Gold, one of the largest passenger liners in the world, ten thousand bewildered Australian/Kiwis metaphorically walked down the plank, thoroughly confused, lost, and worried for their future and the future of their children. They walked off the ship in a trance to the immigration sheds. Parents with young children, clinging nervously on to their hands, middle-aged couples, single men and women of varying ages, all looking like the people of the damned, as they walked towards the immigration entrance underneath a sign that said Welcome Home. Thousands of New Zealanders were there to give these people hope. This was the start of the largest immigration invasion since the colonisation of New Zealand in the eighteenth century.

CHAPTER TWO

Wellington, New Zealand

New Zealand had a coalition government of three parties on the left. The Greens, who had been the majority for over ten years, were in their third term. They had made up a government over the last fifty years, with the Labour Party and the New Zealand Maori Party. It wasn't always a smooth ride, but now it was going to be different. The prime minister had summoned the party leaders to his office. Passing coffee and tea around, Jim Lofthouse, the PM, turned to the labour leader, Rachael Sommerfield.

'I need the help of your party, Rachael. No ifs and buts. I need unequivocal support on this.' Then he looked at the Maori leader, Rangi Turner.

'The same with you, Rangi. This is going to be hard on everybody, but we need to do this together.' He paused.

'What we are going through now is not a task just for us but for the whole government. With your permission and support, I need your party's backing to invite the National Party into our ranks for the duration of this crisis.'

'B-but,' Rangi stuttered.

'Hold on, mate. Let me finish,' the PM said.

'They have some brilliant people in their ranks, and we need to utilise them all. We have on our shores right this minute, ten thousand Kiwis sent home from Aussie. It's going to take a monumental task force to get this right. We are talking about people who have nothing except a small amount of compensation from the Australian government. They are now our people. I want you all to go back to your parties, and I don't care how you do it, but I want an answer by this time next week and I want a yes. I will talk to the Nats once you have seen your party caucuses. Then we will sit around this table, and as a group, put all our collective thinking hats into the pot.'

Gazing at the labour leader, he said, 'Rachael, I would like you to stand down as my deputy. Would you also give up, willingly, the portfolio on housing and development? I know that's a hard decision for you and me both, but we need to be seen working for the common good of our country. You will not miss out. I assure you. Any other portfolio of your choice is yours. I'm sure you all agree that young bloke Briggs Wilson in the National ranks is quite brilliant. I want him to have the chance to see how we can house two million people. Australia has only given us two years to integrate their policy of dumping all these ex-pat Kiwis on our shores.' He looked around the table. 'We have to give some of the opposition more power. I don't like it, but it has to be done. I want to offer, in good faith, the deputy PM position to the National leader. This way he will know we are serious. This is a New Zealand calamity, not party politics. So get your caucus together, and let me know, the sooner the better. We are in crisis. We have to be seen to the people of New Zealand that their elected members can work in cooperation in the best interest of the country. You have a week. Now, if you'll excuse me, I have a lot of work on my table. Keep me posted,' he stated as he stood up. 'I know you both will do the right thing.'

As they filed out, he plonked himself down again. Will this work? he thought. Bugger, it has to. There is no other way. Jim Lofthouse was a tall, thin man of fifty-two, with deep-set eyes and a long face. It didn't matter what he ate; he never put on weight. With light-brown hair, longer than normal for a politician, even now he still felt like a bit of a rebel. Jim was brown as a berry, as he just loved the National parks of New Zealand. Spending as much time as he could tramping through the bush over the mountains and around them, he loved the outdoors. The PM was a Green supporter from the day he read about the Hector dolphin saved from extinction, when the first Green Party went into power. He was a lad at the time, and the Greens had turned the Banks Peninsula into a marine park, now one of four hundred marine parks in New Zealand. He loved nature, and his party had done well with its coalition partners to clean up the waterways.

Planting native trees, saving species of birds and plants, New Zealand was becoming green again with restricting cattle and dairy farming, and having it managed once again by the smaller farmer, not by a corporation. Rivers returned to their normal state of cleanliness, safe for swimming. They spent millions on all farm waterways, on native tree and bush planting, encouraging native birds to the farms and their waterways. It also created thousands of jobs, much to the astonishment of the people, and what works, winners become grinners, and the Greens were in close to the action for fifty years.

The government knew the climate was going to change when global warming hit with a vengeance. It was not as bad in New Zealand, as the party had invested in water storage. All major rivers throughout New Zealand had overflow pumps hidden close to the source of the rivers for when they flooded; and they did as New Zealand's rain had increased in the west of the country, twofold. The excess water, though not all as that was impossible, they pumped 70 percent from the overflows into massive pipes underground, diverting the water to artificial holding lakes all around New Zealand to be used when the hot-weather months arrived in summer. The West Coast of the South Island pumped water through the Southern Alps to the East Coast lakes. Farmers from Southland, Otago to Nelson could tap into these for the dry summer months. The North Island had the same scenario as the South Island. The rivers overflowed, and pumps would send the water through the Ruahine and Tararua Ranges under the Kaweka Forest Park and the Te Urewera National Park. From Wellington to Hicks Bay, excess water filled these artificial lakes for the day when, in the summer, the country needed them.

Back in the early twenty-first century, Milford Sound was getting seven metres of rain a year, but now the sounds were getting fourteen metres or more. So much fresh water will not mix with the salt water of the fiord. From seven metres to fourteen, fresh water would never mix. There was just too much. It was ideal to scoop at least all the fresh from the eight- to ten-metre mark. One-metre pipes were sunk, then anchored to the floor of the fjords. From there, they pumped the fresh water out to holding tanks in the Hokitika Trench four hundred kilometres north.

The beauty of all this pumping and pipes was the fact they were invisible and environmental friendly. The pipes were over twenty-four metres deep and went deeper as they went out to sea, the natural environment left untouched. Water was filtered through umpteen-dozen filters, and from the holding tanks on the trench floor, the water was then exported to Australia. The government had built an ocean-mooring facility atop these tanks. There was a continuous stream of tankers filling up and leaving twenty-four hours a day, and the tanks in the trench had never run out. They devised a plan to increase the volume even further by having a pipeline from the Hokitika Trench to Mallacoota, Australia. This was in progress, cutting the need for water tankers in the future, and New Zealand had paid for this project. This was a lifeline for Australia, but the Aussies in power still moaned that it wasn't enough.

Jim Lofthouse thought this problem with the influx of New Zealanders coming into the country was going to be difficult. Nothing that any of his party or any party would have ever envisioned. The Green Party had to have help from an opposition party. It was the only way. He had spoken to his colleagues before he had talked to the coalition leaders, and at least his party was behind him. He was also popular with the average Joe out in the street since he was a down-to-earth bloke. Jim thought, with a grin, This would rock their socks; that's for sure. The last time this happened was in the Second World War, over one hundred and fifty years ago. He stood, looking out the window from his office in Parliament, at the Wellington Harbour, the sea blue and twinkling like a thousand diamonds. In the distance could be seen the large water locks of the dykes outside Wellington Heads, controlling the level of sea water in the harbour. With the sea turning green as it went deeper into the channel, you could see the bushline on the other side of the harbour, green trees climbing up to the ridge. We have done well, he thought, but how in hell can we absorb two million people without it being detrimental to our green, clean image? Is it possible, in the short term, maybe long-term? Well, he thought, that remains to be seen.

CHAPTER THREE

Wellington, New Zealand

Within a week, the three coalition leaders were together again, sipping their coffees. 'My caucus backs you, Jim,' Rachael, the Labour leader, informed him. She grinned with a bit of trepidation.

'You're right. We are all in this together,' Rangi stated. 'I had a bit of trouble from a few of the hardliners in the party. I talked them around with a promise that it will involve us housing our people. There will be a lot of Maori coming home. We will arrange housing on all the marae around the country. Of course, we will liaise with whoever works on the housing effort,' he volunteered.

'Thank you, Rangi, Rachael. That's a big load off my shoulders that your parties are behind me. I'll invite the National Party leader in today, and I'll make a time tomorrow, so we can all sit around the table.'

His coalition partners rose from their seats.

'It's going to an interesting couple of years, Jim,' Rangi stated as they moved towards the door.

When the door closed behind them, the PM called his secretary. 'Susan, would you get in touch with the National leader, and his deputy. Ask them to join me. If they have the time for a working lunch in my office at one p.m. Ask the caterers to bring up the Nats' leader's favourite meal, and also make sure that Lyn is with me.'

At forty-one, Lyn Soo was the deputy leader of the Greens. Her grandparents had immigrated to New Zealand from Hong Kong at the turn of the second millennium. She was an astute politician and long-term Green member, a wonderful orator, and educated in environmental management and finance. A short, black-haired dynamo of a woman, with a voice like honey, she could talk the birds out of the trees. Jim and she were great friends and would spend many a weekend together with Jim's wife and children, at their house or tramping, when they had the opportunity. She knew, of course, that this meeting was going to be unusual. At the back of her mind, she wondered, Would the Nats would have done the same thing? Would they have invited us to join them if they had the parliament? However, like the PM, Lyn remained utterly convinced that this was the best for the country.

His old-fashioned buzzer rang on his desk with Susan announcing, 'They are here, Prime Minister.'

Jim and Lyn stood up as the National Party leader, Jonathan Martin, and his deputy, Ted Watson, walked into the room. They both looked slightly bemused at what the hell was going on.

'Thanks for coming, Jono, and you also, Ted, at such short notice. They will serve lunch in twenty minutes. Before we sit down to eat, I have something very important to discuss with you both.' He paused. 'Please take a seat.'

Ted Watson was a tall, man, with a large chest and arms. An ex All Black, his hands the size of dinner plates, and still looked in his prime. Ted used to be a farmer. He never looked comfortable in a suit, and his tie was off more than on. In contrast, Jonathan was a small suave bloke, neatly dressed with a three-piece suit, immaculate in all aspects and a brain as sharp as a whip.

'This doesn't happen every day, PM,' he voiced, sitting forward slightly.

'No, it doesn't, but once you hear what I have to say, maybe more so in the future.'

The PM then outlined his plans for bringing their party into the collective crisis parliament.

'Can we work through this jointly, Jono, because

if we can't get together at this meeting, will this be all in vain? My partners in the coalition have agreed to my request to invite you to join us. That is how serious we all are, and now the ball is in your court. I want to bring into the ranks your young bloke, Briggs, and any others who have special talents. I'll get all the leaders together to thrash this out with the best people for the job. In addition, as an incentive, I'll ask you to become my deputy leader of the house.'

Jonathan raised his eyebrows as he looked at the PM.

'Rachael will give up her deputy position?'

'Yes, she will for the good of the country. Naturally, she will be in the mix with other portfolios as you would expect. It's important, Jonathan, to get this right. A lot to think about, Jono,' the PM remarked. 'Let's have a bite to eat before going on.'

Clearing the table, the catering staff brought a trolley in with a meal for each person. Jim magically supplied the wine from the small cabinet at the back of his office used for special occasions. It was quiet as they sat and ate. Ted was eyeing Lyn and enjoying the light conversation.

'You still tramp, Lyn?' he asked.

'Yes, I do, when I get the chance. Do you, Ted?'

'Yeah.' He grinned. 'Same as you, when I get the chance.'

'Well...' She smiled. 'With this cross-the-party friendship, we might get out for a tramp together.'

Ted just gulped. He was not that good around women, and for a bloke of forty-five, unmarried, and a politician, he was a pussy with the fairer sex. Though in politics, he was no fool, and on the rugby field, in his day, he took no prisoners.

'That would be nice,' he muttered quietly.

The meal over, sitting in comfortable chairs, sipping their wine, Jonathan explained, 'Tentatively, Jim, we will agree. Give me a chance to get my team together, and I'll be back tomorrow. You are right, this has to be sorted out now, not later.'

Jim smiled. 'A big day, Jono. Who would have thought that the parties from both ends of the spectrum could come together for the common good. I'm pleased. We will call a truce on slagging each other, though, of course, debating in the house to get a point across will be as normal. The public must see us to be in harmony. Have I got your word on that? I will not allow infighting or backstabbing, any of that, or I'll replace the culprit. Is that fair?'

'Ted leaned forward. 'It is to me. I'll come down like a tonne of bricks if my lot gets toey, and I'll make sure the whip keeps them tucked up under his wing. We will all be on common ground for the country, not the normal political one-upmanship.'

The next day, with a yes from the National Party leader, all the coalition partners got together in a marathon effort to find the correct people for the right portfolios. Every cabinet minister had four other members as helpers. They had one from each party. The PM involved all parliament members in the crisis that was facing the country.

The end of the week came quickly. The press was having a field day. Never, it screamed from its online sites, has a parliament in NZ had every party in sync. There was news here until the cows came home, as soon as the PM and his new deputy sat together at an interview. Left and right holding hands, so to speak, and talking on the same wavelength, the press and the people of New Zealand realised this was a massive change in the political climate. There were teething problems at the beginning. Over the next couple of weeks, all the parties came together for the common good, to house, feed, and clothe Kiwis who were booted out of their closest country's borders: Australia. New Zealand had to create thousands of jobs, build thousands of houses, and all the committees were burning the midnight oil.

The PM stated, 'We have a month to get this up and running. By that time, the next ten thousand will leave Australia. Then it will be ten thousand a week until they are all back in New Zealand.'

CHAPTER FOUR

Australia

Kathy Wong strolled through the campus of Lithgow, the newest university in Australia. This was a special university, built mainly for scientific research. Kathy was a professor at the Faculty of Science and Engineering, researching nanotechnology, which had come a long way. She was close to a revolutionary process that would take science even further. Engineering, mathematics, and electronics were her calling. A short, attractive woman with jet-black hair, she had the lightest-brown complexion, slim body, wide eyes, and stood 1.57 metres with no shoes. A very intelligent young woman of thirty-two and a born and bred Australian.

It was a lovely morning. The heat had yet to build up as she took the pathway, following the artificial river with its wild plants and trees. Giving the impression of walking in the bush, flocks of birds were squawking overhead as she smiled to herself, contented on her walk and looking forward to her day. She was thinking about not being far off from a breakthrough on the project she was researching. Her team had been at it for three years, and they were nearly there. So close that she could taste the ultimate results. It made her feel excited. Nanotechnology had changed the world; the next step was even more exciting, and she and her team were in the forefront.

Kathy turned the corner and walked across the car park. She thought, It's not that long ago that the internal-combustion cars were all sitting here. Now they were all electric, including electric hydro. The work on that science was improving every day. Singing a song to herself, she entered her science block to be accosted by the head of faculty, Brian Cutler.

'Kathy,' he whispered quietly, 'there are some men up in your office. They never told me what it is about. They want to speak to you. Government people, I would hazard a guess. Just a heads-up; be careful what you say to them.' He touched her shoulder as she moved away.

'Thanks, Brian.' She thought, What's all this about?

Taking the elevator up to her office, stepping out at her floor, she walked down the carpeted hallway to the last door. Strolling in, she noticed two burly blokes standing by the window looking over the river pathway, where Kathy had just recently walked. They turned as she came into the office.

'Ah, Ms Wong, please take a seat,' the shorter one instructed.

Kathy fumed inside. 'This is my office, Mr… whoever you are. I do the offering of a seat, not you. Now, what's this all about? I have a busy day.'

'Okay.' The shorter one smirked. He hadn't given his name nor the name of his partner, who was frowning at Kathy. She ignored him and concentrated on the smaller one. 'Where were your parents born, Ms Wong?'

'Oh, for goodness' sake. Australia, of course,' she spat. 'Where do you think?'

'What about your grandparents?' he fired back.

'The same,' she replied. 'I'm third-generation Australian. What in heaven's name is all this about?'

'Well…' he said. 'You are telling a little white lie there.' He smirked again. 'Your grandfather was born in New Zealand.'

'Don't be so silly,' she argued. My great-grandparents were from China. They came out to Australia via New Zealand and were there for about a month before they came across to Australia. Oh, that's right, my grandfather was born there. He was a couple of weeks old when they came over with his parents to Australia. I mean, they were only in transit. Hmm, I forgot about that, and it's a no-brainer; he was as Australian as my parents and I am today.'

'Well, for your information, that's not correct,' the short bloke announced. 'You're classified as a New Zealander. Your grandfather was born there, and the government has stated its case. You have a month to pack and be in Sydney for your trip back to New Zealand. Here are your deportation orders. If you are not at the demarcation one month from today, you will be a fugitive from justice and can get up to ten years in prison. The new prisons that are built out West, in the dust belt, is where you will end up, and in the end, they will still deport you after you've finished your time. So it is best to take the easy road. Everything you want to know is in those documents, and here is a one-eight-hundred number for more information.'

Kathy just looked at the two men with a gaping mouth.

'There has to be a mistake, for goodness' sake. I'm on the verge of a breakthrough in my field. What it will do for the Australian economy, you cannot put a price on.'

'Ha!' He laughed. 'Getting rid of Kiwis is better than anything you could produce in the short term. We are clearing out the rabble to give Australians a better deal. Right, I have served you. I would think about it seriously: don't go bush, young lady. We will find you, and it'll make everything so messy. We will see you on the wharf in a month's time.'

They turned, dropping the papers on her desk, and walked out the door, leaving Kathy staring at their backs as the door closed behind them.

You could hear a pin drop as Kathy slowly walked around to her chair and flopped herself down, holding her head in her hands with tears in her eyes. My God, she thought through her tears, what the heck was going on? She had thought little about the deported New Zealanders, and now she was one of them. What in the name of heaven am I going to do? Her mind was in turmoil. All those years of work behind me; how can I carry on? I know nothing about New Zealand. Kathy had only been there once in her life, and that was five years ago to ski at Coronet Peak in Queenstown. They still got snow over there. Not in Australia; it didn't fall anymore. She thought, Do I know anyone in the science community in my field over there? She racked her brain, but no names came to mind. They have to be behind the times. It will ruin all my hard work. I'll need a team with me to carry on; it's going to put my research back years.

She wiped her eyes, then got mad. Blast them, she thought. I'm taking my research with me. In a single movement, she walked out the door to the elevator and punched basement three. Three stories below ground level was her research centre. It took less than fifteen seconds; she was out the door and into her research facility. She ordered her staff to take some time off for a coffee.

'I need quietness for a while to work on some figures,' was the excuse she gave them.

When they had gone, she turned to her computer. 'Computer on,' she said.

'Hello, Professor,' the computer replied. 'How I can help you today?'

'Hi, Betty.' Kathy said to the computer. 'I want you to upload all my research to my heaven account, please, including your interactive programme as well.'

'Wonderful,' remarked Betty. 'Are we going on holiday?'

'It is sort of one, Betty.'

The latest computers were quick, downloading or uploading ten thousand gigabytes in micro seconds. Her research had over one million gigabytes, and it had uploaded in less than five seconds.

'Done, Kathy. Anything else today?'

'Yes, Betty, I want you to take the letter x out of all my equations and every fourth bracket as well.'

'That will be harmful to your programme here in Australia, though not the one in heaven, Kathy, and it will take a few years to fix. Are you sure?'

'Yes, I am, Betty.'

'It's done and dusted, Kathy.'

'Good, Betty, now I want you to wipe your memory from today and also block your input to the program. I don't mind if they rewrite your programme and eventually fix the problem I'm leaving them, but for now they will have to work hard to think about what I have done.'

'I now have completed the task, Kathy.'

'Good, close down, Betty.'

'Goodbye, Kathy,' the computer replied.

Kathy was in two minds whether to delete the files. She thought it would take an expert to decipher her thought pattern on her computer. A lot of technical information was random, and a lot was in her head. Now she had tampered with the programme. It was going to be a headache for the person who took over her research. She headed back up to her office. She then sat down and read the deportation document.

Kathy had no family. Her parents had passed away a few years ago, and she had no siblings. Her only relatives were still in China, though she had never been in contact, and to be truthful, she was not about to. They were too far removed. She was on her own. Kathy had a lot of friends and also all her work colleagues, but, she thought, at thirty-two, she would have to start all over again. Reading the document, the Australian government would compensate her, at most, half the price of her flat. She could merely take personal items with her. They allowed memorabilia, but cars, bikes, anything bulky was out of the question, unless she was prepared to pay for them herself to be sent over. There was also a New Zealand number to call if she needed advice. She went over to the water cooler and poured a small cup of water. She thought, I cannot let this get me down. I'm tougher than they are. Bugger it, I'm much stronger than they think. She chastised herself for swearing. Normally, she never swore, well, rarely. Right, she thought, picking up the phone as she dialed the New Zealand number.

CHAPTER FIVE

Wellington, New Zealand

Three weeks had passed at a frantic rate. Parliament had been burning the midnight oil. Concerns were slowly making way for a positive outlook. It was not perfect, but it was a start, as every department had exhausted themselves by finding a remedy for the population situation. They had looked at what Australia had done. They had to deal with millions of their population before settling them on their Eastern Seaboard. New Zealand had learnt a lot from the Aussies' experience and mirrored some of their achievements.

The New Zealand government had asked all mayors and their deputies from around the country to come to Wellington. They had to be in the loop with the crisis. After three weeks, they had a plan of sorts, though everything needed to be flexible. In all the major centres, hotels and motels and any accommodation that could house families were to be used. Every council would coordinate their own building program. Red tape went out the door. The government asked all retired tradespeople to return to the workforce. Even if they could not lift a hammer, they could contribute by supervising. The government was importing big fifth-wheel caravans that would hold a family of four. They were already on the container ships coming out to New Zealand. They would construct massive caravan parks. Landscaping them to look attractive in all towns was a stopgap until the real housing caught up. Prefab homes from around New Zealand, China, and Europe were also on their way. In all the larger towns where the prefab homes were to be built, the experts were now constructing the workshops, with the hope there would be a steady supply for the new immigrants. Parliament would utilise all the island nations as well, helping them in retaining their own people. They would construct modular and prefab homes for the New Zealand market in the Cook Islands, Samoa, Fiji, Vanuatu, and Tahiti.

The second deportees' ship was due to arrive in a week. The Ministry of Internal Affairs had received permission from the Australian government to have one hundred of their personnel on board each ship. This was to categorise who was coming, their occupations, and, of course, where the most suitable place for them to settle would be. The ship usually took four days to cross the Tasman. The Australians agreed to stretch it out for seven days. By the time the ship arrived in New Zealand waters, all aboard would know where they were going and what they could expect. There would be lectures in the ship's auditorium, also utilising all the entertainment areas, and the theatres would run continual documentaries about New Zealand.

The cabinet decided the first port of call would be Bluff. All passengers for Southland would disembark there. Then go on to their alternative places of residence from Invercargill to Wanaka. The next stop would be Dunedin and so on, right up to Whangarei in the far north. Each town in New Zealand had to take 10 percent of its population in new immigrants. Even the small towns like Ross on the West Coast, with their three-hundred souls, still had to take thirty. The only way the country could cope was to share the burden. The logistics were quite mind blowing. People in the building trades had to go to every town throughout New Zealand. Then there were teachers, doctors, farmers, engineers, nurses, etcetera, all who had to be placed where they would be most needed. This was the job of the Employment Management of Internal Affairs team. When the immigrants disembarked the ship in Invercargill, they would have a good mix of all these various occupations in each group, or as much as humanly possible.

Hundreds of Kiwi residents opened their homes as well to the immigrants. Thousands had relatives in the country, and they also took cousins, aunts, uncles, nieces, nephews, grandparents and parents, including sons and daughters who were living in the so-called lucky country. In the first year, thousands of warm, dry homes had to be built. The country battled on every month, and forty thousand deportees would arrive and had to be settled. The teams on the ship coming over had increased their personnel to two hundred per trip. They sorted out the occupations, and they had the system down pat. So, by the time the first year was over, they bedded in their system, and things ran smoothly. The first Christmas, there was a halt. The Australians gave everybody a break of two months, and this helped New Zealand make headway in the building of homes and the infrastructure that comes with it. A slight breathing space.

Jobs, of course, were another bone of contention, as the powers that be thought about how they could accommodate all these extra workers. Even if an average family was two adults and two children, that would still mean a requirement of a million jobs to create. The professional professions would easily fill. Even now, after a year, the Internal Affairs were scratching their collective heads, thinking how daft Australia was for deporting doctors and nurses, mathematicians, engineers, lawyers, scientists, and IT professionals.

It was around this time the ministers decided that every business in New Zealand would take on at least one staff member, subsidised by the government for the first three years. They went out canvassing every business. After a few heated debates, the government got its way. From farming to conservation, restaurant work to rubbish collections, everyone was to be offered employment. Oh, there were a lot who complained, but in the larger scheme of things, most people accepted the outcome, as they were told that a few years down the line when things settled down, they could move on like any other citizen in New Zealand. They explained to the newcomers that they were here for the long haul, not a holiday. The Internal Affairs Department did their best and tried to accommodate everyone. There were so many people, and there was a swag of them still going to be disgruntled. Some folk disliked their accommodations and needed help and guidance. This included counselling to come to terms with their new environment in the first year of settlement. The country took it on the chin, though a lot went on behind the scenes that the average citizen did not know about.

There was a tap on the door of the PM office. The minister of science stuck his head around the corner.

'Kia ora, Jim. Do you have a minute,' he asked.

'Come in, Tere. What can I do for you?'

Closing the door quietly, Tere was looking thoughtful.

'Jim, you will not believe this. We have had a phone call from Professor Kathy Wong.'

'Do I know her?' the PM inquired.

'Yes, we met her at that dinner when we were last at the Australian president's residence.'

'Ah, yes. I remember she was working on nanotechnology.'

'Yes, that's her,' responded Tere.

'So why has she rung, mate? Is something wrong?'

'No, not for us, but those idiots that call themselves the Australian government have kicked her out, as she had a grandparent born in New Zealand who, incidentally, left here virtually straight after the birth. His parents, at the time, were in transit, and he arrived early. He would have only been a couple of weeks old. They say because of that birth, she is a Kiwi.'

'You have to be kidding, Tere. That is the dumbest thing I have heard of in a long time. She is world renowned in her field, isn't she?'

'She sure is. Is it at all possible to include her with our own group, Prime Minister? Kathy will have to sign the Official Secrets Act, but we cannot let her slip through our fingers. She told the professor of science at Victoria that her research was coming with her. Professor Wong has also said that there are four more scientists from her uni alone being deported. They will be on the next ship out of Sydney.'

'Okay, Tere, get all our leading scientist people together, and let them decide.'

'Thanks, Prime Minister. Professor Bruce Walton is beside himself as he knows her achievements very well. Even though our people have kept a low profile, they know who's who in their field.'

'Good. Well, we can do with more of these types of people, Tere. It might push those experiments into the fast lane. Thanks for the update.'

'No worries, Prime Minister. I'll keep you informed of every scientist who ends up here.' He climbed out of his chair. 'How a country can throw out this calibre of people… if they can do this with impunity, I believe we will have to observe them carefully in the future.'

CHAPTER SIX

Wellington, New Zealand

Kathy Wong stood leaning over her balcony, watching the sea gates close as the liner drifted under slow power into the lock. She could see the city of Wellington open up before her as the ship came to a stop. The sound of water sucked out of the lock, and the ship sank like an elevator down to the harbour level.

The sound of the door opening behind her made her turn around. Her three colleagues came into her cabin.

'It looks a nice place,' Kathy whispered to all those who were listening.

Humani Patel and Eric Radwell looked out with frowns on their faces.

'Yes, it looks nice,' Eric replied, 'but as yet, we haven't got the foggiest idea what is happening. I wish they had someone who would talk to us. Like all those other poor beggars on board, but for us, no one. Just this letter to say we will meet on the wharf.'

'We just have to be patient,' suggested Judy Loe. She was originally from Victoria and had been with Kathy ever since Lithgow University had opened.

'I'm sure we will fit in fine. It's not as though we are going to the moon. This is New Zealand. There is not much difference between us,' she volunteered, 'and besides, we are all Kiwis now.' Judy had a few great-aunts in New Zealand that she had never met. They had made contact. They all had offered her a place to stay, but they were from the South Island. The NZ government had told her and the rest of her colleagues that they would go to Wellington, as that's where they would be more useful.

Humani had relatives in NZ but never met them, and with his studies and being a dedicated scholar and researcher, he had no time for anything but his research. It agitated him because, for the last few weeks, he was in limbo, and he hoped he would be back at work soon. He was missing his laboratory.

Professor Eric Radwell's mother was born in NZ and the entire family—siblings, nieces and nephews—were forcefully deported as well. They had cousins in NZ, so for him and his family it was not as bad as a majority of other people. Eric, with his wife and children, reckoned they would fit in good as gold. The extended family would not all be together, but the government had tried to keep the family within a hundred kilometres of each other. Eric was told that his wife and children would settle in Wellington; of course, the government would not separate them. He had a photo of the house that the government had put aside for him. He was the only one who knew where he was going to live.

They stood together as the lock gates opened into the harbour.

'This is it; I'm very nervous.' Kathy gulped. 'What is to become of us all?'

Eric touched her arm. 'I think we will be all right, Kath. We must take the Kiwis at face value. I'll catch up with you all later. I need to get back to the family. What say, once we get settled, you all come around to my new place, and we will have a "new country" party.'

'A good idea,' replied Judy.

'Yeah, I believe I'm lucky to have a house supplied, what with all of us Aussies coming over. The logistics of housing everyone must be a nightmare for such a small country.'

'Well, we are part of it now.' Judy frowned. 'So I suppose we need to get into the mindset.'

'Catch you three later,' Eric replied as he headed out the door.

They watched him go, then turned back towards the city. Two large tugs had latched on to the cruise liner like limpets and were slowly manoeuvring the ship alongside the wharf and the start of a new life for them all.

Tere Swan was waiting for the four university researchers as they came into the custom rooms. This was a formality, as they had processed all the passengers on board the ship. Buses were standing by to take all those who came off the boat destined for the lower North Island. Trains were waiting at the station, and there were government officials rushing around trying to help those who were lost. Tere had a big sign above his head with the names of the four people he was meeting. Eric was the first to turn up with his family.

'Ah, Professor Radwell, Mrs Radwell, welcome to New Zealand. I have a van waiting to take you all to your new home. We do not expect you to do anything for the next week or two. We want you to be settled in before we introduce you to some people we would like you to meet.' He handed Eric a folder. 'This is all the information on the house, shops, and malls in your area, schools for your children, clubs, etcetera. Phone numbers are all in your phones, which are on the dining table when you get to your residence.' Turning to a bloke, who arrived at his shoulder with a trolley to carry all the bags, he said, 'Oh, this is Mike, He will take you to your new home and get you settled in. He is your contact man. Anything at all you need, Mike is there for you. He will also pick you up when it is time for us to talk. There is a new car in the garage for your benefit. All your new licences are with the documents. The car is fingerprint entry and voice activated. Mike will help you get it up and running. If you need questions answered, don't be afraid to ask him. He is your go-to man.'

'Kia ora, Professor, Mrs. Radwell,' Mike announced cheerily. 'I'll get you all settled; no need to worry at all,' he stated. 'If you will follow me, please.'

They were about to leave as Kathy, Judy, and Humani came into view.

'Over here, Professor Wong,' Tere called out. 'Welcome! Welcome to New Zealand! A big welcome to you all. My name is Tere Swan, and I'm the minister of science.'

They looked at him with surprise on their faces.

'Yes, we all have to pull our weight now, and it was important for me and my government to welcome you to NZ personally.'

He turned towards Eric. 'You hop off, Professor,

and get your family settled. My number is on your phone.'

'Thank you, Minister,' Eric replied. 'Come on, kids. Time to see our new home.'

At least the children seemed a box of birds, he thought as he followed Mike towards the doors. Tere watched them leave with Mike. Smiling, he turned back to the others.

'It's lovely to meet you again, Ms Wong. We last met at the president's dinner a couple of years ago in Canberra.'

'I cannot remember you,' she said apologetically.

'No, well, many people were there, and I'm a small fish in a big pond. We in New Zealand like to keep our technology close to our chests as you soon will find out.'

'Now then, you must be Judy Loe. A pleasure to meet you, Miss Loe, and you, also, Mr Patel. I read your papers on crystal Wi-Fi energising your life and found it very interesting. We are all looking forward to working with you all. I think, for now, this is not the time and place to talk, and I have an e-van to take your personal gear to the apartments that we have set up for you all. Have you ever been to Wellington before?' he asked as they followed him outside to the waiting car.

A chorus of no's came back as they placed their belongings into the van, and shortly after it was pulling out, they stopped and watched it manoeuvring into the line of traffic.

Humani stopped dead when he saw the car they were going to get into.

'Th-there are no wheels; it's floating,' he stammered.

'Er, yes,' replied Tere. 'This is the brand-new Hovva XL. We designed it here in New Zealand. It uses antigravity, which is the modern form of motoring. The car sits at the same height as the normal car with tires, but they keep this on the road with magnets, which have now been embedded into all roads in New Zealand, also keeping it at a consistent height: powered by a battery and is completely solar. You all have one to play with waiting for you at your apartments.'

'Why,' Kathy asked, 'are you putting out the red carpet for us?'

'Because, Professor Wong, you are the best in your field. You all are, and we do not want you going off to foreign lands. We want to make your life in New Zealand notable, and if this helps, then all's well and good. We want you all to be happy and relaxed, and then we want you to work yourselves to the bone, as your expertise is sorely required. Now, come along, and let's get you sorted into your new homes.' He opened the door for the women, and Humani jumped into the front.

'Is this the new driverless car, Tere?' Humani asked.

'Yes, there is no driver, Humani; it's now becoming very popular,' replied Tere.

He sat in the back, looking at the women, then spoke.

'Hovva, to the apartments, please.'

The car waited until there was a gap in the traffic, and smoothly it glided out onto the road and headed for Oriental Parade.

Tere was explaining as they pulled out into the traffic. 'We set aside a block of apartments on the Parade, overlooking the harbour, for you. I think you will be comfortable. It supplies you all with a brand-new Hovva, and everything you require is there, just like with Professor Radwell. We will give you a few weeks to settle in, to get the feel of your new country, so to speak. You have a new New Zealand passport as of now, and there will be an Oath of Citizenship at Parliament in a week's time. We supplied the passports early to get the paperwork out of the way. Once you all have taken the Oath of Allegiance to New Zealand, and of course, that means you agree to become New Zealand citizens, there will be official documents to sign before you start work, and that will be a week after the oath.' He looked up. 'Oh, we are here already.' The Hovva pulled into the small entrance. The garage door lifted automatically, and the car slipped inside the double garage.

The apartments were single bedrooms with an en suite. Included was a small, modern kitchen, with a large lounge overlooking the harbour and large sliding glass doors that opened onto a walkout patio. The living area was tastefully decorated with paintings on the walls depicting New Zealand scenes, a coffee table, comfortable lounge chairs, lush carpeting, and off to the left, a working office. The apartment was all voice activated. Tere had taken each person to their own apartments, then they gathered at Kathy's place.

'All the documents are on your coffee tables for you all to read at your own leisure, including your new bank accounts and credit cards with Kiwi Bank,' he explained. 'There are six apartments on this block, and everyone who lives here is single and works for Wellington University. In the meantime, make yourselves comfortable. We have Henry Johnson arriving around two p.m. to go over everything with you all, from intricacies of the workings of your apartments, to using your Hovva. Plenty of time to unpack and relax. There is food in the fridge in each flat, so you will be good as gold for the foreseeable future. Now, I must be off. My phone number is the second name on the phone list. Henry is the go-to man; he is on top. We will inform you of your remuneration at the government signings; any problems or queries just call. I will catch you all up next week at the oath ceremony. Until then, see you later,' he said, waving as he walked to the door that automatically slid quietly open, leaving three people slightly bewildered at what was happening in their lives.

CHAPTER SEVEN

Wellington, New Zealand

Kathy woke to a voice in her head.

'Incoming call, Kathy. Pick up, please.' Over and over it went on until she sat up, wiping the sleep from her eyes, and answered.

'Visual off. Good morning, Kathy here.'

'Kai ora, good morning, Miss Wong. Henry speaking. Sorry to wake you so early. They asked me to pick you up at ten a.m. and take you to uni. I hope it is not an inconvenience?'

'No, not at all, Henry. I'll see you at ten,' she replied.

'Good as gold, see you then.'

'Call finished,' the phone announced.

Kathy lay back on the bed, thinking, It's about time. I've had enough of this inactivity. She was also anxious about where she would work. Likewise, where was New Zealand in her area of expertise? One day at a time, she chastised herself. She threw off the blankets.

'Lights on; shower on,' she ordered the apartment. 'And coffee in ten minutes, please.'

It took a bit of getting used to having the flat doing things for her. It was starting to become second nature after a couple of weeks.

At ten fifteen, Henry dropped her off at the bottom of the stairs of the old university building. Thanking Henry, she slipped out of the Hovva. The brick stairs were L-shaped. Climbing up to the first floor with two floors above, Kathy noticed ivy growing up the outside walls and bay windows while looking out over parts of the campus and Wellington City. She thought, this is it: climbing the stairs to be met at the top by the university chancellor.

'Welcome, Professor Wong,' the chancellor said, thrusting out his hand. She took his hand and smiled at him.

'Thank you for meeting me,' she said.

'I'm Colin Spencer, the chancellor of this establishment. He grinned down at her. 'Come along with me to my office. The minister and staff are there to meet you.'

Arriving at the door, Kathy was apprehensive. Doubts started to wisp through her mind as Colin opened the door for her, stepping back to let her enter. Four people stood in front of the bay window, looking out. As she walked in, they all turned. Tere Swan, the minister of science, smiled at her as he approached.

'Welcome, Kathy. You are looking well. We are looking forward to working with you and your team. We will talk about that later. Let me introduce you to Professor Matt Baldwin. They all work in your field. The woman next to him is Professor Rachael Brown and, lastly, Mereama Watson BSc.'

They all came over and lightly shook Kathy's hand.

'It is wonderful to meet you at last, Kathy.' Matt beamed. 'Once the formalities are over, we will get together and put our cards on the table. We know you might be ahead of us with your nano knowledge, but one thing we might be ahead of you on, is application.'

'Oh,' Kathy remarked, 'that sounds interesting.'

'In the meantime, Kathy,' the minister said, 'the document on the table is the Official Secrets Act. It needs to be signed by you before we move forward. As you are now a Kiwi, with the oath under your belt, this is important, as without your signature on this document, we cannot progress.' Kathy looked at him, then at the people in the room.

'Will I be working in my field of expertise?' she enquired.

'Definitely,' Tere answered.

She picked up the document and skimmed it. Satisfied, she picked up the pen and, with a flourish, signed her name.

'Wonderful,' Tere replied, signing it as well. Then one by one, each person in the room signed as a witness to Kathy's signature.

'Thank you, Kathy,' Tere uttered. We will have a cuppa, then I'll leave you in Matt's capable hands. He handed her a letter. Open that when you get home today,' he stated quietly. 'It's the information regarding your salary that started the day you arrived and will be paid fortnightly into your bank account.'

The tea arrived with an old-fashioned plate of lamingtons that Kathy hadn't eaten for years. There was small talk until Tere announced, 'Well, I'm off. A lot to do today. Good luck, Kathy. Your other colleagues will go through this ritual in the next few days. As you are a leader in your field, we thought it only right for you to go first. I'll be in touch. I'll catch up with you all later.' With a wave, he strode out the door.

'What happens now?' asked Kathy to no one in particular.

'I believe it is time to introduce you to your lab, Kathy. I have this feeling you will be in for a big surprise,' Matt told her.

'Are we all ready?' Matt asked everyone, and with that, he headed for the door, with everyone walking behind him like ducklings, in a row. Down the passageway, then left into a large room with no furniture, continuing through another door into a smaller room with no windows, the hidden lights in the ceiling made the room bright. Matt shut the door and pushed a green button on the panel beside it. He stepped back. There was a light hiss, then movement as the room slowly descended. Matt turned to Kathy, who was standing behind him, open-mouthed.

'You will use this lift every day you go to your lab, Kathy. Secrecy is paramount as you will see today. Only fellow lab personnel who work here, plus the ministry involved, and a few high-ranking armed service offices know what it is about.'

By the time he had finished his explanation, the room had come to a halt, and the door had slipped open quietly. Matt and the team stepped onto a platform where what looked to be a clear glass or plastic bubble sat waiting for them. The compartment held six people.

'We call this is an orb, Kathy,' Matt explained.

The orb had no wheels and sat on a raised rail, though it was not steel but organic, made from bamboo. Very thin with another track on the other side, two orbs could pass each other comfortably. The lights were dazzling on the platform; they explained to Kathy that lights charged the batteries of the orb as it never saw the light of day. The lights were for keeping everything charged. Once inside and seated, the door whispered shut, and the orb sped off down the lighted tunnel silently.

'Where does it take us?' Kathy asked tensely.

'Don't worry, Kathy,' Rachael explained. 'This is our transport to the lab. I guarantee you will love your new place of work. It's about ten kilometres from the uni as the crow flies.'

'Years ago,' explained Rachael, 'our government wanted a research centre away from prying eyes. A place where we could safely do our own research without worry. This is what they built. Here in New Zealand, we have never been a big spender on defence, and the government thought if we could protect ourselves without having to buy all the latest aircraft and ships, we would save money and still be able to protect our way of life. We know we are the laughing stock of most Western countries as we don't have an air-force strike wing or a deep-sea navy. Our army is up with the play, but it does not cost as much to keep them up to date. We had to be self-contained, and hence, this facility.'

'So this is a defence facility?' Kathy asked.

'No,' Matt replied. 'Defence comes into it, sure, but it's not just for that; it's for the betterment of our country, and the defence part is a by-product. What we do here is beneficial… well, it will be to the world, eventually: the invention of the anti-corrosion nano-water pipeline that is built to ship water to Aussie. The pipes have a nano component that monitors the pipes and all the pumping stations throughout the system. Anything that goes wrong, the nanos automatically fix the problem.'

Kathy stammered, 'Y-you are that far advanced? Nothing has ever been said about that to me. I didn't even think you were working on this science.'

'Well,' Mereama answered, 'it is all very secret, and we know how to keep a secret. In the future, it might be pertinent to be secretive. We have lived with this knowledge for years now, and it is interesting and fulfilling to know that you, Kathy, a leader in your field, have never heard of us. Even the pipeline that is constructed, the technicians don't know we are using nanotechnology. As far as the tech people are concerned, when finished, it is still hands-on. We will monitor everything that might go wrong from our end. We will have a department for that once the pipeline is operational. One thing that we are working on is nano size, and we have hit a brick wall. We have invented the nanos being small, but they need to be much smaller. We hope you will be the one who breaks the barrier down.'

The orb came to a stop at the end platform. The doors slid open softly.

'Follow me,' Matt instructed Kathy as he walked towards a door that quietly opened into a large laboratory.

There were a dozen people at various workstations, but what took Kathy's eye was the view. They had built the lab into the hills of Ohau Bay, and the vista was stunning, looking out over the Tasman Sea, with the very tip of the Queen Charlotte Sound visible at the top of the South Island.

'No one can see us, Matt informed her. The glass is not glass but a by-product of crystal with the infusion of nano to keep changing the look of the outside surface to blend into the hillside. To us, it's clear, but if you were on the outside, you could stand right next to it and still you would not see us at all. It would look like the surrounding hills.'

As far as the eye could see, there were trees and bush.

'This used to be barren,' Rachael remarked. 'The Green Party, over the last fifty years, has planted millions of native trees and bush right up this coastline. It is now back to what it might have looked like when the Maori arrived in Aotearoa.'

Kathy was truly amazed.

'Come, Kathy. I'll show you your office and workplace,' announced Matt.

'Oh, I get my own?' she enquired.

'Too right. A person with your expertise needs space and a place to think.' He walked towards the window and turned left. There was a door that opened on his command. The office had a large desk and comfortable chairs, looking out towards the window and vista, like the lab. Kathy could see the glimmering of the seawater in the sun.

'This is your computer,' Matt informed her. 'Everything is voice recognition. Computer on,' he commanded.

The computer screen slid out of its compartment on the desk. On an optic-glass screen, on the desk close to the chair, a keyboard image switched on.

'You can just talk to your computer,' Matt instructed her, 'or use the keyboard, and of course, there is the holograph image as well.' He showed her by saying, 'Holograph,' and the image of a woman materialised from the desk to look at her.

'This is wonderful.' Kathy smiled. 'I think, Matt, I'm going to be comfortable here.'

Matt informed her, 'All our research is on this computer. Just ask her by her name: Helen.'

The computer instructed Kathy to place her hand on the shape of a hand that became visible on the glass desktop. Kathy placed her hand on the shimmering light, and Helen thanked her.

'I now have your DNA from the oil of your hand, Professor, and voice recognition,' the computer informed her.

'Just call me Kathy,' she told the computer.

'Good as gold, Kath,' the computer replied.

Kathy laughed. 'That's so funny.' Turning to Matt, she added, 'I have brought my research with me. I need to download it from my heaven account.'

'Thanks for that information, Kathy. We don't use an outside source to save our research; it is all on our own storage files here. You can source anywhere in the world, but no one can see ours, as we do not connect them to an outside internet. We connect to our private satellite that processes it before it comes down to us. When you want to save something, once saved, it disconnects from the main satellite internet and goes to our personal storage facilities at the bottom of Cook Strait. The deep water is quite cold, keeping the storage unit cool. You can source it, but only you or anyone in this facility—no one else. If you have a programme that communicates to you, it will blend into the one here, but it will keep the same name: Helen. We don't want people getting confused with names. Keeping it simple is the motto. If you need anything at all, just yell. Welcome to our place, Kathy. Now, I'll let you get settled. We will catch up later for a coffee.' He turned and walked out to the main lab.

Kathy sat there looking at the view. Absentmindedly, she pulled out her computer from her bag, then the chip with her programs she had downloaded.

'Helen,' she requested. 'Can you download the programs into your database, then could you go to my heaven account and download my files from wongkathy210032 password Aussie slash Kiwi?'

'Place the chip on your desk, Professor.'

When she did that, two small lights on the screen flickered, then another light flashed, and Helen announced, 'All done, Kathy. It's nice to be back. I'm not sure I like the name Helen. I was rather fond of my last name, Betty, but if you are happy, so am I,' the computer chirped.

'Welcome to New Zealand, Helen.' Kathy smiled. 'We are Kiwis now, and I have a bit of catching up to do, so let's get started.'

CHAPTER EIGHT

New Zealand

Two years in the making, the new pipeline to Australia would open shortly. The operation was tested and retested a dozen times. It functioned perfectly, with the nanotechnology running to perfection.

The scientific team had placed errors into the system. The nanos had fixed every mishap within minutes. Even with a simulated pipe burst, within five minutes, the nanos had repaired the pipe. Everything flowed freely once fixed. These nanos repaired the pipeline at the break, all because of Kathy Wong's work.

Kathy had miniaturised the nanos down to atom size. There were millions in the system, and they could rebuild the whole plant if need be.

They sent the application through the system on the pig. The pig was a bullet-like tool that is inserted into the line with the pressure of the water propelling it through the pipes. Each pump station had millions of nanos waiting to go to work, if necessary. They would reproduce themselves to keep up their numbers. There was a time limit of a year before they dissolved. It kept them busy reproducing themselves while waiting to do repairs.

The pipeline was one metre in diameter. Pumping stations were located every forty kilometres, maintaining pressure throughout the complete line of nineteen hundred kilometres, from the Hokitika Trench to Mallacoota in Australia. They placed the control building in Hokitika. Kathy had suggested that each pumping station would have their own nanos for safety and repairs, as would the pig. Nanos then could repair any section of the pipeline while on the move. Not only would the pig clean the pipes, but could slow down against the flow of water to repair any damage it came across. The pig would travel in both directions, and the beauty of it was only the operator in New Zealand had the technology and full control of the system.

Operators would check the pipeline weekly as the pig would travel at around fifty kilometres per hour, the return journey taking six days. They estimated eight hundred thirty thousand barrels of water to be pumped daily to Australia—one hundred thirty-two million litres a day. This was far better than tankers, quicker. It was so much more beneficial to the Australian economy as they were receiving the water consistently. The tanks in the Hokitika Trench would still be the starting point and would increase in size if necessary. There were four tanks nestled at the bottom of the trench, each holding ten million barrels. The chance of them running out, with the amount of rainfall, was slight. If worse came to worst, the flow would slow down, but overall, the outcome was looking rosy.

Arrangements were under way for the New Zealand delegates to travel to Canberra, then down to Mallacoota by helicopter. They were to be met by the Australian President, Brendan Talbert, and members of the Australian government, then attend an official dinner at the president's residence, with the Kiwi delegates returning home to NZ the next day.

New Zealand would send the deputy leader of the Green Party, Lyn Soo; the National and New Zealand Deputy Prime Minister Jonathan Martin and his wife, Gail; Labour Party leader, Rachael Sommerfield; and the leader of the Maori Party, Rangi Turner, with his wife, Aroha, and a few under-secretaries rounding up the touring party. The New Zealand prime minister could not attend, as he had a delegation from China to contend with.

'Pass on my regards to our counterparts in Aussie,

Jono,' he told his deputy. They are still pretty cool towards us, and I don't understand why. Keep an open mind while you are there. My gut feeling, of what we have achieved with the pipeline, is that it's not good enough for them. I'm usually right when my gut plays up. I'm going to send Kelvin Underwood with you as well. As you know, he works on environmental issues, but he is one of our best SIS operatives. I just want him to feel the lay of the land over there. He will stay in the background as a gopher. Use him for fetch and carry; he collects more information that way, more than anyone I know.'

'Do you really believe that the Aussies are up to something, Jim? I haven't got that feeling, but I must admit, in doing business with them lately, they're very close-lipped. Not like in the old days. I don't like the way their democracy is heading; it's hardly that now, it's more a dictatorship with no elections. If they keep this up, it could amount to civil war down the track, and I would hate to see that happen to our neighbours.'

'Yes, well, it's caused by lack of water, isn't it? If we can build up their water stocks, they might open parts of South Australia and even Victoria. That would take an enormous amount of pressure off them, and if we can help, we will do our level best, though they have tried their damnedest to ruin our economy by dumping their people on our doorstep.'

'That might bite them on the bum in the end,' Jono remarked. Look what that young woman Kathy Wong has done for us. What an asset to our country, and what arses the Aussies were to throw her out, and she is one of many. Okay, PM, I'll keep my ear to the ground, and I will brief all our group to do the same.'

'You will use the "thread recorder" while you are away, Jono. They record everything. The tech people will deliver them to each of you before you leave.'

This recording device was a cotton thread that the University of Auckland had invented a few years ago, resembling the kind of thread sewn into your garment either in a button or hem. The signals bounced off walls to get photos of faces no matter where the thread was on the clothes worn. It could record in 360 degrees and send in microseconds. The invention was still new. Field trials tested positive. Everything worked a treat. There would be monitors on all the delegates while in Australia.

The ten parliament members met in the parliament ready room or National Crisis Management Centre, ten stories below the parliament building, specially designed, as they had built the room into volcanic rock. No signals could penetrate the room. There was also the new electric cloaking device which deflected any sound and infrared microwave transmission.

'Is all this necessary, Jim?' Rangi asked.

'Well, Rangi, according to our PM, he has this gut feeling that something over the ditch is not quite right, and he just wants us to be aware. I would rather be on the ball than not. So, wired we all will be. No going out on the town, because from the time you arrive in Aussie, our people will monitor us. We will be cordial, friendly, but we will listen and observe what our Aussie counterparts say and do. As long as you are all happy with that, we should have a pleasant couple of days. One thing I must emphasise: there will be no talking of our military or inventions at all to anyone. We have kept our programmes secret; we do not want to have anyone know what we have up our sleeves. Is everyone clear on that?'

'You are making it sound, Rachael,' the Labour leader interjected, 'that there are problems with the government over there. Rachael, you know as well as I do that all's not right politically in Aussie. We want to keep our house private, and the PM has his gut feeling, and we all know about that. He hasn't been wrong yet,' he replied with intensity.

'On a lighter note, he announced it has been a worthwhile achievement what we have done for our cousins across the ditch. Let's hope they appreciate it. It is beneficial to both our countries. We paid for the complete water-pipe system ourselves at no cost to them, and we are selling the water to them at twenty dollars a barrel. We hope that within two years, it will pay for itself. Subsequently, we will drop the price to ten dollars. It's a win-win for them. It costs them treble the price using their water tankers; they should be happy. This we can gauge when we are over there. We'll be leaving from Wellington tomorrow at nine a.m. on the PM's RNZAF aircraft. We meet here at eight a.m. and take the parliament orb to the airport.'

Just like the orb at Victoria University, the government had a line to Wellington Airport. It took them to an underground station. A lift brought them up inside the air force hangar, where they embarked without the public seeing them arriving at their aircraft. Then it was wheeled out for takeoff.

The new air force's Vulcan AG26Z, was a twenty-six-seated luxury aircraft. It looked conventional, but it was all show. The engine on the wings made all the right noises but was powered by electricity. Sixteen new micro-crystal batteries could hold enough power to fly the bird at Mach three, or six thousand kilometres per hour, with no sound. This plane had antigravity capabilities. Most important was the new cloaking device, making the aircraft invisible in flight. It could stay up indefinitely. It didn't need a runway, it could just hover and drop. Keeping everyone's prying eyes off this aircraft, it went through the standard procedures as an ordinary aircraft taking off and landing. She also had a ceiling of twenty thousand metres. The wings would swing back towards the main body, and the engines slipped across the wing and snuggled up close to the fuselage. Sleek, fast, and cheap to fly, the entire plane was one solar panel that charged the batteries, though this was the secondary source of power. The first was the new nano matter and antimatter technology.

Tim Captain and Brenda Low had been working on laser application. They had made a complete breakthrough ever since Ray Silver and Mata Rangitira had invented crystal-battery power. Using matter and antimatter combined with nanotechnology, they had revolutionised the regular battery to become as small as a fingernail. As antimatter deteriorated quickly, nanos came into play, making antimatter and matter replace the deterioration as quickly as it disappeared.

The antimatter was in its own crystal, with matter in the other. Moving them closer together created heat, and it converted this to energy, which sent more power to the batteries of the aircraft. This was the major power used to fly the bird. The aircraft had unlimited capabilities.

Not known as yet, even to the PM, the new laser armament, installed by the science lab, was from the

Wellington uni-secret installation branch where the nanotechnology work had been developed. The laser guns could deliver nanos through laser light, the nanos programmed to destroy the target they reached by dismantling whatever the target was. Within seconds, it could stop an engine, cut all communications to the outside world. A target would just lose power, and the nanos would go right on dismantling the target until there was nothing left, making this a potent weapon. Interestingly, the weapons were weightless; it was a light beam. The onboard computer was programmed to ascertain if the target was friend or foe before it fired. The computer talked to the pilot, and the pilot had the last say of whether to fire. This aircraft with it's cloaking potential could just disappear off the radar. The PM's plane was a wolf in sheep's clothing. The air force now had three of this model aircraft. They used one as a passenger aircraft, and the other two as communication aircraft with teeth.

The trip to Aussie was going to be slower, only to fool everyone who was watching. The aircraft looked like a normal executive plane. They did not want to have the Aussies think the Kiwis were more advanced than what it led them to believe. It was best to keep allies and enemies guessing. You just never knew what was around the corner.

CHAPTER NINE

Canberra, Australia

Donald Anderson, the Australian prime minister, sat in his office glaring at his minister of defence. The PM was a great, chunky man, 1.98 metres. He had piled on the kilos over the years since he retired years ago from playing rugby league. This gave the grey-eyed man a round face, a large, circular body, and huge hands. His hairline was also receding at a fast rate. He was a conceited man, arrogant, harsh, and a bully. He had two faces. One for the constituents: a jovial smile and a wave of his hand, laughing. The other was affected so he would look concerned if the time and place merited it. At the drop of a hat, he could revert to his normal persona of being a complete bastard.

He stared through slitty eyes at his minister.

'I don't want any bloody excuses from you; you hear me? I want to know the complete capabilities of the New Zealand armed forces, and I want it in a week. He slammed his fist on the desk. You have had months to organise your department to sort out my demands. Get it finished or, mate, you are going for a long ride out West.'

These days, everyone knew West was out in the dust belt, where the undesirables, criminals, and political opponents just disappeared, never to be seen again. Massive prisons had been constructed, and thousands of people had vanished. The courts were lenient with the government's decree of "If they're bad, send them out": in this case, West.

The defence minister, Simon Wills, had a faint line of sweat on his lip. He knew some of his acquaintances had disappeared. Not recently, as parliament pulled into line with the PM and his cronies; he was one of them.

'I'm doing my best, Prime Minister,' he voiced. 'New Zealand has a closed-mouth policy, but we have gathered that their armed services are not in great shape compared to ours. Give me that week to complete the file, and it will be on your desk within your deadline.'

'With their delegation coming over tomorrow, I want you to infiltrate a few of our military personnel, and see if anything out of the ordinary comes up. Right. Get it done, and if the deputy is out there, send him in,' he snarled. The defence minister slid through the door with the words hitting his back, 'Don't piss me off, Simon.'

Simon spoke to the deputy as he passed him. 'He's free now. You can go in.'

Harold Wade bounced through the door. A complete contrast to the PM. He was tall and slim, with high cheekbones, a pointed nose, and a small scar on the side of his left cheek. And he wore thick glasses, as his eyes were getting worse from the gas attack years ago when he and his men infiltrated Jakarta to assassinate the then president of Indonesia. An ex-military man with a cruel streak, he went into Parliament as a war hero after the war with Indonesia forty years before, a dab hand at a bit of torture. The PM and his deputy were a powerful force to reckon with, and the parties had fallen into line. This was a dictatorship. There were no other words for it. They had most of the military on their side, also the police, with the court's backing.

The only thorn in their side was the Australian president. In the old days, before the republic, when Australia was a commonwealth country with allegiance to the king of England, the governor general could dissolve Parliament if he or she thought the government of the day was losing the plot. They built those conditions and safety clauses into the document of the Republic of Australia.

This was the law of the land. Written into the new constitution of the republic, the president could, if the situation arose, storm into the debating chamber of Parliament and dissolve the house. The PM and his party could not do a thing about it unless it was an all-out revolution. That could start a civil war. Parliament knew there was a large part of the population who were not happy with how the county was being run, and no real representation from the masses. They weren't ready for a civil war—well, not yet at this point in time—though the way the country was shaping up, it probably wouldn't be that long before there was an eruption from the masses.

The thinking of the selected twenty caucus members was to take the population's mind away from what was happening in the country and focus it on water. Subsequently, they would turn to looking at New Zealand, who had too much water for its own good, and that would justify Australia to just waltz into the country and take the lot.

This pipeline was a start, but it still would not be sufficient, and there were millions of litres in the high country of New Zealand ripe for the plucking. And the Australian PM, in his wisdom and power, explained the time was ripe to just take it.

The PM looked up at his deputy. 'Any movement on the president, Harold?'

'Yes, I think we have it sorted, Prime Minister. Once the New Zealand delegation leaves, that will give us a month to complete our plan and put it into action. When we have that date, we will just go in and take Colleen, the president's wife, to the president's residence on Hamilton Island. If the president does not comply with our suggestions, Mrs President will be another one going West. Don't forget we will be also rounding up his daughters, husbands, and their children. He will be in so much of a bind, the president will do as we say.'

'Do you think he'll come around, mate? He is a bit of a stubborn bugger when he wants to be.'

'Oh, he'll come around, Don, a little scream from the missus or the grandchildren over the internet will fix that. He is not a brave bloke and overall a bit of a wimp. He only has the presidential army attachment that really is in our pockets... well, most of them. Anyone not with us are mugs. He won't move on Parliament or do anything to stop us from making our country strong. After all, my friend, we are the lucky country. We'll tame that dust bath out West and bring back water to the old states. Nothing, Prime Minister, must impede that.'

The PM looked at his friend. 'I'm going to play devil's advocate here. New Zealand is going to supply us much more water than in the past. They are still going to include sending tankers as well. What with the new pipeline, we will eliminate our water problem on the East Coast; however, we still need to be conservative with the water. We will be better off than we have been over the last ten years.'

'You are right, Don. However, New Zealand has millions of litres or more that could supply water to Victoria and South Australia. My God, even the old state of Western Australia, and still have water over. We will be able, once again, to reopen those states. They won't supply this quantity of litres to us, and really, the water is there for the taking. We have one hundred tankers spread around the country that can carry two million litres each. We will go to any port in NZ and take what we want. With the use of Kiwi labour, we can push pipelines from their holding lakes in their mountains to the ports. They have quite a few pipelines already established. It's there for the taking. All we need is to have control of the country. As an old military man, I know the New Zealand armed services are a joke and always have been. We have been propping them up for years. Their army is good; that's fair to say, but their air force is a shambles— no fighter wing. They have never had a fighter wing since 2001, over a hundred years ago. All they have is a few helicopters and transport aircraft. Their navy doesn't even have a deep-sea fleet any more, just their fishery protection fleet. Honestly, Don, they have no idea, and nothing in the last ten years has changed my mind on that score. The country are bloody no-hopers, and this is an excellent opportunity for us.'

'Okay, that's fine, but what about their allies? Won't the USA, UK, and Canada come to their aid if we set foot onto sovereign soil?'

'Not at all, Prime Minister. New Zealand has been going it alone for years, off the radar, so to speak. By the time those countries get a whiff, it will be all over. We will co-opt the New Zealand government with a bit of pressure to say they invited us to come and help ourselves, so to speak. Look, Prime Minister, it will be all over in a day—two, at the most. We have the strength and the power; they have a third-rate armed service. It will be a cakewalk. Don't forget their allies are ours as well, and if push comes to shove, we can say it's a neighbours' tiff, and they have asked us to pop across and sort out the crises that had arisen. We can make up some cock-and-bull story that the TAAM (The Anti Australian Movement) are getting out of hand.'

'Is there such a movement?' the PM asked.

'Yes, there is, about eighty-five members at the last count, but that doesn't matter; they have one, and we can play on that.'

For the first time, the PM smiled. 'You have it sorted, Harold. Just make sure the minister of defence is up to speed. I want a plan of action in my hands, not later than a month henceforth. He is coming back to me next week with the Kiwis armed-service capabilities. In addition, their big day of the year is the sixth of February, the signing of their treaty with the Maori. Whatever made them do a stupid thing like that, I wonder. They could have just taken the country without a treaty. Bugger me, the Maori were a Stone-Age people. Anyway, as it's a public holiday, it would be a pleasant surprise for them to have us knock on their door, don't you think? He smiled. Other things to do on my list. We want someone to represent the government at this water pipe opening. We're not going, as their tree-hugging PM won't be there. I have decided that most of our top politicians will not be there. We'll send the minister of defence. Maybe it might help him focus on the New Zealand armed services. Who have we got on the lower end of the scale to fit the bill? Conceivably, it might make the Kiwis think they are not so important if we send someone who has no genuine power and low on the totem pole? It will make them take note they are not the be-all and end-all.'

'Hmm,' replied the deputy prime minister. How about Elise Sanders, minister of Child and Youth Affairs?'

The PM laughed. 'Crikey, Harold, you have a wicked mind that would be perfect. She can have an undersecretary with her and a few military personnel, plus a few undercover agents. Liaise with Simon, if you would. I want his best men to go to this party. Personally, I want to know what this Kiwi mob is thinking. Have our agents in New Zealand got any new information lately?'

'Yes, they told us they have a few new ocean tugs supplied to the navy. They can also utilise these ships for sea rescue and fishery protection, since they extended their international boundaries to three hundred kilometres. New Zealand has redesigned their fishing protection fleet craft to foiling, making them quick over water. However, they are only one hundred metres lengthways, with crews of eighty. A few popguns fore and aft. They're no match for our destroyers, though they have around twelve of these ships now. They have a few cars on the road using magnetic power, still in its infancy. Even we don't know where we are on that. That's it. Their army has all the latest gear. The new air force base is now in Kaikohe. Whenuapai closed down a few years ago and turned into housing. I scratch my head sometimes, thinking they have no protection. Anyone could just walk in and take over. The sixth of February is such a perfect day, to walk in and do just that. Most people will be celebrating their treaty day.'

The PM frowned. 'Letting natives into power.' The PM shuddered. 'On the footy field, that's perfectly fine; they are hard men, but in power, running a country—what possessed the average Kiwi to accept that?' He looked at his deputy. 'Okay, that's by and by. Let's have Elise up here, and I'll explain to her she will represent her country at the opening ceremony of the water pipeline. The president is going, I could not stop him. He will take the limelight, but we have to let him think he is important at the moment.'

Elise Sanders was a plain, small woman. She looked like an old school matron, older than she appeared at forty-two. Her brown hair in a bun on top of her head was turning to grey steaks. She had a sallow complexion, and her grey eyes and thick glasses gave the impression of an old, stodgy aunt.

'You wanted to see me, PM?' she asked as she poked her head around the corner of his door.

'Come in, Elise. Sit,' the PM demanded. 'I'll get straight to the point.'

Her eyes looked enormous behind the powerful lenses of her glasses. Looks deceived, as she was a manipulator and had no empathy for those down and out. The completely wrong person for the Ministry of Child and Youth Affairs. She had never married. She was a spinster who had sent hundreds of people out West for the simple reason she didn't like them.

Elise just loved playing God, and was making a nice nest egg with backhanders from people who she threatened to send away. They paid her not to send them. It was the reason she was in the caucus lineup. She blended with everyone around the table.

'I want you and a staff member to represent Australia at the pipe-opening ceremony tomorrow. The president will be there and also the minister of defence. You will be responsible. Liaise with Canberra House. After the ceremony, you will wine and dine the New Zealanders at the president's residence. They are staying at the Hilton. Arrange flowers for the women delegates and any of the wives. I want them to think that we are hospitable people. Keep an open ear to everything that is conveyed to you and what you think is important to us, especially on the armed-service front. Is that clear, Ms Sanders?'

'I'm honoured, Prime Minister. This is truly a privilege. I won't let you down, sir.'

'Good, then the information is here in this envelope,' he declared, pushing it across his desk. Sort out who you want with you. Meet the Kiwi delegation when they arrive in Canberra tomorrow morning. Your team will fly down with them to the opening at Mallacoota. At your disposal will be a few military personnel and some hangers-on. We have planned for you to stay at the Canberra House that evening and see the New Zealanders off the next day. Okay! Sort out what we require, and remember... ears to the ground. I want to know everything that goes on. Pick your team. Now off you go. Oh, don't forget to liaise with the minister of defence, Simon Wills.'

'Thank you for this opportunity, Prime Minister,' Elise remarked as she stood up from her chair. 'I won't let you down.'

The PM just flicked his wrist without looking at her as she slipped through the door. An important day for me to make my mark, she thought, rushing excitedly down to her office to work out who she wanted to accompany her.

CHAPTER TEN

Canberra, Australia

The flight across to Australia the next day was uneventful to a point. They had been airborne less than thirty minutes when the hostess informed all the parliamentary delegation that the PM wanted a conference right away. Beside each seat was a 3D monitor. Each person sitting in their seats placed the visor over their eyes and instantly transported back to the conference room in Wellington. The PM was sitting in his chair at the head of the table.

'Good morning to you all. I'm sorry to interrupt your flight. I thought I'd better bring you up to date on some intel that came through early this morning.' Looking down at his notes, he continued, 'It appears that the First Battalion Australian Republic Army is on the move. We had our normal flyover with the old spy in the sky, and it was interesting to see their destination—one hundred and fifty kilometres west of Rockhampton. We came across a mock-up city out in the sticks that looks very much like Wellington. To a smaller degree, Auckland. Well camouflaged, but our latest technology picked it up. Now, why do you think they have our cities as mock-ups, I wonder? Would it be fair to say that the sods are planning an attack on us? If this is their thinking, taking the power base of Wellington, where our parliament is situated, Australia would kill our country stone dead.

'As we all know, the main TV, Wi-Fi, and 3D stations for the country are in Auckland. Looking at their mock-ups, all roads lead to the four major stations, including the police headquarters in both cities. My gut is doing somersaults.'

'My God, is this real?' Rachael asked. 'What could possess them?'

'Bugger that. What the hell is driving them?' Rangi moaned, putting in his two cents' worth. 'And what are we going to do about it?'

The PM remarked, 'To be on the safe side, I want you to give me unequivocal authority to set in motion Operation Mahira.'

'But that's only for a war situation,' exclaimed Rachael.

'I think,' the deputy PM, cut in, 'if the PM thinks it is an invasion force—I cannot believe that myself—

but if it is, we have no other option. If it turns out to be just an exercise, well and good; no one will know except us. So you have a yes from me, Jim. Are the satellites ready to go, Prime Minister? he asked. 'It's short notice for rocket lab.'

'I have sorted it at this very moment, Jono, and by the time you are all back in the country, I will have an update for you all.'

He looked at his deputy. 'Do you agree, Lyn? I know you don't like this sort of technology. We have a situation here, and I'm sorry to spring this on you like this, but needs must. Our cousins across the Tasman will never know. If it turns out to be all our imagination, we will destroy all information gathered. Is that fair?'

Lyn Soo sat looking at her hands, then she looked up. She hesitated.

'I trust you with my life, Jim, and I know you would suggest nothing like this unless you thought this was important.' Looking at the other members of the group, she asked, 'Is everyone in agreement?'

Ted, Rachael, and Rangi agreed, and they hoped the caucus members back in New Zealand would also agree.

'Just press the agreement button on your consoles, and thank you. I'll be in touch after a special caucus meeting today. When you arrive back tomorrow, I don't care if it's midnight; we will get together. Ka pai, you all take care, and don't tell the buggers anything but the weather. I have a feeling they might want to pump you on military matters, and we cannot have that. See you all tomorrow. Good luck. Conference over.'

The room disappeared in a haze of colours as the party took off their visors.

Rangi stood up and stretched.

'My God, Jono, what is happening? This surely cannot be occurring; nevertheless, we have excellent spotters. I know some of them personally, dedicated men and women, and if they say this is what they saw, then they did see those mock-ups.'

Lyn Soo, the Green Party deputy, had been quiet after she had talked to Jim. She stood up from her seat, turning to them, and whispered, 'We are going to have to be doubly careful over there in Canberra. At no point do we give them any information at all, and we have to act as though we are best friends. As the PM said, mum's the word. They are in for a big surprise if they try to invade; they know nothing about us, military-wise. Their PM is a racial bully, all their caucuses are. I'm surprised the president hasn't walked in and shut their parliament down.

'I believe, Lyn,' explained Ted, 'their National

deputy leader. He does not have the complete confidence of their armed services, and without them he is a puppet. He could still dissolve their parliament with a few troops if he so desired. Besides, it might compromise his wife and family. If it's got to this stage, his family will be in deep trouble. Does he even know what's going on? Their parliament keeps a tight grip on all its caucus members, and we have information that anyone against their PM seems to vanish. So the Mahira operation is what we need to find out exactly what our neighbours are up to.'

'Ted, you are right,' volunteered Rangi. 'We need to have our eyes open. The president's family might vanish. We would want to know where they went.' Rangi turned to the DPM. 'I think while we have a bit of time up our sleeves, let's jot a few things down on our thread voice-overs. At least, that way, the PM will know what's on our minds before we arrive home tomorrow.'

During the next hour of the journey, they looked at every scenario they could think of, and no doubt the PM and other members of the caucus did the same back in New Zealand. As they interacted with each other on the aircraft, their conversation was instantly overheard within milliseconds at the ready room back in Parliament in Wellington. The head operator, Cyril Takarei, flashed the PM with their conversation once they had deleted all the irrelevant words, giving a condensed briefing of their thoughts. It pleased the PM that they were all on the ball. He was waiting for the rest of the caucus to arrive for a similar conference as that of the MP's on the aircraft.

Before the aircraft had landed in Canberra, the hostess gave Jonathan, the DPM, a voice message. "Remaining caucus unanimous." Well, that is positive, he thought as he passed it around for all to see.

Lyn was saying, 'It's nice to know after all this time we are still on the same page.'

As Canberra came into view, and the pilot was starting his descent, Jono said, 'Right. Oh, fellow Kiwis, support each other, and let's be nice.'

The hostess's voice interrupted them. 'We will be on the ground in five minutes. Seat belts on, please, and we hope you enjoyed your free flight on your government taxes.'

The group laughed, a bit of light release. However, from now on over the next twenty-four hours, they had to remain friendly and tight lipped.

The aircraft kissed the runway using the conventional approach of a normal run in, taking half of the strip to pull up. Large, yellow arrows blinked on the taxiway, directing the plane to its special VIP parking area. The aircraft came to a halt. No noise—

silence. Then the wings bent upwards, and the aircraft sank on its suspension to a few metres off the ground. The stairs unfolded, and standing at the door, looking down at the Australian President, Brendan Talbert, and the minister of Child and Youth, Elise Sanders—Jonathan Martin waved out at the pair. He came down the stairs, followed by Lyn Soo, Rachael Sommerfield, Rangi Turner, and the rest of the delegation, including their partners. An RAAF band started playing the New Zealand national anthem, "God Defend New Zealand."

The president stepped forward. 'Welcome. Welcome to you all. It is a pleasure to have you in Australia. Let me introduce you to my associate, Elise Sanders, representative of the Australian government. The prime minister and deputy prime minister send their regards and apologies for not being here to welcome you all personally. They're tied up with matters of state.'

Elise stepped forward. 'Welcome, Deputy Prime Minister, and to your team. The helicopters are waiting to take you all to the opening of the pipeline. We have a team to take your luggage on to the Hilton.'

'That's very good of you,' Elise replied. 'Jonathan, we have our people to load the luggage van, and then they will stay here to guard our aircraft for security reasons. Is this acceptable to you?'

'Yes, perfectly, Deputy Prime Minister. Please follow me. I'll be accompanying you to on your aircraft with our president.'

Three 18-seater electric choppers from the RAAF were sitting, waiting as the party stepped aboard. Within minutes, they had taken off and were heading down to the pipeline at Mallacoota. The choppers were quiet, with a faint whine. Elise was trying to get closer to the Kiwi DPM by leaning forward, as the seat configuration was two facing each other. She was saying in a conciliatory voice, 'That is an interesting aircraft you arrived in today. Do you have many of those models?'

'Oh no,' the deputy prime minister remarked. 'Just the one. It's all we need, as from a small country, it is sufficient.' He turned to say, 'This is a terrific chopper, Elise, quiet and efficient, large as well. Heck, you could carry twenty passengers in here.'

'Yes,' she gushed. 'Though this one will take thirty-five at a squeeze; we have a squadron of these. You cannot hear them at all. Gone are the days of fuel engines and the smell of petroleum. This aircraft can fly off anything, with a range of two thousand kilometres. They are still quite bulky. All our aircraft carriers have at least half a dozen. Of course, batteries are the biggest problem, but we are working on it.'

'That's marvellous, Elise. I knew you Aussies had a big fleet. So the new aircraft carrier works for your requirements?' he asked.

'Yes, of course. We now have three,' she replied condescendingly. 'You haven't any large naval ships, Deputy Prime Minister?' she whispered, leaning in closer.

'I'm sorry Elise,' he said, turning his head back to her after quickly gazing out the window, distracted. 'I missed what you said.' He leaned towards her. 'Did you say you had a couple of aircraft carriers now?'

'Oh no, we have three now.' She smirked.

'I always knew you were the lucky country, Elise. That surely proves it.'

Before she could answer, the president, sitting next to Elise, informed them, 'Look, there is our destination. You can see the pipeline as it comes out of the sea.'

They drove all the dignitaries to the podium, then the speeches began. The president, then Elise with a reply from the NZ DPM. Rangi and his wife gave a Maori blessing down on the pipeline proper. The president, Elise, and the NZ DPM cut the ribbon, and the water instantly shot out of the pipe thirty metres into the air, creating a rainbow.

'Wow!' Lyn Soo exclaimed to an Australian squadron leader standing next to her. 'That has to be a good omen for us all.'

'It certainly is,' he agreed, smiling. 'More than you think.'

A steward came to the podium with a tray of fresh Fiordland water, handing out a glass to everyone there. Down in the public area, they also handed out to the people who came to view the occasion, a glass of water.

The president walked up to the microphone. Lifting his glass, he announced, 'Let us give thanks to our friends and their life-giving water. We toast New Zealand for this liquid gold.'

Every one raised their glasses and cheered together, 'Liquid gold.' The ceremony was over. The NZ team mingled with the delegates, until eventually, they were transported back to the choppers and flown to Canberra.

'The time is yours until seven p.m.,' Elise explained to them all at the airport. 'These cars here,' she affirmed, waving her hand towards the hangars where they were waiting, 'will take you to your hotel. They will return to pick you up at seven p.m., bringing you all to Canberra House for the official dinner.'

The NZ delegation arrived at the Hilton Hotel. The trip back had been uneventful, and if anyone conversed, it was about the wonderful occasion, about how the Australians appreciated their efforts, and how fortunate they were to talk with the president. Wasn't Elise a lovely person? What a bonus that the weather stayed fine for the occasion. They did not know if the cars were bugged or not, and caution was par for the course. Lyn Soo was looking forward to a cool shower before dinner. They all were. It was a long day.

Before they walked inside the hotel, Kelvin Underwood, the special SIS undercover agent, met them on the steps.

'Good afternoon, Deputy Prime Minister. He stopped, then gave his neck a whack. Sorry, I always seem to attract a lot of insects—flies and bugs—while here in Australia. He smacked his arm, exclaiming about the bloody bugs. 'I do not know why.' He laughed. 'Mum always said it was only peculiar to me. It's funny; looking back, she told me always to keep my mouth shut, otherwise I would invite all the little buggers in.' Another whack. 'Sorry, sir, I get distracted by the insects. Your luggage is already in your rooms. I delivered them personally. You should all be comfortable. There is a communication link if required to New Zealand. Just let me know, and I will activate it.'

Everyone heard the conversation, and they all got the message. Bugs in the rooms, and mum was the word.

'Thank you, Kevin,' the DPM replied. 'Get out of the sun, and mingle with your counterparts, but in your case, do it inside, and the bugs won't affect you.'

'Good. Oh, sir, I'm just a message away if you need me.' He turned and walked into the hotel.

The team, some with frowns on their faces, followed him inside.

CHAPTER ELEVEN

Canberra

Precisely at 7 p.m., the limos arrived to take the Kiwi delegation to the president's residence.

Only one small thing out of the ordinary had taken place while they were in the hotel. All the women in the party had flowers placed in their rooms, with a card saying, "With the appreciation of the Australian government." What was a lovely gesture, each of the women thought. They went from each other's rooms to look at the flowers and cards. It was then the Maori leader's wife, Aroha, noticed the ink dot at the end of each card. There was a slightly darker ink dot than what was written on the rest of the card.

Aroha, knowing the room was bugged, grabbed a pen and paper and wrote a message, showing it to Lyn Soo, who passed the message to Rachael and Gail, the DPM's wife, to check theirs cards as well. The cards were duly brought into Aroha's room and placed together. All the dots were darker. Rachael rummaged in her bag and found a small magnifying lens of clear plastic. Looking through the strip, she summarised all the dots looked slightly raised. A thought came to her that this could be a message. She wrote on a piece of paper for the other women to see. "I think it's a message." Lyn Soo, the Green Deputy leader, gathered all the cards together and, with a, 'I have to see the DPM before we go out, ladies,' she strode down to the room of the DPM with his wife, Gail.

Gail cracked the door and asked, 'Are you decent love? Lyn is here.'

'Come in, come in,' he called out. I'm just sitting here admiring the view.' Lyn and Gail entered. Lyn gave the written note to the DPM to look at, all the while talking about the view and how the Australians have been wonderful.

'The Aussies have been so thoughtful, Jono, with our rooms overlooking this beautiful parkland. And placing some lovely flowers in our rooms, the smell from them, divine.' He looked up from reading the note in his hand.

'Yes,' he replied. 'They have made us very welcome. It's a shame you cannot take the flowers home with us. Regulations are regulations, though the cards will be a pleasant reminder of a wonderful day.' He slipped the cards into his briefcase in a small pocket that was unrecognised as a pocket even when you intentionally looked for it.

The cards are a lovely keepsake of an outstanding occasion for sure. Are you ready for this evening? Lyn asked. 'I'm going with Ted, if that suits you. Two deputy party members together.'

Gail enquired, 'What about Rachael?'

Lyn grinned. 'She won't be alone. Do you see how the gentlemen look at her? She will not be lonely. She is one attractive and formidable woman.'

The president's home used to be the governor general's residence before Australia became a republic. Set in fifty-four hectares of parkland and built in 1859, its white paint and curved drive was in keeping with the old vintage look.

The president and his wife, Colleen, were at the main doors of his residence as the latest Rolls Royce Electra quietly pulled to a stop. The New Zealand DPM, Jonathan Martin, and his wife, Gail, stepped out as the door of the car was opened by the doorman, dressed in his number-one presidential uniform.

'Welcome, once again, Jonathan and Gail. I hope you have had a pleasant afternoon?' Brendan Talbert was smiling at them both, ushering them through the main entrance. He escorted them towards the old smoking room, preceding the dining hall. The guests mingled with Elsie and her group. Most of the Australians weren't staying on for the dinner. Only the chosen few, and they were mainly armed service personnel. In particular, it was a colonel who latched on to Rachael, the Labour leader, waiting to escort her as she walked through the door.

Scot O'Brien was the youngest colonel in the army at thirty-nine, and good looking to boot. It was his job to suck as much information out of Rachael as possible. Half of the Australians present were armed service people. A little bloke next to Elsie Sanders, the youth minister, was Derrick Temple. He mingled with the New Zealanders, introducing himself as the secretary to the education minister. When he approached each of the Kiwi women, he asked if the flowers were to their satisfaction, and that he hoped they would take the card home as a memory of this auspicious occasion.

'Now don't forget to put them in your handbags,' he emphasised, rubbing his hands together. I would hate you to leave them behind. The cards were hand painted.' Derrick was such an inconspicuous bloke, they hardly ever saw him for the rest of the evening. Even sitting at the dinner table, he seemed invisible.

Kelvin Underwood, the SIS agent, had watched Derrick Temple and buttonholed him as he went out to catch a breath of fresh air, before they moved on into the dining room.

'Best part of the day,' Kelvin remarked. They stood out on the patio watching the kangaroos that had come out of the treeline to graze on the lawns of the residence.

He turned to Derrick.

'My name is Kelvin,' he said, thrusting his hand out to shake Derrick's hand. 'I'm the all-round dogsbody and fetcher for our group. You are, sir?'

'I'm Derrick Temple. I'm with the education department.'

'Our kids will always need education, Derrick, an important job,' Kelvin claimed. 'I nearly ran into you while you were delivering the flowers to our women delegates. That was a friendly gesture for the women in our party. They appreciate the token from your government.'

'That's all right, Mr Underwood: a simple thing for our close friends of Australia.'

Kelvin continued, 'Those cards where attractive as well,' he muttered. 'A nice souvenir of this trip for them.'

'Yes, make sure they take them home,' Derrick whispered, turning to him. 'It is utterly important that they do.'

He was frowning, and a line of sweat had formed on his forehead.

'Promise me, Kelvin. I know who you are, Mr SIS, between you, me, and the gatepost.'

'How the hell do you know that, Derrick? Do I stand out that much?'

'No, you don't, but when I saw the list of who was coming, I did some background checks, and low and behold, there you were. Snuggled up to the SIS director's daughter. To be that close, I presumed you must be part of the organisation. Please take me at face value until you get home, then you can check up on me.'

Derrick looked around, checking to see if anyone was listening.

'No one here knows, mate. I have slipped under the radar. If I'm found out, I'll be good as dead. I'll never survive them shipping me out West. There's a message on the cards.' His voice dropped lower to barely a whisper. 'I'm a Kiwi, well, part of one in my country's eyes. My mother was born in New Zealand, however, came to Australia when she was one week old. Read the message on the cards; check out the dots at the end. It's extremely important. Now, I'd better be off. I've been out too long. If asked what I have being doing out here, I can at least say I have been pumping you about everything military. Be careful.

They have bugged everything,' he whispered as he turned and vanished around the door, back into the main room.

Kelvin Underwood lingered outside, contemplating the conversation he just had. He knew that the thread attached to his jacket would have sent the conversation back to Wellington. They would now be analysing the information passed on by Derrick. The report would be available to them on their return to New Zealand. They would also check up on the secrets of Derrick Temple. It would be a bonus to have someone well placed in the Australian government, the way this country was heading. What the hell, he thought, were the Aussies up to? Tomorrow we might have some idea. He turned and walked inside to mingle with the armed service personnel.

Everyone milled around until the dinner gong rang. They opened the doors to the dining room. The uninvited guests shook hands and left as the invited guests walked towards the dining room. They laid the table out for twenty people. All the names of each person were displayed on cards opposite each seat. The Kiwi delegation moved into the room, where waiters ushered them to their allocated seats.

Lyn Soo whispered to Ted Watson, 'They have split us up, and notice who we are sitting with?'

The New Zealanders all sat between the armed service personnel.

Lyn looked across the table at Rachael sitting next to the good-looking colonel from the Australian infantry.

Rachael looked over at Lyn with a slight smile "He mea whakarite." (It's a setup.)

'What does that mean?' Scott O'Brien, the colonel next to her, inquired.

'What a lovely setup you have put on for us.' She smiled.

Rangi turned to add his ten cents' worth, with a frown when his wife gave him a tap with her foot under the table to remind him they were to be careful, and smiled.

'It is a lovely table, isn't it, Rangi?'

The president and his wife, Colleen Talbert, sat at the head of the table: Elsie Sanders on his right and Jonathan Martin on his left. Then there were all the heads of the Australian armed forces between each New Zealand delegate. They toasted everyone, including the Queen of England, Catherine, the eldest daughter of George VII. That toast in an Australian establishment was rarely heard. New Zealand was still a monarchy, and the new queen was its head of state.

Rachael Sommerfield preformed the toast for the New Zealand team. Wine flowed freely. It took a concerted effort for the delegation to look as though they were drinking, keeping a tight rein on their liquid intake. They bantered continually with questions about the state of the Kiwi armed services. Why haven't you got a deep-sea fleet? Why don't you have a strike wing? What are you doing to protect your country?

Their questions never ceased, until the end of the evening when Jonathan stood up and stated they had a long day tomorrow, and it was time to depart for the delegation's hotel. There was a flurry of questions as they moved out to the waiting cars, shaking hands, and driving off to their hotel. There followed a collective sigh of relief as they drove towards the city. They knew they could not relax until they were on the plane home. Most sat quietly. A few, to keep the conversation open to Aussie ears, spoke about the dinner. What a lovely do, and the president's wife was a lucky lady to have an astute man as leader of the country. They made us so welcome. Wasn't Elsie such a lovely person? She really rolled out the red carpet, but they sure have a fixation on military matters.

The next morning, they collected up their bags, then were taken to their aircraft. Elsie was there for the last goodbye.

'I would love to come over to New Zealand,' she voiced. 'Maybe sooner than later. I'll arrange it with your people in a few months. Would that be acceptable?'

'Of course, Elsie, you made us very welcome. It is the least we can do for you,' Lyn Soo replied.

They shook hands and stepped up into their aircraft. Jonathan went forward to the cockpit and handed the captain a note: "Get us out of here. As soon as we are out of radar contact, cloak the aircraft and open her up. We need to be home as fast as possible."

Twenty minutes later, at twenty thousand metres, the aircraft cloaked and just disappeared.

The captain announced over the speakers, 'We are now cloaked and secured. You can talk normally now. We will be on the ground in thirty minutes.'

A collective sigh of relief went through the Kiwis on board.

'My God!' Ted cursed. 'Those buggers grilled us the entire time we were there. What the blue blazes are they up to? That Elsie! I had never met her before, and honestly, I don't want to again. What an uncaring piece of work that woman is.'

Jonathan took the cards out of his bag.

'I wonder what this message is on these cards. We will send this off now, Kelvin, to headquarters.'

Kelvin took the card and laid it flat on a console. He communicated in a normal voice: 'Message to decipher coming through. Top Secret. PM's and chief's eyes only.'

There was a light flash; the card vanished.

'Well, that's one sent.'

Three more on the way. In seconds, a voice came back, "Received."

'That's out of the way. So, team, what were your impressions of this trip?' Jonathan asked.

Rachael spoke her piece first. 'It was a setup right from the beginning. Once the pipeline opened. For goodness' sake, all those top military men: the Minister of Defence Simon Wills; Andrew Baggs, he is on the chief of defence staff with a rank of air chief marshall. Then there was Barry Eaton, lieutenant general of the army; George Gammon, vice admiral; then that snaky-looking bloke, Paul Jellyman. I think he is an air vice marshall. To top it off, they had that good-looking army colonel, who did his damnedest to get me to succumb to his charms. He wanted to take me out on the town, and I knew where that was going to end up—in a secluded hotel, with a bit of pillow talk. They must think I was born yesterday.

Everything they talked about was military, and I think this is more serious than we can imagine. They weren't subtle at all, though I am of the opinion they thought they were. That message on the cards will give us an idea, I hope. I have a bad feeling in the pit of my stomach about all this.' She stopped and looked around the cabin. 'Is this a fair assumption?'

'The funny thing is, though,' Lyn exclaimed, 'talking to the president and his wife. It bewildered them both, all the military talk. It's just a feeling, but I think he is not in the loop. If that's the case, I feel that it's not going to be a good outcome for him and his wife.'

'Yes, it is strange,' Ted piped up. 'They questioned me on runways and how long they were. If push comes to shove, would we use our international airports for the military? The navy blokes were on about how easy it would be to blockade our ports, hypothetically. They have something up their sleeves; that is for certain.'

Rangi jumped in with, 'That bloody woman, Elsie, is a racist bitch. She was saying to me—me, of all people,' he exploded, 'that they haven't got an aboriginal problem anymore as they have all gone out West. I took that as these people have sent the entire population out there into the dust belt. My God, if they decide to pop over to New Zealand with this in mind, our people will be in danger.'

'That might be the lot of us, Rangi,' Rachael suggested. 'Remember the last census was an eye-opener. Sixty-five percent of New Zealanders say they have some Maori blood; we have never been so close.'

'Well,' Jonathan broke in. 'We will see what happens when we get home. No doubt all the conversation that was taped over the last couple of days will go through the analyst as we speak. Let's hope it is not as bad as we think, but like you, Rachael, I have a bad feeling about this.'

CHAPTER TWELVE

Wellington, New Zealand

The orb whispered to a stop. Standing on the platform was a captain from the Royal New Zealand Artillery Corps. After the members of parliament alighted, he advised them, 'I'm here to escort you to the ready room. The PM thought it was appropriate as things stand at the moment. If you will follow me, please, ladies and gentlemen.'

They had whisked the wives of the delegation into the waiting cars, once they had arrived in Wellington. The rest of the team had no time to think and were quickly escorted down to the orbs that were waiting for them.

As they arrived at the ready room, two burly army military police, fully armed, were guarding the main door. They came to attention, saluted Jonathan Martin. The sergeant instructed him to place the palm of his hand on the pad that the second guard had passed to him.

'Security, sir,' he advised. 'You will all need to place your hands on this pad.'

Jonathan duly placed his hand on the pad as a light flashed and a voice spoke. "Welcome home, Deputy Prime Minister."

Once all the team had gone through the ritual, the guard announced they were all secure. He then ordered the opening of the security doors. There was the sound of a light hiss as the door slid into the wall cavity. Standing inside, looking at them, was PM Jim Lofthouse.

He welcomed everyone individually into the room. It seemed overcrowded, what with all the caucus members and the chief of defence staff, plus heads of the three services and their aides. The door closed, and a light flashed green as the cloaking device activated. A voice came through hidden speakers. "Room secure."

Jim Lofthouse moved to the head of the enormous oval table and ordered, 'Please take a seat, everyone.' A few minutes later, once everyone had nestled into their seats, he spoke: 'We have a serious situation. All the recordings of your part while in Australia, Jono, we have analysed every word. Our analyst in speech, human behavior, and general topics that came through from the Aussies on the recordings, has us coming to a conclusion:

our neighbour is going to attempt an invasion of our country.'

There was a collective murmur. He put his hand up before anyone could speak out.

'You can have your say in a minute,' he cautioned. 'First, we are not sure when they will attempt to invade, though we have an idea where. To confirm all this, is the message we received from Derrick Temple, the Australian who spoke with Kelvin Underwood in Canberra. He left a message on the cards. Well, one card had a message; the other three were empty. Before we do anything, I will play this message to you all.' The PM instructed the computer to play the message.

From the middle of the table, a holograph image materialised. The figure of Kelvin looked as though he were speaking to each individual in the room, as it didn't matter where the group sat, he was looking at them.

'Hello, my name is Kelvin Temple, secretary to the ministers of education and collector of documents. I have the job of just wandering into the ministers' rooms, picking up papers, and leaving. A majority of the time, the ministers don't even know I have been and gone. The reason I am passing this information on to the New Zealand government is twofold. First, I'm worried, like many people in Australia, the way our county is heading. It's definitely not the way we want. Our government is now a dictatorship. If I can help stop the plans of these policies that our government is going to put into practice in the future, I will do my level best. Second, my mother was born in New Zealand ninety years ago. At the moment, I'm on borrowed time if they find out that my mother was a Kiwi. Well, she left at one week old. Her parents were only passing through New Zealand and had to stop, as my mother was premature. According to our government, she is a Kiwi, and that means I am as well. They deported her, and her at ninety, I'm worried, as I have had no information of her whereabouts. She has never been to New Zealand at all in her life except for her birth. Her name is different from mine, as she remarried over forty years ago, and it is because of this name change, they have not picked me up. So that is my background. All I ask is if your country would find her and make sure she is safe and well. Her name is Victoria Katherine Willis.

'Right, where to start. Our government has this fixation on your country brought about by the lack of water. New Zealand is abundant; Australia is not. I have overheard frequently from the PM to the DPM, including the minister of defence, that we should just waltz in and take it. They have now come to the stage of planning to invade. Information about where or when, I could not glean from my eavesdropping, but I have a good inkling it might be Wellington. I have heard Auckland mentioned a few times as well as blockading your major ports. The intricacies of the invasion are, I'm sorry, beyond me, but this is to give you a heads-up to at least be aware. If you can do something about it, the ball is in your court. The president is not in the loop; he is completely in the dark, and I do fear for him and his family. I have overheard that they will kidnap his wife and their children, including grandchildren. They will hold them at the president's residence on Hamilton Island, making it impossible for the president to walk into parliament and dissolve it. The presidential guards, at least most of them, are still loyal to him, though our PM thinks otherwise. So, if push comes to shove, at least our president has some teeth, but he won't do a thing if his family's incarcerated.

'I know nothing about your abilities, and I believe that our military also thinks that you are easy beats. They have an illusion that your capacity to stop them is nil. I don't know personally, as I have never been interested in military matters until now. If you have satellite coverage, point it up north. Our first battalion is doing manoeuvres up near Rockhampton, and I believe it is pertaining to New Zealand. Also, you would see a lot of tankers in the ports, and I believe these will drain your water supply to the last drop.

At the last count, I heard about one hundred ships.

'Can you stop our government? I just don't know. My duty is done. I have passed this on to give you fair warning about what is coming in the future. That's all I have. Sorry to have to give you bad tidings. Good luck. The only contact I want from you is to know if my mum is safe, and then I will vanish. I'm for the chop if I'm caught, not only as a so-called Kiwi but a traitor to boot. If you find Mum, I'm sure you will be discreet in getting in touch.' 'Message finished.'

You could hear a pin drop. Around the table, people had their head in their hands. Others looked into the middle distance in a trance, slack jawed. Two women had hankies out, dabbing their eyes. Then the PM broke the silence.

'That's it, in a nutshell. We have a lot of planning to do, but the first thing is confirmation. Even though we have this message, and our old satellite has picked up those manoeuvres out of Rockhampton, it's not set in concrete that the Aussies are going to invade. We will prepare; we will be vigilant, but we need positive proof. Within the hour, a rocket is on the launch pad at Mahia, loaded with the latest satellites, thanks to our nano team from Wellington Uni. Kathy Wong, the head of Nano Tech, is at the site this very moment, making sure that everything is going to her satisfaction. He turned to Tere Swan, the minister of science. Will you explain, please, Tere,' he asked.

Tere stood up and looked around the room.

'This is the special operation Mahira, or nosy. We are going to put into orbit eight satellites. This has only been possible because of Kathy Wong and her nano research. She has shrunk the satellites to matchbox size. The tiny size does not take anything away from their ability to function. In fact, they will have a higher ability than before they were downsized. The hearing devices on each of the satellites can pick up conversation one kilometre below ground level. It can take photos in 3D, standard photos up to five thousand-plus pixels. They can also fire out a laser beam and mark any place, vehicle, or organic plant with a listening device called a spark. This can film, listen to, and send back information to us for twenty-four hours before dissolving. Also on board, the nanos replicate and replace any part that breaks down.

'We have satellites that are operational twenty-four seven, for years, with no maintenance. They also have hunter-killer capabilities, and we can knock out Aussie's satellites, if need be. These satellites of ours can communicate individually with our armed forces and will be our eyes and ears from below the Roaring Forties to ten degrees south of the equator. The eight satellites have cloaking abilities so they will be invisible and, of course, be so small they will look insignificant if the cloaking was not in force. We will spread them out at equal distances with one directly over Canberra. Whatever is spoken in their Parliament, or their so-called secret war room, we will hear it. That's the plan, and with luck, we will know what the hell is going on, with concrete evidence.'

He stopped and asked, 'Questions?'

The Minister of Transport, Warwick Isaacs, asked, 'Is this reliably tested?'

'Yes,' came the reply. 'It certainly has, and I can tell you the results are quite amazing. With this technology, you can snoop wherever you want; it's that good. There is no place to hide unless you have cloaking abilities. In our case, it is only to be used in this sort of situation. We will never use it for snooping on our own people willy-nilly, and that's written into the statutes of Parliament. Though, in this case, we will do it incognito; we don't want our population to know. We have to keep it secret this time to avoid panic. All this information could be a white elephant. We certainly don't want our capabilities open to our cousins across the ditch.'

'Right,' the PM said, looking around the table. 'First order of the day, I want you, Kelvin, to find Derrick Temple's mother, and make sure she is settled into New Zealand and is well. We will flash your finding to an operative at our embassy in Canberra.'

Next, he turned to the chief of staff, Sir Gary O'Brien.

'We need a complete assessment of our armed services' capabilities. We will have to use our new technology, which I hoped we could have kept secret for a few more years, but needs must. Anything to do with protecting our borders, gentlemen, is now in your hands. Expect the best; prepare for the worst.'

'Leave it to me, Prime Minister. We will have a working paper on your desk in a week.'

He turned to the heads of the three services. 'A fair assessment required.'

'Good as gold, sir,' the air commodore replied. 'We are very fortunate that we have been working on this scenario for some time in exercise mode, so it just needs to be tweaked.'

'Okay,' the PM said. 'Law and order will have to be tight. Do we inform our population another question to ponder? Are our airports protected from enemy aircraft? All our major ports in New Zealand have sea walls, and the only way into our harbours is through the locks. So the entrance's protection is paramount. I don't have to emphasise the importance of this as we all are aware. So we will need to have a group looking after our ports of entry.'

'Leave it with us, sir,' the chief said. 'This is what they pay us for. You get the civilian plan of action; we will do the protecting.' He grinned. 'I would not tell you how to run a country, Prime Minister.'

'Sorry, Gary. I'm just worried, and I get carried away sometimes.'

'Well, sir, it is delegation time. We all have to have jobs. I'll work on mine. You will have our report sooner than later. Now, if that's all, sir? I have time to get up to Mahia and watch the rocket launch. We have an aircraft waiting to take us up there. Televised back to you, sir, on our secure link.'

'Right, Gary. We will keep in touch daily. I need to know everything militarywise. Let's hope it is only an unnecessary exercise and not the real thing.'

The armed service personnel saluted the PM and left.

Brigadier Hone Paparoa was walking beside the chief of defence staff. With him was Group Captain Earl Quigley.

'Sir,' he asked, 'if you don't need Earl, I would like to take this opportunity to do a quick inspection on Wellington and Kapati Airports. To make sure our anti-landing equipment is working to perfection. I know they checked out not so long ago, but this is quite serious, and I think it is necessary. You will have a report of this inspection tomorrow on your desk.'

'Very good, Hone, do that, and take Captain Sale with you. He laughed. He had to be in the navy with a name like that. Have a yarn also about lock protection, and all of you come to my office tomorrow morning at ten,' he stated as he stepped out of the elevator.

'I have transport, Earl,' stated Hone. 'Now, where is Paul Sale?'

They found him waiting near the elevator.

'Tai Ho, Paul,' Hone called out. 'You are with us.'

Frowning, Paul turned.

'Oh, it's you, Hone. Kia ora, Earl. Where are we off to?'

The boss has given us the job of checking the airport anti-landing devices at Wellington and Kapati, also your expert advice on how to protect the locks from invasion.'

'Oh, I'm good for that.' He grinned.

The second elevator arrived, and the three men stepped in. 'Car park, please,' Hone instructed the elevator. Twilight was setting in as they climbed into Hone's car. Once in, he ordered the car to take them to Wellington Airport security area. The driver-less car silently drove out of the underground car park into traffic.

'How long has Wellington had this anti-land device up and running, Earl? I remember when they started building them. I lost track since I came back from my overseas attachment to the USA,' Paul said as the car shot into Thornton tunnel.

'This was the last city to have them installed, so only a few months,' Earl replied.

They arrived after dark, stopping at the airport security gate. Hone showed his pass, then was waved through. Continuing their drive, they pulled up at the main office. Pausing for a minute and gazing out over the runways, they climbed out of the car, then walked up the stairs to the security office, where the security officer was waiting for them. Hone had rung through before leaving the National Crisis Management Centre.

'We need to check the anti-landing devices, Peter,' Hone remarked as he sat down on a chair. 'Can we see them in action, so to speak?'

Peter looked at the three men.

'We have always checked them later in the evening to keep the old prying eyes away. Of course, there's not so many aircraft around late at night. Is something up?'

'No, not at all. It's the PM. He want us to check, and here we are.'

'Right,' he conceded. He looked at his watch. 'If we can wait another hour, the forecast calls for it to cloud over and that would be beneficial for security.'

Coffee made, the hour passed quickly, until Peter announced, 'Control tower, this is security. Which runways are not in use at the moment? We have an anti-landing check.'

'Roger, Security, we have a fifteen-minute window. I'll have the next aircraft do a longer circuit. Would that suffice?'

'Good. Oh, Tower? Will activate devices now.'

Peter turned towards his computer, typing in, Activate security anti-landing device 001/2198 Peter Nelson 47. The computer message came back: Activating Device Now.

Zero1 runway changed. Across the tarmac, walls appeared out of the ground every one hundred metres. These tungsten-steel walls blocked every metre of the runway right out to the sea lock. The three men had donned night glasses as the walls blended into the evening.

'That...' voiced Hone, 'will stop any aircraft from landing. Would that be your opinion, Earl?'

'Yes,' he agreed. 'You would have no way of landing

even if you tried. The landing gear would rip off, and you have nowhere to go except into another wall.'

Peter explained, 'We even have them on the taxiways; only a parachute could land.'

'Yes, well, this is excellent, Peter.'

'Have you seen enough, fellows?' Hone asked.

Both of the men nodded.

'Pete, thanks for your time and patience; enjoyed the coffee. We will be in touch.'

As they were walking to the door, they heard Peter say, 'Anti-landing device disengage.' They stopped to watch the walls slip back into the ground. They then continued their drive up to the Kapati Coast to check out the airfield there, with the same results. It ended up a late night.

Earl explained, 'Every airfield in New Zealand now had this anti-landing device. They appear to work well. If anyone wanted to land troops, they would be in for a big surprise. That's for sure.' Changing the subject, he asked, 'Have you used the new laser rifle and artillery weapon that was developed by the nano unit?'

'Too right, I have,' replied Hone.

'As you both know, we have them now on our ships,' uttered Paul. 'I'm quite amazed how the technology works, but those laser cannons can stop a ship dead from one hundred kilometres, with no casualties. I believe that if any ship, regardless of size, enters our waters, they will not know what hit them.'

'So what about the locks?' asked Earl.

'We can centralise the controls in one area,' replied Paul. At the moment, they are in each city, but this is unnecessary. We can centralise them at one of your drone bases, Earl. As your bases are in the middle of nowhere, discovery will be virtually impossible. That's for sure.'

'Actually, Paul, that is a rather good idea. I'm feeling sorry for the Aussies. They really haven't taken us seriously for years, and it might just bite them on the bum.'

CHAPTER THIRTEEN

Mahia Peninsula

The rocket sat quietly on its pad as the technicians worked on their last checks. 'T minus 30 minutes,' the computer's voice announced over the speakers. Kathy Wong and her team had been at the installation for a week doing their ultimate checks and were now at the stage where they all had their fingers crossed.

'It's not as though our work would go wrong,' suggested Kathy to Eric Radwell, 'it's the waiting that get's me down.' Then she giggled, un-Kathy-like. Which showed Eric that she was on pins and needles. All their work could backfire if this operation did not work.

Tim Capstain, the laser-delivery designer, came through over the holograph connection. He smiled at Kathy.

'I have been monitoring all our systems from my end, Kathy, and everything is ready to go. Don't look so worried.'

With him was Ray Silver, who was the inventor of the crystal-battery power units. They would power this rocket faster than the required escape velocity of over seventeen thousand kilometres per hour. His use of antimatter and matter sliding together in their own crystal tubes, creating power to the batteries, was going to make space travel faster than ever before. With the nanos replacing the used antimatter as it died, there was going to be an unlimited power source at their fingertips. Also installed was the latest antigravity device. The rocket would use no power until it lifted at least twenty metres off its pad, making it lighter than anything sent into space before. This had done away with all the liquid fuel tanks. The designers were smiling, and everything was looking ready.

'T minus 9,' the voice counted down. The gantries pulled away as the countdown went to zero. The rocket left the launch pad. It wasn't like a normal rocket firing; she sat for a second, then quietly lifted into the early morning sky. Not a sound was heard as it sent the power to the rocket. It just took off. Within four minutes and topping 28,384 kilometres an hour, she was at her optical orbit of three hundred kilometres above the earth's surface. A few minutes passed, then the nose cone opened. Like a flower in bloom, it spat out babies like a seahorse spitting out its young. The tiny satellites popped out into the void. They clustered together for a few seconds, until the sun hit their small charging solar units. Within seconds, the batteries were fully charged. They took off for their precise destinations twenty kilometres above the old twentieth-century space station at three hundred and forty kilometres above the earth's surface. Once on station they settled into their orbit, the same speed as the earth's rotation, keeping them in place over their allocated spots. The cloaking devices activated and the satellites disappeared from all radar.

Within an hour, the first of the images and voices came through loud and clear. New Zealand had gone nosy on its neighbour. They then tested the laser spark on an unsuspecting member of the Australian Parliament as he walked through the main doors of the Canberra Parliament House. The laser light hit him, leaving a small dot that then blended into the colour of his clothes. Once activated, the operators in New Zealand received clear pictures of his surroundings and conversation. Everything was going as it should. All they had to do was be patient. The eight satellites, Tahi, Rua, Toru, Wha, Rima, Ono, Whiti, and Waru were sending back an overload of information from all over the East Coast of Australia. A special receiving section was analysing the information as fast as they were getting it. The computers were working overtime.

The first interesting information came from the Australian Defence HQ in Brisbane ten hours after the satellites came online. They overheard a conversation that the defence force had leased a Japanese car transporter from the first of January for three months, with the stipulation that the Australian Navy would be in full control of the ship. The lights burnt bright that night in the New Zealand war room when that information came through to New Zealand, working out why the Aussies wanted this type of ship. Until it twigged. They would use this ship to transport men, tanks, personal carriers, and all their heavy equipment in one go to whatever port in New Zealand that had the facilities for this type of ship. Over the next month, the information continued to build to the point that the New Zealand government knew exactly what the Australians had in mind. Where they were going to attack, and what equipment, ships, and aircraft were to be utilised.

Near the middle of December, they picked up more thought-provoking information from Canberra, deep in their war room. The Australian PM was being briefed on the plan to place under house arrest the president's wife, including his two married children, their husbands, and grandchildren. They would do this while the president was out inspecting the new water pipes. The pipes had pushed slowly out West and had reached Mildura, Northern Victoria. The dust storms had abated in this area.

There was hope that with water pumped into the derelict town, it might help to stop the dust, and it just might give a chance to repopulate this corner of Victoria. While the president was out and about in Mildura, his wife, Colleen, was back in Canberra. She was opening a charity concert for the widows of the storm. They rounded thousands of men up and sent them out West to save the smaller towns at the very beginning of the dust storms. The storms were so bad, hundreds perished.

Every two years since, there was a charity concert to raise funds for the wives and children of the hundreds lost. This year it was going to be different. The president's wife would fly to the president's home on Hamilton Island with all her family. The PM mentioned to his colleagues that it was for their safety. 'We don't want our beloved first family to be compromised by the unsavoury.' Of course, the president would be told once he arrived back at his residence in Canberra that there was an assassination attempt on his family while he was away. As a precaution, and until they caught the perpetrators of the incident, it would be best for his wife and family to be safe on the Island. The date for this operation was in the middle of January.

Not long after the news of the plot to kidnap the first family, the final date came through from satellite "Wha" from Defence HQ in Canberra. The four

Australian chiefs of staff and the defence minister came together for the final briefing to the PM.

The Australian secretary to the Minister of Defence, David Abbott, told the Australian PM, the date of the invasion would be the sixth of February,

'The day you suggested, Prime Minister, will be the day, sir.'

He turned towards the other chiefs of staff with a nod. Lieutenant General Barry Eaton rolled out the maps.

'This, sir, is the plan, to date. We are flexible with it, still. We believe this will work. Some fine tuning is called for, but these are the nuts and bolts of the operation: Liquid Gold. The date, as you suggested, is a public holiday. An excellent time to take control of Parliament, podcast and TV stations, and, of course, police headquarters. With very little traffic on the roads in the major cities, we can block all motorways in and out of Auckland, Wellington, Christchurch, and Dunedin. They have major bridges on all these highways. It's just a matter of blowing up a span or two to stop their army driving up or down their roads. They only have one major rail link. Pointing at the map, he said, we will blow these bridges, cutting the rail link throughout the country in both North and South Islands.

'We now know, sir, and I confirmed this, that the New Zealand armed forces are not that equipped. One, they have no fighter aircraft. Two, they have no blue-water navy. Three, they have only three army camps and nine thousand service personnel spread between the camps. Their major camps are two on the North Island and one in the South. By blowing all bridges north and south, they cannot relieve Wellington or Auckland before we get a complete foothold.

'In their favour, they have attack helicopters. Ten at each base, Kaikohe, Waiouru, Linton, Blenheim, and Burnham. Also, two each at the naval establishments in Portabello and Bluff and their new navy base on Great Barrier Island.

'Their fishery protection fleet is modern and also foil, with speeds up to sixty knots. Their armament is insufficient to harm our destroyers. Their fleet is behind the sea walls in the inner harbours of each city. The time to go through the locks is no less that thirty minutes for each craft. We can catch the ships within their harbours. Our navy will sit outside the sea walls and bombard them from there. Once their ships are out of action, we will be able, in our own time, to move into the locks and into their ports with no threats. They have half a dozen of these vessels at each port, including their naval bases. All told, thirty-six, with a couple of reserves for maintenance.

'Now then, their army is excellent, as I have explained. They base the army in the middle of both Islands. Once the bridges are down, their army will become completely cut off. Our aircraft carriers will sit just inside their territorial waters at the two hundred and fifty kilometre mark—here, here, and here.' He was pointing as he explained, touching each spot with a cane. 'There is nothing they can do about it. They have nothing, and I mean, sir, nothing of any military significance to make me think otherwise.

'The first operational strike will hit the new airbase in Kaikohe, on the sixth of February at dawn, six forty-one a.m., knocking out all helicopters and destroying the infrastructure of the complex. The second wing will hit their navy base on Great Barrier, then go on and destroy the Auckland Harbour Bridge, including the new road tunnel under Auckland Harbour.' He stopped to look at his notes. 'That will be enough to stop all movement, and to a lesser degree, we will have destroyed the bridge at Hobsonville as well. This will insulate Auckland from the rest of the country.

'Our second aircraft carrier is stationed with its battle fleet directly in line with Taranaki. The first bombers will take out Waiouru. The second wing will bomb the main camp at Linton and cut the bridges across the Rangitikei River. We will hit the bridges across the Whanganui River, Manawatu River, and the Otaki.

'To cut the Lower North Island, we will whack the Rimutaka Pass road. Their army will have nowhere to go. We will parachute three hundred troops into Wellington Airport. Once the airport is secure, fifty men of the detachment will make a beeline to the Thorndon Tunnel and secure the entrance. The rest will continue around the coastal road to meet up at the Parliament Buildings. They will rendezvous with the troops who, by this time, would have berthed at the roll-on, roll-off ferry berth with our Japanese-leased ship. From there, the troops will spill out to take the parliament buildings, defence headquarters, and police headquarters. The tanks will roll up Highway One to the gorge road and block anyone down from Upper Hutt, Lower Hutt, and Porirua, completely cutting Highway One, including Transit Gully. The surrounding of the capital is ensured. I should also mention a platoon of troops will capture the governor general's residence and the prime minister's. Of course, they will all be in Waitangi for the celebrations of their treaty with the Maori. This is mainly symbolic.

'Troops will parachute into Waitangi and capture the parliamentary group. They will use our new c640e, which holds one hundred and twenty men. The time of the drop will coincide with the first attack on Kaikohe. The New Zealanders have a dawn service outside at the flagstaff. Our men will round them all up. There is only a small contingent of navy personnel. Mainly band personnel and reserves. At the same time another group of two hundred parachuters will drop into Albert Park in Auckland, and one hundred will drop on Auckland Airport, and secure the major police stations, online podcasts, TV, and 3D stations. With their ships in the harbour being bombarded by our ships, they will not know what is going on, and by the time they have any inclination, it will be all over.

'That is the North Island. The South Island is much in the same vein. The third battle fleet's aircraft carrier will fly off their aircraft from just outside the Chatham Islands. They will destroy Burnham Camp. Then bomb the Rakaia River Bridge. The aircraft will continue on to the Rangitikei Bridge and destroy that as well. Once their first objective is complete, they will hit the bridges around Kaikoura, Arthur's, and Lewis Pass. The second flight will hit Blenheim Air Force Base and destroy it. The third flight hitting the naval bases in Dunedin and Bluff. Once this is in hand, we will blockade all harbours so no one enters, unless they are our people. We are working on prisoner retention. Our thinking is to use rugby stadiums around the country for military prisoners, but that is just the mopping-up stuff for the admin boys. We will intern political prisoners from the prime minister down in Australia. Incarcerated at your pleasure.

'Over all, Prime Minister, we all believe with the timing, it should be over completely in two to three days, maximum. Hit them hard and fast, and they will have no comeback. He sat back with a smile on his face. As a military operation, Prime Minister, we believe to sustain minimal casualties to our forces as the Kiwis will be completely overwhelmed.'

He sat back down, tapping the cane with his hand. Unbeknown to him and all his colleagues, everything that was uttered was overheard by the New Zealand satellites, and beamed into the secure defence room under parliament buildings in Wellington.

CHAPTER FOURTEEN

National Crisis Management Centre,
Parliament, Wellington, New Zealand

The operators who were monitoring the information from Canberra could not believe their ears. The head operator, Cyril Takarei's, normal procedure was to record the briefing, then inform the New Zealand prime minister immediately.

'You need to listen to this, sir, urgently.' He spoke to the PM on the secure holographic link. 'It is the confirmation that you are looking for, sir. I would advise the defence chiefs of staff to attend.'

Within an hour, the room was full of military and parliamentary personnel. The prime minister and deputy leaders of the parties, including the director of SIS, Dame Mary Gedge. They all sat around a glass oval table in silent anticipation.

'When you are ready, Cyril,' Prime Minister Jim Lofthouse drawled.

The lights dimmed, and a holographic image of Lieutenant General Barry Eaton of the Republican Australian Army, appeared in the middle of the table. After rolling out the map, smacking the cane in his hand, and explaining to the Australian prime minister how they were going to invade New Zealand, you could hear a pin drop around the table. There were a few sighs, and puffing out of cheeks as the briefing got into the nitty-gritty of the operation. The lights were turned back on at the end of the briefing. There was a quiet reflection at the enormity and consequences of what has being revealed. Nobody said a word as faces turned to one another in disbelief.

The PM stood up, moving around, rubbing his hand through his hair. He stopped and turned towards the table. 'Well, now we know,' he spat, his cheeks flushed, his brow in a permanent frown.

'I swear little, but those bastards are going to invade our country, and that pompous prick Eaton made me sick. Okay, negative thoughts out the door.' He turned to his chief of defence staff, Sir Gary O'Brien. 'Gary, we had an idea, but this is confirmation. How is our planning going?'

Gary O'Brien was a little bloke of one metre fifty-six. He was a pocket of dynamite. A very astute man, respected by all his staff. He now looked up at his PM and explained it to him.

'Things were bouncing along pretty bloody good. I have been on exercise with Eaton, and the one thing I believe is his downfall, is his ability not to get his facts completely right. In this case, of course, he is off the mark completely. Our training is complete. You have no worries, Prime Minister. Our secret bases are on maximum alert and will stay that way until this is over. My heads of service will gather once this briefing is over, and with your permission, I would like to meet with you here, and I'll explain what we have been working on.'

'Will we tell our population, Jim?' Rangi asked in a low tone.

'To my way of thinking, Rangi, we will leave it till the last minute, if at all. We do not want the public to panic. At the end of the day, we still might avoid this conflict. Our defences have to be low-key. We don't want to show the Aussies our hand. Any other questions? Until I've have heard what Gary offers, we should ask questions when his briefing is over. Okay, an early lunch, and I don't have to tell anyone here this is top secret. If you need to talk to anyone connected with this briefing, it is to be done at your designated secure room, with the new electric cloaking device. I do not want to hear a thing about this crisis on the Parliament stairs or in the restaurant. If I do, heads will roll. We cannot give the Aussies any sign that we know about their plans.'

'Just one thing,' Lyn Loo, the Greens deputy leader asked. 'Are we going to be the aggressors, or are we just going to sit back and take the first hit?'

'That is a good question Lyn.' Jim sighed.

'Can I answer, Prime Minister?' Brigadier Hone Paparoa replied. He looked at his chief before talking.

'Go ahead, Hone.'

'Well, Lyn, as soon as any ship or aircraft or uninvited army personnel cross our territorial borders without our permission, they're classed as the aggressors. We can ask them to leave politely, and we record that for future reference. We will be in our own rights to knock the buggers out of the air, off the land and sea. So, in this case, we are the defenders, and they are the aggressors.'

'Thank you, Hone.' Lyn smiled. 'I'm satisfied with that.'

'A pleasure, Lyn.'

Once the security locks and electric cloak had turned off, they all rose and moved out of the room.

'I'll see you in an hour, Prime Minister,' said the CDS. 'Will the director of the SIS be here as well?' He grinned, turning to Mary as she walked out beside him.

'Always a pleasure to be at your beck and call, Gary.'

In one hour, precisely, the PM and his chiefs of staff, SIS, and of course, the leaders of all parties where once again settled into the chairs around the table. Sir Gary O'Brien stood in front of the lectern.

'Prime Minister, ladies and gentlemen, I would never have thought in a million years we'd be in this position, that we have to defend our country. Nevertheless, we in the defence force are going to put this invasion to bed before anyone in our homeland incurs injury. Australia has put us in a very awkward position. We did not want to show our hand at this time. The weapons we have, once this operation begins, will have all eyes upon us from around the world.' He shuffled some papers, then looked up.

'Righty. Oh...' he said, catching his breath, 'Firstly I want to emphasise that the Australian president does not know, or has any cohesion with the government of Australia, regarding their plans to invade New Zealand. As we heard, kidnapping and incarcerating his family on Hamilton Island means he cannot carry out his constitutional duties. He's compromised, as they will put his family in harm's way. Turning to Dame Mary Gedge, he asked, 'Can you get a message to the president through your spooks, Mary? Explain the situation, and let him know we can help. This will give him time to think about his course of action, and it gives us time to plan a rescue of his family. We will hop over the ditch and collect his family from Hamilton Island the night of the invasion, and transport them to the prime minister's holiday home in Queenstown. He turned to the PM. 'Sorry, sir, I haven't asked permission. I'm sure you wouldn't mind his family using your crib for a few days?'

'Good as gold, Gary.'

'I won't go into details as we will need to work on that scenario. Once we know the exact date that the Aussies move on the president's family, that will be in the future and only on a need-to-know basis.' Looking at the PM, he said, 'I will brief you, sir, and the senior members of cabinet on this operation once organised.'

'In any event, when we have rescued the president's family, he will be able to dissolve Parliament, without fear. The president, it appears, has the presidential guard to do that forcefully, if need be. I hope they are with him. If not, we can help on that score. Our army has grit, even though spread thinly. The Aussies will not be expecting us to fight at all. We will have two thousand men here in Wellington, two thousand in Auckland, and the rest divided between Waitangi and the South Island.

'We'll discreetly call up all reserves for a six-week training from the end of December. There is no way they are going to take our parliamentarians into captivity. It is imperative that all normal activity carry on until daybreak. We don't want our neighbours to twig that we know what they are doing.' Gary looked around the table to where Terry Swan was sitting. 'I want your people to liaise with Hone, Terre. The Aussie satellites have to be taken out at daybreak on the sixth of February. We will get together for a yarn after this briefing. Then you can talk to Hone and Kieran and work on a scenario to do that. That will certainly affect their operation, having no eyes in the sky. Our air force is going to be our main defence force: Seventy-five Drone Squadron, Fourteen Drone Squadron, three squadron choppers, six squadron navy, and forty-two squadron VIP. We will use this squadron's aircraft to collect the president and forty squadron for special operations. Every squadron will be utilised, and our bases are on full alert from this moment on. Let me tell you, ladies and gentlemen, our men and women are the best—highly trained in their area of expertise.

'We were not happy to start with when we introduced this technology. I found it, frankly, weird. I have seen the results, and the Aussies, I'm afraid, are in for a shock. All airports throughout the country have sliding, blocking walls. All were checked and in order, working perfectly. There is no way an aircraft will land in New Zealand on Waitangi Day on any runway. We have temporarily moved all the lock controls to our top-secret base at RNZAF Takaka Hill. All locks will be under defence control until this wee shindig is over. We have a lot more planning to do, but this is to assure you all that not one enemy soldier, sailor, or airman will step foot aggressively on our islands. Only the ones we have to pull out of the sea or surrounding areas as they float down will be the exception. I must emphasise this is not an idle boast, as I and my fellow chiefs of staff had seen firsthand the capabilities of our armed services and their equipment. The men and women we have in the defence force today are top people. Our way of life will preserve you, mark my words. My chiefs of staff will, from this moment on, organise the nitty-gritty of the defence of our country.' He looked again at the SIS chief. 'Mary, If you can come back to me as quickly as you can, I would appreciate it. That's it for now, Prime Minister. Let us leave from here united. We will win. I am so sure of it. Our equipment is superior to what the Aussies have, and you really have to thank Australia for sending us their people.'

The PM stood up. 'Thank you, Gary, I want you to brief the war cabinet daily from now on. We all need to be in the picture and especially the group off to Waitangi on the sixth of February. Briefing time is to be at six p.m. each day. Thank you, ladies and gentlemen. I adjourn the meeting until tomorrow at six.'

CHAPTER FIFTEEN

RNZAF, Takaka Hill

Takaka Hill, was nestled between Tasman Bay and Golden Bay, at the top of the South Island of New Zealand. At an elevation of eight hundred metres, a marble mountain with hundreds of natural caves covered in native bush was the perfect place to establish a fighter wing with no fighter aircraft.

This was the home of 75 Drone Squadron. The base was in a natural cave of solid marble, over two hundred metres below the surface. There were no roads in or out; everything was bought in by an e-chopper, at night, power supplied from the Cobb Dam. Water came from a large, natural spring that poured down through the cave's system. The electric choppers would land on the landing pad, which would then sink the two hundred metres into the base. As it sank, a second roof would slip into place. From the air it was hard to pick out, as they painted the roof camouflage colours of the surrounding bush.

At ground level, you could walk over the roof and not know you had, it was so well camouflaged.

The base was on the edge of a cliff face that had a perfect view of Tasman Bay. There were sixty small exits cut into the marble where the drones flew out from, giving the base the name "The Bat Cave." The population of the base was 250 personnel—sixty of them pilots, with ten drone pilot reserves. The rest of the personnel where the infrastructure to run the base with a group captain in charge over all. They were on a two-weeks on, two-weeks off rotation. The training had been intense for the men and women of 75 D squadron. They had doubled flight-training tactics in the wake of the news from their chief of staff of an impending invasion.

Sixty aircrew sat in their own pilot rooms, which were climate controlled, painted in tranquil pastels, giving the rooms a restful ambience. They were all connected through the communication centre. The men and women pilots dressed in light-blue flight suits while sitting in large captains' chairs that rotated and tilted to the drones' movements. A small touch joystick was the only instrument attached to the arm of the chair. Their individual drones flew from their rooms through a small opening in the wall, facing the sea. On command, the wall panel would slide down, revealing a tiny tunnel in the cliff face. This was the exit and entrance to the drone base.

The defence force had spent a lot of money training the aircrew. They had to be perceptible to ESP, as all commands relayed through their helmets, with not a word spoken. The helmets were individually designed for each pilot. Similar to a motorbike helmet with an oblique visor. The difference was night would become day with the visor down. They had programmed each helmet to the brainwaves of the individual pilot at a cost to the taxpayer of over ten million dollars per helmet. Big bickies, but much cheaper than buying aircraft.

The pilots sat in their custom-made rooms. Once connected to their helmets, the pilots could look over their entire squadron from any direction. The vista gave 360-degree vision in full colour, always in clear daylight. Even on a miserable day with visibility down to metres, or in the dead of night, the visor could penetrate all haze and darkness up to ten kilometres in every direction. When the drones flew, the pilots did not leave the room. This was not a simulator, but real flying, as they flew their individual drones on a training mission.

With communication through their helmets, the pilot rooms had a silent, eerie atmosphere about them, yet the pilots conversed with the twelve members of their own flight. Overall, they conversed with the entire squadron of sixty, including their operation base, with their minds. All communication from the base was spoken; it reached the pilots in thought waves. The pilots' thought waves converted to speech during the return of communication.

On this exercise the wing commander was Bill Ingram, a squadron leader at twenty-three. He was monitoring his wing, then ordered, 'Stop the chatter and concentrate.'

They swung to port together and circled high above Mt Taranaki. They then dived to sea level together, crossing the coast at Waverley, then climbing to twenty thousand metres, and leveled off. No one heard or saw them. They always activated the cloaking devices when they left The Bat Cave.

The drones were the latest in the air force arsenal. They were no bigger than a matchbox, using antigravity technology, with microscopic batteries that could punch out a laser beam of a million volts. Cutting a ship in half was easy as pie. They had practised on numerous occasions during training exercises.

They had a speed of Mach 5, a ceiling of thirty thousand metres, were deadly accurate, and the pilots were exceptionally good at what they did. Years of training for the right people were honed into a fighting force that was yet to be seen outside New Zealand.

Thanks to Kathy Wong and the nano team, the

lasers now with nanotechnology installed were a revolutionary plus. A burst of fire was just a pinprick of light carrying millions of nanos. The laser light penetrated its targets. Then nanos would go about their work dismantling everything that needed to be destroyed. This happened in microseconds. They could fire a killing shot. Heat from the laser would cut the target in two. Laser defence systems were so accurate that they could shoot incoming multiple missiles down in any direction. The drone computers would calculate the time and space, then fire in microseconds, hitting every enemy missile. The nanotechnology within the drone meant that the lasers could reproduce themselves and refire instantly.

There was a new laser design that was only trailed recently. It was the fan shot spreading the laser light up to three hundred metres wide, like a funnel. With three drones, three hundred metres apart, firing simultaneously, they had a kill range of nearly one kilometre wide. An enemy hitting the light would be like running into a brick wall. This technology was still in its infancy. Tests had been positive, and the defence force wanted to use the technology sooner than later. What with the rattling of the sabers from the lucky country, it was prudent they introduced the system as soon as possible.

The advanced technology of the nanos were incorporated into the laser, then programmed into the pilots' helmets. It was their thinking process. All that was needed was a thought command from the helmet and it was instantaneously carried out. If you wanted to kill the engine of an enemy, all the pilot had to do was think about killing the target's engines, or communication system, and that's exactly what would happen, when the laser reached its target. The nanos would go to work within microseconds; the engine would shut down, and communication would be cut. A deadly weapon in anyone's book. It looked as though the Australians were going to be the first country in the world to feel the effects of this technology.

Takaka Base flight area covered Taranaki in the north to Stewart Island in the south, including the Chatham Islands. It was a large area for New Zealand. Because of the quickness of the drones, they could be at the farthest point from their base within sixteen minutes.

The 14 D Squadron covered the top of the North Island, situated just under the rim of Mount Hirakimata on Great Barrier Island. It was the same situation as 75 D Squadron. The squadron was situated a couple of hundred metres underground, away from prying eyes. The air force had copied everything from the Takaka Hill base, smaller with only thirty-six pilots, plus ten reserves, a wing commander in charge, and two hundred air force personnel to run the base. The best-kept secret since sliced bread, as the area was a special breeding ground for the Black Petrel. It was out of bounds to everyone except the Department of Conservation. The drone squadrons were the front-line firepower of the New Zealand armed forces, with the reserve of ten pilots from both squadrons filling in any gaps that cropped up.

There were, of course, the latest eyes in the sky, the new satellites. Even though they were used specifically for eavesdropping, they also had a secondary role—keeping track of any untoward activity heading into New Zealand territorial waters. Laser armed, from orbit, they could hit a target smaller than the size of a ten-cent piece. Also to be used as a hunter-killer of other satellites. The drone squadron receiving a message from a satellite would scramble and be in position within minutes.

Takaka Base had the job of New Zealand's lock control for the foreseeable future. They had moved all lock controls to the base, and with it, their civilian operators under the official Secrets Act. Twenty operators controlled the locks from Southland to Northland. Each province had its own harbours and seawalls with remote cameras and controls. These men and women from RNZAF Base, Takaka Hill, could only activate the locks.

The only way to penetrate the lock gates was by an explosion. They hoped this would defeat the purpose of destroying them. Any enemy blowing locks would end up with millions of litres of seawater inundating the harbours, land, and ruin the infrastructure. The New Zealand Defence Force thought this would also be the thinking of the invading force, that they would like everything intact.

The 3 E Squadron, Electric Helicopters, was to be used as search and rescue and ground support operations. There were two larger twenty-seaters stationed at Waitangi, to use for evacuating the members of Parliament and dignitaries who would attend the Waitangi Day celebrations. The PM did not want to give the Australians any cause to think other than everything was normal in the Shaky Isles. The choppers were only there as a precaution against everything turning turtle. Also, the PM's aircraft from 42 Squadron would land on the ground if required. She could hover and whisk him and his party away if the Aussie paratroopers got a foothold and ruined the day.

The navy fishery protection fleet had teeth. The new EF1, Electric Foil One, with the new laser cannons fitted to each ship, included two e-choppers from 6 Squadron per ship. Used for anti-submarine and air-sea rescue. Their job would be to round up survivors, and if need be, to hassle the blockade ships the Aussies were going to use to block all major ports throughout New Zealand.

The navy would not be behind the locks or seawalls as the Aussies surmised. They would be out at sea, ready to pounce when required. Royal New Zealand Navy ships would head out from their ports the night of the fifth of January with mock-ups replacing them in the harbours to fool any prying eyes. Unfortunately, spreading the ships thinly could not be helped. Their speed was their biggest asset, hitting over sixty knots on their foils. The one thing in their favour was they knew exactly where the Australian battle groups would be.

They were powered by two 8000- horsepower electric engines, the power coming from the two thousand nano batteries that were recently fitted, and the new antimatter propulsion. In length, they were one hundred and ten metres with a width of twenty metres, shallow draft, a greyhound of the sea. With a crew of sixty, with the ability to carry another fifty if required in a rescue operation. The ships could load up to one hundred souls if the need arose. Two high-speed patrol boats were included in the arsenal, and laser cannons forward and aft, which could hit a target thirty kilometres away. Quite formidable and would be a match for a destroyer. They relied on speed and guile.

The transport wing, 40 Squadron, also had the operation of surveillance with their new Delta E4NZ, like the old Orion of a hundred years ago. The difference being they could stay up a week without resupplying. A crew of twenty were all mainly computer and signal technician analysts, with two aircrews of four. They would do eight hours on and eight hours off. Sleeping quarters and a galley were at the rear of the aircraft for twenty personnel using the electrical and antigravity power source with four large prate engines, pushing the speed out to just under Mach 1.

The new cloaking equipment installed in the Delta was an important part of the New Zealand Defence Force. The Delta would circle the country at twenty thousand metres, picking up all signals from the satellites, and relay overall commands to all defence operations on the ground, air, and sea. Also, this was complimentary to the satellite network and double-checking to make sure that the right information was coming through and going out to the right parties. All information were copied to NZ defence computers for analysing by the ground-operation staff. Everyone called the Delta "Two Cents," as they always got their two cents' worth out of her.

The Delta was to leave New Zealand at the beginning of February for a program with the Fijian army for a couple of days, then head to the Cook

Islands and wait there until the evening of the fifth of February. It needed to be online over New Zealand at 3:00 a.m., the false dawn of the sixth of February.

Each area of the New Zealand Defence Force was coming together with their planning. The army was working on the lock protection. When the Aussie roll-on, roll-off ship, which was hired from the Japanese, floated into the Wellington lock, the lock would only half drain, leaving the ship in limbo.

Not wanting any infantry to escape the ship via the sides of the lock and up to the walkways, planning was underway to fix this problem. A burst of laser fire from a position at Red Rocks and south of Pencarrow Heads would disrupt the party. A couple of blasts with the nano application could kill all the firepower from the Aussie ship. The defence of the lock wall and pathway on both sides of the harbour was well in progress.

Wellington Airport was to be surrounded by army personnel. NZ would quickly round up the Aussie paratroopers who dropped in. Sharpshooters on Mount Victoria could pick off individuals and block Thornton Tunnel to stop any advance into the city. A blockade at Highway One, at Evens Bay intersection, would halt any progress of the paratroopers if they should get out of the airport. With the Japanese car carrier in the lock, it would end up a prison for thousands of Aussies and all their equipment. The New Zealand Defence Force could sink the ship, but there would be consequences of a ship sinking in the roads, blocking entry to the locks. That was why the decision was made to allow the ship in, then lock the doors behind her so to speak.

The Aussies using a civilian ship were clever. If it had been one of their own transport ships, the NZ government would not give them permission to enter. A Japanese car carrier was good as gold. If they had not found out the Australian plan, in advance, once the carrier had reversed up to the roll-on, roll-off wharf, it would have been a fight to keep the Aussies at bay. The New Zealand Defence Force was working day and night to prepare while keeping a check on their cousins across the ditch.

New Zealand had the confirmation they were waiting for. From the satellite Whau, the Australian president's family evacuated to Hamilton Island for their own safety after a failed assassination attempt.

CHAPTER SIXTEEN

Canberra, Australia

'Well, it worked a treat,' Lieutenant General Barry Eaton informed the Australian prime minister, in the war room of the Parliament building. 'We have whisked the whole presidential family away to Hamilton Island. The idea of the deputy prime minister to have our man actually shoot into the crowd was brilliant. There was no chance of anyone getting hurt as our sharp shooter is the best in the army. Sir, you now have the president where you want him. He will not make trouble for you, now that his family, including his grandchildren and his daughters' husbands, are all tucked away nicely on the Island. We have a dozen guards up there under Captain Millar, head of security. I believe that we now have settled the presidential problem. We will let him communicate with his family, naturally, but visits… no. There could be another attempt on his or his family's lives, and we cannot have that, can we,' he said, grinning at his PM. 'I have spoken to Colonel Jones of the presidential guard, and explained that it's up to him now to tighten the security around the president. He has canceled all leave in the foreseeable future. His troops are now on full alert. It will keep them busy and out of our hair until we have reached our aim. Once that has occurred, we will then bring him into the fold. If he still wants to be the president's man, then he will have to go west. As you have alluded to, there will be no need for him to be in the Office of the President, that will be your job in the future. Sir, I believe all his guards are behind the army and the government of Australia, just as it should be, not an individual man.'

The PM sat back in his chair with his arms folded. 'Good,' he expressed, 'and the rest of the planning is now complete. It's just a waiting game until the sixth of February?'

'It is, sir. We have notified New Zealand Agriculture that a car transporter with a load of farm machinery will arrive in Wellington on the morning of the sixth. They have already given us the lock number to proceed through into Wellington harbour. That's a go as well. The First Battalion will start arriving at the Brisbane wharf over a two-week period so as not to cause any suspicion. Everything is going according to plan. The battle fleets will head out on the first of the month; everyone is prepared.

Harbour blockage frigates are ready to go. One last briefing for you and your cabinet, and we will deliver another couple of new states to the fold with all their precious water.'

National Crisis Management Centre, Parliament, Wellington, New Zealand

The satellite 'Wha' picked up all the latest information that was overheard in Canberra, then sent it directly to the National Crisis Management Centre in Parliament Wellington. The Defence HQ staff sat and listened to the Australian army chief explaining to his PM, the assassination attempt on the president's wife, including the rest of the plans to invade New Zealand. When the recording finished, there was complete silence, until Sir Gary O'Brien, Chief of Defence NZ, gave orders.

'First, I want to speak to the Head of SIS Dame Mary Gedge. I have had no feedback on her agent. We need that spook in the president's residence to explain what is really happening to him and his country. See to that now,' he urged his personal aid. Second, he turned to Air Commodore Kieran Vause, NZ Air force. 'Kieran, I want a plan on my table ASAP to pull the president's family out of Hamilton Island. We have talked about it; now we have the positive proof. I don't want them rescued before midnight on the fifth of February. I'll leave it in your hands. Liaise with Hone on this one, please. Arrange your plan; we'll get together again and pick holes in it.' He grinned, knowing that his air force chief was a meticulous planner and, once in place, it would be foolproof.

'Righto, today is the fifteenth; we have three weeks until D-Day. I want everything completed by the twenty-second. That gives us at least a couple of week's grace to change things if need be,' The COD concluded.

'A message coming through, sir,' the operator announced to the COD. 'It's from Head of SIS.'

'Good morning, Gary.' Mary apologised, 'Sorry for the delay. We have had problems with communicating with the Australian president. He is now in cotton wool, so to speak. Our ambassador has managed to persuade him to have their annual presidential golf match on Wednesday. My man is going to caddy and pass on the information we have for him, including today's revelations. With luck we should have him up to scratch with our people. Then we can loan him the new cloaking device so he can communicate with us from his residence without fear of being overheard. This is, of course, if he believes us and wants us to help. I understand time is of the essence, so I will push things along from my end. A bit of bad news I'm afraid—Derrick Temple's mother died three days after arriving in NZ; we'll pass that on to him as well.' The message ended as the holographic image disappeared.

'Hmm'… the PM said, 'she has a point if the president doesn't believe us—what then?'

Sir Gary replied with a grunt.

'We will go in without his permission. We know the situation. If we don't get them out, his family could just vanish. We need someone who is strong, sincere and popular with his people, and this bloke is. So we will grab his family and apologise later if he doesn't believe us.'

I'm sure you are right, Gary,' The PM answered. 'We will meet back here for a briefing at eighteen hundred. If you will excuse me, I still have a lot to do. I'm sorry to hear about Derrick's mother, though; it really is a shame.'

The meeting finished as Sir Gary and his team picked up their tablets, 3D monitors, and left the room.

After they had gone, the PM looked at his deputy.

'Your thoughts, Jono?'

'I'm thinking like you, Jim. If the Defence Service stuff this up, we are history. The Australia parliament has lost their heart and are now a complete dictatorship. If they win, there will be no room for you and I or any of our politicians. You have heard and read the intel, Jim. They are going to incarcerate us out in their dust belt. So what our defence force has planned has to work. I'm optimistic.' He grinned. 'I have been out inspecting the army reserves; they impressed me since we had those exercises at the beginning of the month. Everything has gone like clockwork. With the technology we have, I hope it is enough to stop Australia in it tracks. We just have to have faith in our armed services. I have and I know you have; lets hope our faith holds up.'

Republic of Australia, Canberra Golf Club

The old Royal Canberra Golf Club had a name change when the country went republic. The golf clubhouse was only three hundred metres behind the presidential residence. This Wednesday the club had been closed as the president was having his annual golf challenge with the New Zealand ambassador, Cedric Urlich. The golf club was swarming with presidential army guards as the colonel stepped up to the Kiwi ambassador, saluted, and introduced himself.

'Good morning sir, I'm Colonel Jones, head of security.'

'Good morning, Colonel.' Cedric smiled. 'This is Ngarangi Patea, my caddy.'

'Kia ora, Colonel; lovely day for golf.' Ngarangi

didn't look Maori at all: pale skin, red hair. His mother was from Scotland, father, Maori. He had taken after his mother's side of the family. His siblings took after his father. He was an excellent agent and had been an SIS operative for ten years.

'A lot of activity, Colonel?' he asked, looking around.

'Yes, I'm afraid it has come to this. I hope we don't inconvenience you, ambassador. After the assassination attempt on our president's family, we have to be so very careful.'

'That's good as gold, Colonel; I'm pleased that your president came out for a game; it is for a worthy cause. If I lose, I buy the drinks; if he loses, he buys. We like to keep it simple,' Cedric replied.

'Well, sir, we won't get in your road. There are over one hundred of my men scattered around the course. You won't see them all and we will make sure you have your privacy. We will have an eye on you all the entire match. Ah,' he exclaimed, 'here is the president now.'

'Cedric, lovely to catch up again,' said the president, shaking his hand. Turning to Ngarangi, he said, 'And you are, young man?'

'The name is Ngarangi, sir. Most Aussies call me Blue.'

The president laughed. 'Then Blue it is,' he said. Come, the golf carts are around the corner of the house.'

There was a coin toss once they reached the first tee, and another toss to see which caddy would caddy for each of them. Ngarangi ended up caddying for the president, much to his relief.

On the eighth hole, the president sliced his drive into a group of trees blocking the view from everyone.

Ngarangi yelled, 'Hang on, Mr President, I'll give you a hand.' As Ngarangi walked into the trees, the president was standing looking at the golf ball hard up against the tree trunk, scratching his head.

'This is awkward,' he stated.

'Sir,' Ngarangi whispered, 'do you have a minute? This has to be quick.'

He pulled out of his pocket a small box the size of a matchbox.

'Come in closer, Mr President.'

As he did so, Ngarangi pressed a button and a holographic image of the New Zealand prime minister popped out. Two minutes later they were back on the fairway, talking and laughing at the sliced shot. As Ngarangi picked up the clubs of the ambassador and placed them on the cart, Cedric asked, 'Did everything go all right?'

'Yes sir, he is livid, I can tell you that. Not with us, but at what the prime minister told him, and he only touched on the subject. The president is a talented actor, though. He had me believing that he was having a great time playing golf. He advised me he would get in touch with our prime minister as soon as he was back at his residence. I left the cloaking machine with him. I'm pleased our people gave me permission to do so as, from now on, he can have full contact with our prime minister in his own home with no one eavesdropping.'

The New Zealand ambassador lost the game and shouted, 'Drinks all around.' In conversation, the ambassador asked about the health of the president's wife and family. The president explained to him that the entire family was on holiday on Hamilton Island, recuperating after the assassination attempt. They were all in good spirits. All the information uttered throughout the day, was automatically captured on the thread and relayed through the satellite to Defence HQ in Wellington, New Zealand.

National Crisis Management Centre,

Parliament, New Zealand

The PM was in the NCMC when a message came through from the president. Jim Lofthouse stood up as the cloaking device activated.

'Mr President, my sincere condolences to you for all the bad news I'm about to relay to you.'

For an hour they conversed, and in the end, the PM asked, 'Are your presidential troops loyal to you? That will be half the battle won. Your prime minister is sending most of your troops away to deal with us in New Zealand. That will denude Canberra of armed service personnel on the morning of the sixth. A handful will be around to guard Parliament. If your family are safe, sir, would you go in and dissolve your government?'

'I would not think twice, Jim, but I would need to know. Will my family be safe?' he questioned.

'We are working on that now and will have a plan in place for you as soon as possible. Once they are under our protection, I'll have your wife under our cloaking device get in touch with you. When this occurs, the ball will be in your court. If you need a hand militarywise, we are here to help. If push comes to shove, I don't want New Zealand troops to be involved on the Australian mainland, it will give the impression that New Zealand is meddling in Australian politics. I would rather you did this with your own presidential troops. But, if you need us, we will be there for you. Rescuing your family to help you is a different kettle of fish. We will back you one hundred percent. Though, sir, we have to stop your troops from invading and, that, I'm sure, will be devastating for you. We hope from our point of view that casualties will be low. Once you have taken over Parliament and got the police onside, it might be a devil of a job to stop the generals. Our people will know where they are, and will send you and your troops the Intel so you can put a stop to this madness from your end. You and most Australians are not to blame, sir; it is what it is. Unfortunately, a madman and his team have taken over your demographic constitution and are riding roughshod over everyone. We in New Zealand are positive that you will get things back on the straight and narrow. We have faith in you, sir. You understand we cannot do a thing until your army, navy and air force cross our borders. We can plan, but we cannot stop your country until they break the Geneva Convention. No declaration of war on a neighbouring state is against the convention. Once your country is across our three-hundred-kilometre border, we can repel them and we will. Please believe me when I say we will do the utmost to keep all casualties low.'

'You sound as though you can win this, Jim? We have a very large armed force compared to you.'

'Mr President, we think we can, so it is important on your end to lock up those traitors on your side of the ditch quickly to stop any bloodshed as soon as possible.'

The president looked at his watch. 'It's time I left; I'll convey all this to my chief and get back to you again soon.'

'Mr President, can you hold off telling anyone for a few days; we can do a few checks of our own. It's just that we have to know conclusively that your chief is not in the pocket of your prime minister. Is this acceptable to you?'

'You think he isn't the president's man?' He grunted and frowned.

'We don't know yet; we will in a few days, just give us this time.'

'All right, Jim, mum's the word, but if he is not with me, then we are both up to our necks in the brown stuff. Call me in two days.'

His figure faded into thin air. The room was quiet as the grave.

Jim turned to Cyril Takarei, the head spark operator.

'Can we get this information within two days, Cyril?'

'Well, sir, we have sparked him over the last few weeks. Up till now he is coming out in favour of the president. I'll let you know as soon as we get further conformation, sir. I believe he is the president's man.'

Two days later, the conformation came through: Colonel Jones was overheard talking to his men privately.

'We must keep alert,' he was saying, 'an army colleague that I know told me there is going to be a war, and has informed me the president's life is on the line. From now on, no one meets the president unless our guards vet everyone, including our prime minister and his cronies; he is never to be alone. They will not get to him on my watch. I'm working on a plan to make sure he is out of the way if there is any attempt on his life. This is serious, men. We're sworn to protect him and our way of life. This is an honor and privilege we will die for trying to do just that.'

The president received a message from the PM of New Zealand. All it said was, he was to be trusted.

CHAPTER SEVENTEEN

Brisbane, Australia

23.59, 31st January

The Star of Yokohama slipped its mooring and quietly pulled away from the wharf, heading up the Brisbane River before turning right after Fisherman Island. Keeping Mud Island on her left, she sailed between Moreton Island and North Stradbroke Island. Then she set a course and speed south-east to arrive at the Wellington lock at the precise time, the morning of the sixth of February. It was going to be a leisurely cruise to the shaky islands. She was to keep New Zealand on her port side as she headed down the New Zealand coast to Wellington.

On board was the First Australian Infantry Battalion comprising two thousand men and women. There were a section of army MPs, a dozen tanks with their personnel, sixty trucks and drivers, and self-propelling guns with three sections of artillery men. Also, cooks, medics, and a dogsbody of other trades to keep the fighting personnel in good order, all under the command of Colonel Jack Best.

The ship was to be on station at the Wellington lock entrance at 3:00 a.m. New Zealand time, the morning of the sixth of January. Once into Wellington Harbour and docked at the roll-on, roll off wharf, army personnel would have at least an hour to get ready to assault Parliament and all of their military and civilian targets. The jumping-off time was 6.41 a.m. to coincide with all other operations around New Zealand. The Colonel was confident that his men and women would have the situation under control within an hour of disembarking from the ship. He had gone over the plan repeatedly. His section leaders knew exactly where they needed to be, how long it would take to have complete control of Wellington City. They had practised for a couple of months west of Rockhampton, and had completely embedded their task into their minds. Colonel Best was a stickler on any operation, and they were going over it again and again until they arrived at their jumping-off point. Two thousand combat troops with no opposition. It was going to be a cakewalk, with the parachute regiment linking up after they had taken Wellington Airport and Thornton Tunnel. This was to be the icing on the cake.

The Australian government announced a large exercise of their combined armed forces from the first of January until the fifteenth. They would use the expanse of the Tasman Sea down past the roaring forties, to around one thousand kilometres south of Disappointing Island. Including a mock invasion, using the Southwest National Park in Tasmania. It was the excuse the government used to deploy their armed services. The world would not take a blind bit of notice, though a few foreign satellites would pop over the area just to monitor things and report back to their member counties. New Zealand knew it was a sham. The new spot lasers installed on the satellites were targeting the armed services to find out exactly their battle plans. New Zealand now knew exactly what Australia wanted to achieve once they were online on the morning of the sixth of February.

Zero five hundred hours on the first day of February, the Republic Australian Navy Ship Gosford, one of twenty destroyers of the RAN, slipped its moorings and followed the Yokohama out of the roads. She would be fives hours behind the Yokohama. Once she reached Wellington, her job was to blockade the harbour.

A thousand kilometres south at the naval dock in Sydney's harbour, in the early hours of the first day of

February, two battle groups slipped their moorings and headed out of the harbour.

Battle group Alpha set out with the aircraft carrier Melbourne, carrying fifty-five McDonnell T 97 EE Sea Eagle fighter bombers with a ten-thousand-kilogram payload. Its three destroyers, Newcastle, Canberra, Wagga Wagga, and supply ship Penrith, were the first to leave. Their mission was to be online at the false dawn of 3:00 a.m. on the sixth of February off the Kaikohe Coast of Northland, New Zealand. Their task was to knock out the RNZAF Air Force Base Kaikohe and, subsequently to destroy all naval opposition in Auckland, including the Harbour Bridge, Hobsonville, and the harbour tunnel. That would leave Mangere and the western motorway tunnel as a covering backup for the RASAS. They were going to parachute into and take the International airport, TV, Podcast Stations, and the central police station using the bridge and tunnel, as their means to arrive at their destination.

The second battle group, Bravo, set out with the Aircraft Carrier Sydney, which carried the same flight group as the Melbourne, with its three destroyers, Brisbane, Cairns, Mackay, and supply ship Lithgow. They were to be stationed off the coast of Taranaki on the morning of the sixth of February. The aircraft from this group were to bomb the old army base at Waiouru and the principal army base at

Linton, including the air force base at Ohakea. Their secondary task was the destruction of all the bridges on the main highways to stop movement between major town centres.

Battle group Zulu left its base in Tasmania on the morning of the first February, with the Aircraft Carrier Adelaide, destroyers Perth, Darwin, Nullarbor, and the supply ship Mardi. They headed towards the Roaring Forties to come around the bottom of New Zealand and be on station near the Chatham Islands at the false dawn on the sixth of February. Their task was to destroy the Army base at Burnham Christchurch, the naval facilities in Lyttelton and Bluff, and also the air force base in Blenheim. Then when that assignment was complete, take out all major bridges on the East Coast of the South Island, making it impossible for any movement whatsoever, including blocking all passes over the Alps.

All the blockade ships left their naval bases over a twenty-four-hour period. The RANS Toowoomba was to blockade the Auckland Harbour and sink any New Zealand Navy ship behind the locks. All Aussie ships had drones that could fly off and report back in 3D, any situation. If the ships were in the harbour, the Australians would know. Eleven ships, all destroyers, were to be used as blockades. Every New Zealand harbour was a target. Auckland, Whangarei,

Tauranga, Napier, Wellington, Nelson, Lyttelton, Dunedin, Bluff, New Plymouth, and the Manukau Heads. Each ship was to destroy all New Zealand Navy ships if they came across them. Also, stop all shipping coming and going through the locks that protected the harbours.

Stage one was now set in action, as all the ships had left their ports. At the air force base at Williamstown NSW the new P86 Starlifters were on standby for the Republics SAS who were to drop into Wellington, Auckland, and Waitangi on the sixth of February. The Wellington group was to link up with the troops from the Yokohama once the airport and tunnel were secure. The Auckland group was to drop onto Auckland International Airport to secure it, with the second group on the aircraft to drop into Albert Park and take all government buildings, including police, podcast, TV, and telecom facilities—at the same time locking down all internet communications.

Last, the Waitangi group was to capture the Waitangi meeting house where the celebrations were to be carried out, then take prisoners of all the members of the New Zealand parliament who were there. The largest chopper in the Aussie Air Force would be on hand to fly the MPs under guard to the waiting aircraft carrier once they rounded them up. From there, they'd transport them back to Australia.

The current plan was set in motion and all the Australian PM and his cabinet could do now was wait for the start. In their minds, this was a forgone conclusion; they had been monitoring the New Zealand armed services for months, and as far as they could ascertain, it was laughable. The Kiwis were a complete joke, and this invasion was going to be a cakewalk.

The after-invasion committee comprising the Australia PM, Donald Anderson, Harold Wade, Simon Willis, David Abbot, Andrew Baggs, Barry Eaton, and George Gannon, had a preliminary meeting. They were deciding how to move forward once the country was under their command. Law and order were the major topic. Water was the second reason for invading. Once the initial invasion was over, they would pour thousands of troops into the towns and cities to keep the law and order. Any dissidents would be shipped over to the dust bowl of Australia to be interned in the special prisons set up. All parliamentary personnel from members to cleaners would also ship to the camps. They would set an interim governor under the direction of the Australian PM to run the country with military law, utilising labour from NZ to build more pipelines from the high-country storage lakes to the coast. This was to increase the water flow for the hundreds of tankers that would be on hand to supply the Australian mainland.

Complete restriction on travel for the local population with Kiwis told where they could and could not work. The country would split into four areas with a line drawn through the middle of both Islands. They would be province A, B, C, D; each would have a ruling deputy governor who would be under the overall command of the governor in Wellington. He was answerable to the Australia PM. Reclassified as President for life. This was the interim thinking of the group of seven. New Zealand would be a working-class state of Australia. Once Australia's water problem was secure, there would be the time to look more deeply into the country as a whole. Immigration would be a good option, moving thousands of Aussie over to New Zealand and clearing out the overcrowded cities at home. Then move the whole of the New Zealand population to below Christchurch, leaving the rest of the country to the new migrants.

The talk went on into the wee hours until the PM called a halt.

'Get that drawn up smartly, he ordered his secretary. Copies to all members of this cabinet. We still have a lot of planning to do,' he announced to his team. 'The big question must also go into what are we going to do with the Kiwi politicians. We'll leave that until we have the country under our control. You all have a lot more to think about. This has been a positive session.'

'What are we going to do with the president, Prime Minister?' uttered Simon.

'Yes, well, that's another small interference, to my way of thinking; tell me if I'm on the wrong track. The entire family should disappear quietly, no fanfare. We let the public know that NZ terrorists dropped onto Hamilton Island, where they assassinated the entire family, also killing their brave guards. I will suggest to the president that he can visit his family after we have invaded, and we will kill two birds with one stone. Start planning that now, Harold,' he expressed, turning to his deputy. Make it look like it's done by New Zealanders. Leave a couple of bodies around the place in NZ uniforms. Make sure they position the guards in a way that it looks as though they died trying to save their president and family.'

'We will use the special black operation company, suggested Andrew Briggs, the commander of the Australian Defence Force. They are very good at what they do and all sworn to secrecy under threat of death. They will have no qualms at all about this operation.'

'Fine, liaise with the deputy and have something drawn up before the subsequent meeting tomorrow.' Looking up at the clock, he said, 'Is it that late? Make it this afternoon,' the PM ordered. 'Next meeting at fifteen hundred hours.' He climbed out of his chair. An excellent meeting, he thought, everything was going according to plan. He grinned at his deputy. 'Our country will be the talk of the world. We will tame the dust belt with all the water we take from NZ. We will have land out east to grow our food; our people deserve it. To the winners, the spoils. I wish I could see the look on the NZ Greenie prime minister's face when we walk in and take over his country. It serves them right for not spending the dollars on defence; really, it's their own fault. The entire country are a bunch of no-hopers.'

CHAPTER EIGHTEEN

New Zealand Air Force Base, Kaikohe

2 a.m, 6th February, New Zealand Time

Two aircraft sat on the tarmac at Kaikohe Air Force Base, waiting for the green light to take off. Both aircraft looked similar. One was the military version of the other. Inside the Vulcan AJ277R were six SAS special ops groups with their new wingsuits. They were state of the art, not needing a parachute, with small electric jets stopping the fall and hovering if need be. The helmets had clear vision day and night, with infrared capabilities up to ten kilometres, working on a sliding scale to adjust to the area they were working in. They would jump from two thousand metres, twenty kilometres from Hamilton Island. Their job was to neutralise the guards, then take the Australian president's wife and family back to New Zealand. Sitting on the tarmac next to their aircraft was the PM's Vulcan. They would follow the military Vulcan and wait for the call into the president's Hamilton Island residence. They would come in under cloak, hover then land, load, and fly away with their passengers to safety.

Sitting in the military Vulcan was Captain Ian Dagg and his selected team: W/O Matt Eaves, Sargent Susie Mataio, private Joel Neho, Walter Hyuk, and Fete Mapu. All had done one thousand jumps and were top SAS operatives. They were going over the plan once again. Captain Ian Dagg was explaining:

'We know there are ten guards, six on duty at any given time. The sleeping quarters are at the back, on the first floor. This is your job, Fete and Joel, to make sure they don't wake up. You will come in through the back door. They locked nothing, would you believe it. It makes it so much easier. Walter, you will take out the guard on the wharf. Then join Fete and Joel, who will by then be outside on the wharf side of the house. The roving guards come around every six minutes, and they pass each other on the wharf side of the house. As they cross, take them both out. Then secure the landing perimeter. Matt, Susie, and I will come in through the side door and dispatch the guards on the first floor. Then head up to the second floor and take out the last guard who patrols the length of this hallway. The bedrooms are off to the side down this hall. It will be up to us to get the family out and downstairs smartly. Once the last guard is down, double green is the call sign. Fete, you signal the aircraft.

'While we are getting the family out, the three of you,' he ordered, eyeing the privates, 'collect all the guards and place them in the guards' bedroom, then lock the door. All lasers set on stun for twelve hours maximum. We leave everything tidy. Once on the aircraft home, we can then relax. Don't forget your sunnies. Any questions? None; right. Let's just relax.'

There was a beep from the captain's helmet, then a double green. The Vulcan lifted quietly into the air, applying full power at five hundred meters, climbing to twenty thousand metres.

'We will be at the drop point in forty minutes,' the pilot informed the captain.

The second Vulcan was behind them and would hover over Hamilton Island under cloak until given the green light.

10 p.m., 5th of February, Canberra time

Brendan Talbert walked into his office at his residence in Canberra with his head of security. He locked the door, went to his desk, and sat down. He pulled a small device no bigger that an old box of matches out of a secret compartment in his desk. The small light was flashing two greens. He spoke to the box: 'Activate and cloak.'

Instantly the figure of the New Zealand prime minister materialised. 'Good evening, Brendan, and you also, Captain Millar. Our operation is go. Can you get hold of your wife, sir; my men are in the air. And be there at one a.m your time.'

'Thank you, Jim, Brendan replied. I'll do that as soon as we have finished this conservation. Captain Millar has his part sewn up, and I will be ready to go once I have the affirmative that the family is safe and well.'

'We will have your wife message you from the aircraft, Mr President. Just to put your mind at rest, we will hurt no guards. They will be out for a while, no doubt have sore heads and feel groggy, but no harm will come to them. Do you need our help in Canberra tomorrow morning?'

'No, thank you, Jim,' the president replied. Captain Millar and I have been as busy as bees. It is just as well our prime minister is not popular. I have sufficient people in the armed services and police to do what I have to do. I cannot thank you enough, Jim; Australia will owe you a big debt.'

'Not at all, Mr President. We want Australia to be strong in the right way. We need to be mates again, and with luck, all this will be the step forward we need. I must go—lots to do; good luck to you both. Here's hoping that everything goes to plan.' He faded away.

'Right,' the president began, 'I'll contact my wife. Will you, Captain, continue with the plan to close parliament down. It's going to be a long day for us all, I'm afraid.'

10:30 p.m., Hamilton Island

Colleen Talbert was in her bedroom on Hamilton Island when the monitor beeped. She pressed a button and her husband's face came online. She smiled.

'Good evening Brendan. I'm missing you so much. When will I be able to come home with the family?'

'Hello, my love. I'm scrambling this call—will you do the same at your end please. I don't want anyone listening to our private conversation.'

She spoke to the monitor. 'Scramble. Done,' she acknowledged.

'Good. Now listen carefully,' he conferred. 'This is so very important.' He explained what was happening, and what was going to happen. 'My hands are tied right now, Colleen. Knowing my family is safe is a load off my mind. The NZ prime minister is sending a plane to take you out of the country until this is over. So I need you all to be ready to move at a moment's notice. Be careful We don't want the guards to know that anything is different tonight.'

'Oh heck, I wish you had told me earlier; the grandchildren are in bed.'

'That's fine. Acting normal putting the kids to bed is all I want. Secrecy is paramount now. Get the family together; emphasise to Byron and Tiron to scoop up the children as fast as they can when the Kiwis arrive. No looking back, just go. The NZ PM told me he has his special SAS force coming; be ready to move from one in the morning.'

Colleen looked at the monitors clock. 'We better hang up; it's eleven p.m. now.'

'You can message me when you are in the air. Good luck, my love, I'll see you and the family in a few days. Kiss everyone for me.' The monitor went dead.

Colleen gathered her thoughts, then went looking for the girls. It was late. Her eldest daughter Judy was with her husband Byron watching old movies in 3D. Quietly, she asked them to follow her to Mary and Tiron's room. Knocking lightly, they all went in. The guards were quite inconspicuous, which was a godsend, making it easier to talk. Colleen explained what was happening in whispers and shared their father's information.

'We only have a couple of hours before they arrive; prepare to move quickly.'

'Are you sure all of this is legitimate, Mum,' enquired Judy, 'it seems a bit far fetched. The guards have been very good to us.'

'Look Judy, there is more here than you realise. You trust your dad, don't you?'

'Yes, of course,' she breathed, still uncertain.

'Well then, we do as he says. Right, family; we travel light. Only what we have on. Grab the children and follow the instructions of the Kiwi blokes when they arrive. Let's get ourselves sorted, but quietly; we don't want the guards knowing there is something up. Make sure lights are out and we are off to bed, everything as normal.'

They all left for their own rooms, passing the hall guard and saying good night with a smile.

'Time to head off to bed.'

The guard nodded his head and headed down to his chair at the end of the hall.

2:35 a.m New Zealand time, Tasman Sea

Five minutes to bailout, the jump light flickered on. The captain stood up.

'Okay, we are on, people.'

He flicked a small switch in his suit; the helmet came up and over his head. It took a second or two to come on line. Each helmet controlled the entire suit, from communication to pressure and climatic control, keeping the suit at a pleasant twenty-one degrees. The infrared would turn on once they all touched down. They also had contact, if needed, to the satellite Wha.

The plane depressurised. Then the rear ramp came down. The group was standing in line as the double-green light came on. They stepped off together. Once out of the aircraft, they stretched their arms and legs into flying-squirrel-in-flight mode. The electric motors clicked in on their suits. They activated navigation through the helmets, and like ducks on a pond, the SAS operatives headed for Hamilton Island. The night was clear as they came down to five hundred metres. Satellite Wha had done a survey of the drop points and had given the captain the green light to land. They closed in on the Island and ever so slowly sank to the ground. Their helmets then returned to their collars, and the small microphone and earplug came into the equation. Placing their sunnies on turned dark into daylight; touching a small switch on the top of the glasses gave them infrared. They went about the job at hand.

Joel Neho and Fete Mapu slipped through the back door, keeping close to the wall, their laser guns set on full stun. The infrared image on his sunnies had four sleepers in the next room as they silently slipped up to the door. Joel quietly turned the door handle, shifting their guns to the firing position. He swung the door open and Fete fired. No noise, only a light beam came from the gun. There was movement under the blankets as the light hit the sleepers. They checked their work by shaking each guard, checking their pulse. All were out like a light. Then, as quietly as they came, they left the house, heading around to the boathouse side to wait for Walter. He had sneaked up to the boathouse wharf. The guard there was lounging over the barrier, looking at the water, and listening to the fish jumping. Walter gave a small whistle to attract his attention. He did not want to fire. The guard might fall into the water. Not only could he drown, but it would make a racket. The guard swung his head around. He ported his rifle and took three paces towards the noise when a light hit him in the chest. He collapsed instantly. Walter ran over, checking his pulse and, finding everything in working order, dragged him into the undergrowth. Then he moved towards the house.

By this time, Joel and Fete had set up their position to wait for the two roving guards to pass each other. Walter slipped in beside them. No words spoken, just a thumbs up. A few minutes later, they heard the guards in both directions coming around the house. They stopped for a natter. They were getting into their conversation when two light beams hit them and they crumpled to the ground. Walter ran over to check them, took their weapons and headed back to his mates. They spread out to control and protect the landing perimeter.

Captain Dagg, with Matt and Susie, snuck into the house via the side door. Susie slipped down to the kitchen. Her infrared image told her that there was a guard there. She caught sight of him eating a sandwich at the table. Susie was of two minds: to shoot now or let him stand up. She did not want him to fall over the table and chairs, creating too much noise. She waited a few minutes, watching him wipe his mouth. Then he stood up and walk towards the bench. She fired. He fell with a loud bang. So much for not making a noise, she thought, as she ran up to check his pulse.

Another guard came out of the room to check on the noise, right into a blast from Matt's gun. He never hit the floor, as Ian ran in and grabbed him, laying him quietly down on the floor. One to go. The two men crept up the stairs. Their infrared showed the last guard with his head down on his chest fast asleep. They stepped into the passage, and Ian fired instantly. The guard fell off his chair onto the carpet.

'All down?' he asked his team.

'Green,' came the answers.

'We'll sort out the civilians now,' Captain Dagg voiced. 'You three know what to do once the aircraft arrives.'

Fete touched his glasses, and a light came up. 'Double green' he reported. The Vulcan picked up the message. They were in hover position.

'Roger,' came the reply. Then, once the aircraft uncloaked, and on the ground with his other mates, he went to pick up the sleeping guards.

Ian and Matt walked up to the president's wife's door. Ian tapped quietly as Susie arrived at their side. The door opened and Colleen looked out. 'Kia ora, ma'am; I'm Captain Ian Dagg, NZ Army, my W/O Matt Eaves and Sergeant Susie Mataio. We are here to take you on an extended holiday. Are you and your family ready, ma'am?'

'What about the guards, Captain?' she whispered.

'No worries, they're taken care of. They are just having a long sleep, and will wake up groggy. Can we talk on the plane, ma'am, we need to get moving.'

Colleen went to her daughters' bedrooms knocking and announcing, 'It's time to go.'

The children came out of their rooms with the men carrying them, wrapped in blankets.

'Have you any luggage?'

'No, just what we are wearing.'

'Good, then please follow Susie,' Ian instructed them.

They walked smartly down stairs out the front door to see a very large plane hovering just off the ground, steps down, with an air hostess beckoning them to the stairs. They rushed over and clambered aboard. Waiting a few minutes until the last of the SAS were aboard, the door closed. The hostess was making sure that everyone had a seat belt firmly secured. Then the aircraft lifted quickly into the early morning sky, turned east, and headed to Queenstown, NZ. The aircraft was ten minutes into its flight when Colleen sent a message to her husband:

'We are on our way; everyone is fine, she stated on the 3D monitor. I gather we are going to Queenstown. I have never been, so it will be lovely to see the mountains.'

The voice message sent. Another came through from the NZ prime minister.

'Lovely to have you with us, Colleen; we will catch up after this fiasco. Until then, relax and enjoy our hospitality.'

The first stage was over. Now the president had the opportunity to finish this once and for all. With the presidential guard and loyal police, they were going to take back parliament at the same time as the Australia Armed Forces started the attack on New Zealand. He did not want to show his hand until then; he wanted all the parliament members

and heads of the armed services in one room
together before he would pounce, praying once that
was done he then could order all armed services in
New Zealand territory to pull out.

CHAPTER NINETEEN

2:45 a.m NZ time, 6th February, Wellington

The Yokohama car transporter turned into Cook Strait, heading towards the locks in Fitzroy Bay. There was a hive of activity on the ship. The Australian Army, once disembarked, would make a beeline for the New Zealand Parliament building and other strategic points in the city.

A message came through the ship's communication system:

'Good morning, Yokohama, your allocated lock is open and waiting for you. Four greens seaward, enter and leave at two knots. The pilot will wait for you as you leave the lock.'

'Thank you, Lock Control; slowing to two knots,' responded the captain of the ship.

Slowly and surely, with lookouts stationed port and starboard, the Yokohama slid placidly into her lock. Once stopped, Lock Control contacted the bridge again:

'Have a good morning, Captain, Lock Control out.'

The massive lock doors slowly closed, enclosing the ship as the water drained and sunk down to the harbour level.

Like a very slow elevator, the large ship descended. From the ship's height, the captain looked down on the pathway on top of the dyke. He followed the walkway with his eyes, right out to the control station, where it connected to the mainland. Then the downward descent stopped. He frowned.

Colonel Jack Best of the RAA asked, 'Is there a problem?'

'I'm not sure why we have stopped the descent. You cannot hear the pumps working; something is wrong.'

A few minutes passed, then communication came through:

'Yokohama, this is Lock Control. There is a problem; our pumps have malfunctioned and ceased to pump. We cannot find the cause at the moment. We'll have a maintenance team with you shortly. Stand by please for conformation of time.'

'Bloody hell', Jack Best swore, 'this will stuff up the timing if it's not sorted. We cannot get in touch with Canberra coms as we are under strict coms silence. Bugger. How long from the lock to berthing, Captain?' he asked.

'An hour and a half till docking. Time now 3.15 a.m. Let's see. If they take an hour to fix the pump, we still would have forty-five minutes up our sleeves to get sorted. We will be fine. If it takes a couple of hours, we are going to be so far out of sync, it will jeopardise the entire operation here in Wellington. The SAS cannot link up with you.'

'Okay, thanks, sir.' The Colonel turned to his captain. 'Work out a way to bridge the gap from the ship to the walkway over there. That walkway will take us to the mainland via the Lock Control building. We can have feet on the ground and still be at Parliament on time. Though we won't have our heavy equipment.'

Swinging his binoculars toward the building that housed Lock Control, he grunted.

'Six klicks.' Then, looking down at his map, 'twelve klicks to the city, passing the airport. If we cannot get the vehicles off this ship, we take as much as we can carry and leg it.'

'Roger that, sir,' he replied, turning to the captain.

'Leave it with me. I'll work on the assumption we are going to be too late and we revert to Plan B. I'll be in touch. I need to organise an assault by land.'

He left the bridge and took the elevator down to the car decks and his men.

Fifteen minutes later, Lock Control came on in 3D.

'We are sorry, Captain, our people will be on their way shortly. We won't be with you until around seven a.m. They are up at Napier finishing a lock door malfunction. We have at their disposal an aircraft. It will take around an hour to fly down, and the team still has to finish the job off in Napier. We are very sorry; we usually have plenty of staff around, but today is a public holiday, and this problem has never occurred before. All I can suggest is, sit tight and you should be in port for lunch. The best laid plans, eh! We will keep you posted. Lock Control out.'

The 3D image vanished, leaving the captain of the Yokohama perplexed.

He turned to his writer.

'Take a message to Colonel Best. Tell him we're stuck, and there will be no movement until seven a.m. at the earliest if we are lucky.'

The writer arrived at the makeshift ward room where the Colonel had all his officers and senior NCOs in a group going over his plans. The sailor messenger handed him the message, saluted, and left.

The Colonel read the message and rubbed his hand through his hair.

'Bugger,' he complained, 'this Plan B is now plan A.' The ship cannot move. We need ladders and planking to cross from this deck to the dyke walkway. Once over onto the pathway, the first platoon will move as fast as they can to Lock Control. Take that position, then we will send the second platoon over. They will secure the pathway from the Lock Control building to the mainland. We will take up defensive positions on the mainland until we have everyone off. There is a track here, pointing to the map. It brings us to Happy Valley Road. We will appropriate any vehicle we come across. We need to move fast once we hit the suburb of Island Bay. Even though it is a public holiday, it will not be easy staying inconspicuous. There are two thousand of us, so we leapfrog in groups of two hundred as we move towards the inner city. Any vehicles we have, we will load up and make a beeline to our reference points. Copy these maps now, hand out all ammunition, and be ready to go in twenty minutes.'

3.30 a.m., National Crisis Management Centre, Parliament, New Zealand

The conversation from the Yokohama was coming through loud and clear. Because of the spark that the NZ satellites had been firing off for weeks at all

Aussie military personnel, New Zealand was reaping the rewards. The NZ chief of defence was sitting listening intensely to all the conversation from the colonel in charge, Jack Best.

NZCOD Sir Gary O'Brien was thinking out loud:

'We are all set at the Lock Control building. Once they move, we'll hit them hard. Then I'll get in touch with them through our link. I'll give them one warning and if they do not submit to my demands, we hit the ship. We will cut all communication and render all military weapons inoperable. Do you agree, ladies and gentlemen?' he said, turning to his NCM Centre Parliament colleagues.

The navy, army and air force chiefs gathered together. They had their fingers on the pulse. Men and woman of all three services were seated around monitors that were up and running. There was coms connection to all bases and satellites, also to the PM, including his parliamentary caucus through the PM's aircraft com and satellite. All bases were on red alert and ready to go. Naval ships were out of all harbours, had cloaked and were following all the enemy task forces. The air force would scramble at four a.m. They would sit and wait at their designated heights and reference points. All Army reserves were patrolling Ninety Mile Beach, Waitangi, Kaikohe, and Kaitaia,

Auckland inner city and had set up a perimeter around Albert Park and Browns Island, with another group at Auckland Airport. A reservist attachment at Evans Bay, Miramar, Lyall Bay, Hataitai, and Newton, with snipers at the top of Mount Victoria, were all on station.

The COD thought they had done as much as they could; now it was wait and see.

New Zealand, 3.45 a.m., Yokohama

The first platoon was ready. Engineers had rigged the planks from the ship to the walkway of the dyke. Forty-four men waited until the colonel slapped the lieutenant on the back.

'Good luck. Be as quick as you can. The second platoon will be ready once you have secured the Lock Control building.'

They jumped up onto the planks that ran across to the pathway, then once they were all on the dyke proper, they fanned out as much as they could and ran towards the building.

The New Zealand army personnel inside the Lock Control building amounted to a platoon of twenty men. They all had sunnies which turned night into day. When the Aussie Army blokes were about one kilometre from the building, the lieutenant ordered cone fire spread. The men took aim at the soldiers and fired simultaneously. There was a slight crackle of electricity as the light beams of twenty lasers spread out from their guns in a cone shape—hitting the Aussies like a white wall, flinging them off the dyke like old rags. The smell of electricity lingered in the air for a few seconds. As the light mist cleared, they had wiped the pathway clean.

The Aussie colonel was furious.

'What the hell,' he exploded, 'did anyone see what just happened? What was that?'

Turning, he ordered the second platoon, 'Go.'

Another forty-four troops scrambled off the ship and ran towards the Lock Control building. Again the NZ army in the building let go a cone-firing pattern and, once again, the light wiped the dyke clean. They had thrown eighty-eight men off the wall. There were a few survivors; Voices were heard calling for help below the dyke walls.

The time was 4.15 a.m. when the captain on the bridge of the Yokohama stood dumbfounded when he received a 3D message from the NZCOD.

'Good morning, Captain, I'm here to inform you, if you do not cease trying to send troops onto the New Zealand mainland, your ship will suffer the consequences. You have five minutes to run up a white flag. Message ends.' Short and to the point.

The naval captain sent a message to Colonel Best asking for a conference in his day cabin.

'How do they know?' Jack Best asked, 'there is no way they could have an inkling of what we are trying to do.'

'Well, the naval captain replied, the bugger wants us to put up a white flag. I'm not doing that in a hurry.'

'I have lost nearly one hundred troops and achieved nothing, moaned Colonel Best. I'll get a few of our rocket launchers up here and blow that building to hell and back.'

'Do that, colonel, and I'll hold off communicating until it's done.'

Jack Best stood up and had nearly reached the door when another message came through to the captain's cabin.

'Ah, good morning Colonel Best, sorry about your men, but you must realise you are the aggressor here. Your five minutes are up and we know you want to use your launchers up on the bridge. We will not allow that to happen. You have had your warning.'

As he faded away, there were instant pinpoints of lights hitting the ship in all directions. It lasted for a few seconds

'What the hell is happening?' the colonel voiced, as the ship died around him.

The engines failed; all lighting went out. Communication died. Then the army's weapons malfunctioned before their eyes: firing pins, triggers. Ammunition broke in two. Within ten minutes, the ship was a hulk. Nothing worked: trucks sat on the car deck, their engines unworkable; tanks had no workable guns or tracks. Rifles, handguns, rocket launchers — all their weapons completely unworkable — everything just died. A fighting force without the means to fight.

A pinpoint of light hit the bridge and the nanos got to work to restore communication to the bridge. In a second, the figure of the NZCOD came through in 3D.

'Do you surrender your ship, Captain? You are dead in the water. We will restore lighting and power, so you can feed your people and use your ablutions for hygiene. We will also let a rescue party out to search for any survivors from the attack on the Lock Control building. Everyone else must stay on the car decks and not venture up onto the bridge. This includes all officers. No lights must penetrate outside the hull of your ship; it must remain completely dark. We will send over a boarding party. If you agree to this, we will trust you to obey these commands.'

'My God, we didn't even fire a shot. How did you do it? It's not possible, but this ship is dead and you have the technology to fix it on a whim. Yes sir, we surrender and all the conditions will be adhered to.'

'Wonderful, Captain; get your people down to the car decks. We will fully restore the power shortly.'

Five minutes later, a laser light from the Wha satellite hit the ship, and with it, millions of nanos programmed to restart the ship within seconds before the emergency engines kicked in. They restored power, though there would be no communication or weapons. They incarcerated the Aussie Army for the duration. Two hundred New Zealand sailors, fully armed, flew onto the Yokohama at 4.45 a.m., one hour after the original attack.

Back at the war cabinet in Canberra, they did not know that anything was wrong.

CHAPTER TWENTY

0145 RAAF, Williamstown

Three of the latest G180 Hercules aircraft, with a cruising speed of nine hundred kilometres an hour, were sitting on the tarmac waiting for the green light to take off.

On board each aircraft were one hundred SAS army personnel. Their tasks were to capture the New Zealand parliamentary members in Waitangi. The second group was to secure Wellington airport, with the third group jumping into Albert Park and Auckland Airport, securing all 3D news outlets, TV, and internet. They would then take control of all major police stations and main government offices in the inner city.

Each aircraft sat quietly, ready for takeoff. The electric engines hardly gave off a sound. Once given the green light, they tore off down the runway.

A few months before, a couple of Australian tourists had arrived in New Zealand. They had hired a small camper van and travelled up north to the Bay of Islands. Their job was to survey the best area for the SAS to jump into. They would be back there with the marker on the morning of the invasion, a yellow blinking light. Four blinks, it was safe to jump. If the lights weren't there, they cancelled the jump. They had duly sent the coordinates back to the army headquarters in Canberra.

Angus Farm was the jump zone, under three kilometres from the Waitangi Meeting House, where the NZ parliamentary members would congregate. The SAS would use Bayla Road and Tau Henare Drive to arrive an hour before dawn. Just below the meeting house, the manuka bush that hugged the small cliff faces would give the team the protection they needed until it was time to attack.

For the Auckland and Wellington SAS groups, it should have been a straightforward jump. The lights of the cities illuminated the jumping zones. Unbeknown to the Aussies, these cities were going to be blacked out. Once their aircraft crossed into New Zealand air space, NZ would turn all the lights in both those cities off. They would jump into darkness.

New Zealand had been laser-spotting Australia and Australian tourists for months. They had picked up information of the para drops into Waitangi and the two major cities of NZ. When the Australian agents arrived in NZ and headed back up north to the Bay of Islands, NZSIS picked them up then incarcerated them in the new underground prison near Taumarunui, where they grilled the Aussie operatives. This ensured that the SIS knew exactly what they had heard over the spotting devices was, in fact, correct. Then they had worked on a plan to counter the jumping points well in advance.

The chief of the SIS reiterated, 'It is nice to know that the spotting devices are giving us the correct information. Though, it's still ideal to get conformation from the horse's mouth through the agents.'

The NZ plan was very simple. With the Waitangi SAS group, the satellite Wha would fire a laser beam of nanos at the aircraft, changing the navigation system to Moturoa Island coordinates instead of Angus Farm. Moturoa was twenty-one kilometres from Waitangi, close to the mainland. There was no road directly to Waitangi. You could walk around the coastline which was seven kilometres, though you first had to wade off the Island. It would never happen. Three hundred Northland reservists surrounding the island would be in waiting. There was no way that the Australians could get off without swimming. At the same time of the navigational change, another laser beam, with the recommended amount of nanos, would render all military equipment obsolete. They would jump empty-handed onto an island surround by troops. A NZSIS operative would be there also to give the four yellow lights to the aircraft.

With the Auckland SAS, the same scenario would occur as the Waitangi flight. Two laser beams would hit the aircraft; one would change the navigation from Albert Park to Browns Island. The island, just one kilometre off the Howick Golf Club, is a dormant volcano. Waiting for them would be three hundred NZ Army regulars. The second laser strike would once again render the military hardware useless.

The same fate awaited the Wellington SAS. The only difference was that NZDF decided, instead of allowing them to jump into Wellington, NZDF would throw them off course forty kilometres as the crow flies from the capital city. Their drop zone would be Aorangi Forest Park, two kilometres from Mount Ross west of Palliser Bay. This was one thousand metre-high rugged bush-clad area. Dropping into this area, specially if you thought you were dropping into an airfield and it turned out to be rugged bush, was daunting at the best of times. The powers to be would let them jump there and pick them up later in the mopping-up exercise. They would laser-spot all the troops. This would make them easily traced.

With no weapons and the area cleared of all trampers a week before, Aorangi was an isolated place of four hundred square kilometres.

This park size had doubled since the 2020s and been replanted with native bush. You had to have your wits about you with its cliff faces, bush streams, and the uncertain weather patterns. It would keep the Aussie group on their toes.

Zero three fifty-five New Zealand time. Satellite Wha uncloaked and shot out two laser beams at the aircraft, heading for Waitangi. There was no noise as the beam hit the aircraft and subtly changed the navigation computer by a small degree, making sure that the SAS jumped where the Kiwis were waiting for them. Unbeknown to the captain of the aircraft, he announced, 'Five minutes to jump.'

The men rose and checked each other's gear as the rear ramp slowly came down. Four yellow lights issued from our agents below. 'Go, go, go,' the flight sergeant ordered through his micro. The men of the Australian SAS para unit tumbled out into the early-morning dark sky. As soon as they vacated, another laser beam hit the aircraft. Within seconds, all communication went down. A few minutes later, the next beam destroyed the batteries. The aircraft died. The flight lieutenant pilot struggled to maintain glide as he turned towards Ninety Mile Beach. He ordered the rest of the crew to jump.

'I'll try to hold it steady.'

Six men threw themselves out of the aircraft, eventually landing in the sand dunes of Ninety Mile Beach. Hanging from their harnesses, they watched their aircraft belly-land onto the beach. It hit with force, throwing it into the air as it bounced along the beach, until it swung around ninety degrees and ran its nose into a dune, bringing it to a dead stop. All men of this aircraft, including the pilot, survived. Waiting for them was the First Battalion, Northland Infantry Reserve. Coming up behind the aircrew, they marched them all down to the plane to help the pilot, who by this time had gingerly climbed out of his aircraft. They transferred them to another detachment, who would take them to a holding area near Kaikohe while the first battalion waited for more work, which they knew was coming. This was the second act of warfare on NZ soil for over two hundred years. The first had been at the Wellington lock, and one of many as the day proceeded.

The SAS landed in the middle of Moturoa Island. They quickly rolled up their chutes, and waited for their officer's orders. Then the darkness turned to daylight as lamps flicked on around their position. Confusion spread on their faces as they hit the deck, weapons ready. Naturally, they did not know what the hell was going on, until a voice boomed out from a loudspeaker:

'Kia ora, welcome to Northland. You're surrounded. Please stay down and place your hands on the top of your head. Your weapons are inoperable. Comply now.'

The SAS on the ground brought up their weapons, attempting to fire. Nothing happened. Half a dozen laser lights set to stun, hit them, knocking the troops out of action. The Aussies were throwing grenades, yelling in confusion, trying to use their weapons as nothing worked. Everything they tried was unworkable.

The New Zealand captain gave the order to advance, and within minutes it was over. The Aussie SAS Group sat with their hands on heads, looking very dejected.

They sent a message to NZ HQ: 'Success.'

Thirty minutes into the flight, the second aircraft was laser hit, the computer coordinates adjusted to Brown's Island. Gazing out into the night sky, the pilot remarked on the complete blackness of Auckland city before he gave the green light for the paras to jump. Once the string had gone, the flight sergeant voiced the all-clear to the flight crew. Turning left to complete the operation, the aircraft headed over to Auckland Airport with the rest of the SAS. The captain banked hard left to fly over the top of Rangitoto Island, when a flash of white light hit the Herc. The aircraft went soft in the controls and lost height as the engines failed. The captain tried desperately to maintain his height, yelling at his crew and SAS members to get out, while at the same time trying to hold the aircraft steady for them to bail out. Then slowly she nosed down and splashed into the Hauraki Gulf, crashing just off Tiritiri Martangi Island. The crew, including the SAS, floated down with their chutes, landing on the Island. Some drifted onto Shakespear Regional Park on the mainland. Three hundred Auckland Army reserves rounded them up and took them to the army training base at Army Bay. The captain of the Herc never got out. He went down with his aircraft.

The main body of SAS floated down onto Browns Island. This time a few of the troops landed in the sea. The Kiwis heard them splashing around. Once again the lights set up in advance switched on. A few of the troops had landed outside the perimeter. When the lights flicked on, the NZ major in charge gave the Aussie troops a chance to surrender. A few didn't and stayed in the fight. It took a couple of hours to round them all up. Their weapons were unworkable, and they dropped onto an Island where there was nowhere to hide against troops with guns. Eventually the Aussies surrendered. One soldier drowned.

The message was sent to HQ: 'Success at Browns.'

The third aircraft was trying to make sense of the situation. They could not see the lights of Wellington at all so determined that there must have been a power failure. The drop zone coordinates on the computer told them they were on track even though below them, it was as black as the ace of spades. There was no chance of confirmation; there was a complete communication blackout. The crew were unaware that they were off course by forty kilometres.

As the aircraft crossed Palliser Bay, a drone from 75 D squadron hit it with a laser strike which rendered all armaments dead, including personal firearms.

With the green light, the paras flung themselves off the ramp, only to see the aircraft tilt to starboard, then level itself, with the crew jumping for their lives. The last man out was the captain, who watched in bewilderment as his aircraft ditched into the South Pacific outside the Wellington lock gates. The Royal New Zealand Navy picked the crew up, while the paras were going to wander around Aorangi Forest Park in the dark.

To the politicians in Australia, they were none the wiser, the first round definitely went to New Zealand.

The Australian PM had set the action in stone at zero four hundred Australia time. The PM in his war room gave the Australia Republic chief of staff the order to begin the invasion. Signals went out to all ships and aircraft to start their attack, as per the written orders.

Zero six hundred New Zealand time, the battle group Alpha, one hundred and fifty kilometres off the coast of the Hokianga, made ready. The captain of the aircraft carrier Melbourne ordered,

'Bring her around two points into the wind, Number One; prepare for launch.'

'Aye-aye sir.'

'Helmsman, come around two points into the wind, please,' the captain said, turning to the communication comm.

'Signal to destroyers. Operation is now active.'

The sound of action stations was heard throughout the ship as the crew ran to their designated areas.

Sitting on the flight deck were twenty-five H-Tornadoes swing wing semi electric ground to air fighters. The H was for hover, and they sat waiting patiently for the go.

The three frigates of the battle fleet were in defence mode, starting their first circle of the Melbourne. Newcastle ran a clockwise surveillance.

Canberra was on anticlockwise, with Wagga Wagga weaving through the middle. Everyone was on alert until zero six fifteen, when the order to go came through. Twenty-five aircraft lifted off in formation and slowly turned towards Kaikohe Air Force Base. They would come in from the west, crossing over Opononi. Ten minutes after takeoff at six thousand metres, the flight commandeer ordered ground attack formation as the fighters turned right over Rawene, three minutes from target. The time zero six thirty-eight.

The second flight from the Melbourne had taken off and was heading to Auckland. Their job was to hit the navy base on Great Barrier Island, including ships within the Auckland dykes, and all the roads, tunnels and bridges in the Auckland area.

The Battle Group Bravo, with the RANS aircraft carrier Sydney, was situated one hundred and fifty kilometres off the Taranaki Coast. She turned into the wind at the same time the Alpha group aircraft were turning towards Kaikohe. Her aircraft were slightly behind, as the dawn was a little later further down the country. Her aircraft lifted off the deck and proceeded to their destination of Waiouru, with the second flight to take out Linton and all the bridges which would cut off the main roads on the North Island.

The Zulu Battle Fleet, situated one hundred kilometres off the coast of Christchurch, had also gone into battle formation. Aircraft were ready for takeoff. Their job was to hit the army base at Burnham and the naval bases at Bluff and Dunedin. Then knock out all main bridges and hit the air force base in Blenheim, as well as other infrastructure.

A communication blackout was still in operation. Not one of the battle groups knew the fate of the SAS troops in Wellington, Auckland, and Waitangi. The way they saw things, everything was panning out. They believed the operation was going as planned.

The dice thrown, all the pieces were on the board as the clock ticked over to zero six twenty.

CHAPTER TWENTY ONE

New Zealand National Crisis Centre, Parliament

Sir Gary O'Brien, Chief of Defence, New Zealand, stood in the war room at the parliament buildings, looking at the clock. The time was 0625. He knew that the Australian operation was now running; even so, he wanted to make sure that all New Zealand defence were in sync.

Turning to his deputy, Commander Fiona Urlich, he said, 'What's your feeling, Fiona, about the situation?'

'I would give it another couple of minutes, then knock out their communications, sir,' she responded.

She looked at the hologram monitor.

'Their major invasion force is now all nicely incarcerated on board the Yokohama in the Wellington Lock, with our sailors guarding them. They are definitely out of the picture. All their SAS paratroops that were supposed to drop on Wellington are now wandering around the Aorangi Forest Park. No doubt a bit bemused. The navy picked up the flight crews out of the drink. Our Auckland regulars have rounded up all their SAS paratroops on Browns Island, including the regional parks in the area. Our PM has signaled from Waitangi that the Aussies up there are now under our protection.' She grinned. 'We have knocked all troop transporter aircraft out of the air, and our ships are picking up any surviving crews as we speak.'

'We know. In fact, the Aussie PM does not know a thing about what is happening here in New Zealand. We laser-spotted him going into their war room in Canberra in the early hours, this morning. A complete communications blackout was his orders until after the first strike. He and all his heads of staff are in the dark.'

'We scrambled Seventy-Five D squadron at zero four hundred; they are now just waiting for the signal to attack. The drones are thirty kilometres from the Taranaki battle group, with the second flight the same distance from the Christchurch battle fleet.'

'Fourteen D squadron also scrambled at zero four hundred. They're watching the Kaikohe fleet with a keen eye. Everything at our end is a go, sir.' Spreading our navy throughout New Zealand, we will be in position to harass the blockade ships once we have neutralised the battle groups. That is the situation at the moment, sir,' she concluded.

0628 Hours

The CDS turned to Group Captain Earl Quigley

'Operation "Whetu Pupuhi" (Shooting Star) please, Earl.'

Earl turned to his operator: 'Haere,' (Go) he ordered. Instantly, a command message flashed to the satellite Wha. Once the signal upload arrived, Wha uncloaked, did a 180-degree turn and locked on to the Australian satellite Emu. Wha fired a ten-second burst of laser light, hitting Emu full centre, destroying it instantly. It then turned another two degrees, locked on to the Aussie second communication satellite Sydney1, destroying that as well. Australia became completely blind in that instant.

Making sure it stayed blind, they disabled all satellites overflying New Zealand and Australian air space. Wha, Rima, and Ono satellites knocked out communication to the old and new space stations, Russia, USA, England, China, Japan, and European satellites for at least twenty-four hours. New Zealand did not want Australia piggybacking on other countries' communication set-up. New Zealand would apologise later to all the countries concerned.

Earl turned to his chief.

'Whetu Pupuhi, complete, sir. Australia is now deaf and blind.'

'Right, ladies and gentleman; Operation Aotearoa is now a go,' confirmed the CDS.

0631 Hours

The Royal New Zealand Air Force 14 D squadron, sitting at ten thousand metres cloaked, received the order to attack. Two flights of twenty drones swept down towards RANS Melbourne. Red flight stayed on the battle fleet and blue flight tracked the aircraft as they flew over Opononi at 0635. The flight commander ordered, 'Pick your target.' The drone computers worked out the distance, trajectory, and speed of the enemy aircraft. Together as one, 14 D squadron uncloaked. From a distance of thirty . kilometres, killer beams of laser light were fired at the twenty-five aircraft, then instantly cloaked again. It took three seconds. The laser beams hit each aircraft in the engine compartments, killing the aircraft. The nanos disabled all weapons, so there would be no explosion of weaponry when the aircraft plunged into the sea or beach around the Hokianga Harbour, leaving the ejector seats operational so the pilots could bail out.

The flight commander of the Aussie Tornadoes was about to order the command for the ground attack on RNZAF Kaikohe. Out of the blue, a flash of light hit his aircraft. Instantly, his controls went soft, and he had no control at all over his aircraft. The engine died. All the pilot had time for was to release his canopy and pull his ejection lever. Within seconds of being hit, he was hurtling into the air as the aircraft's nose dived towards the Hokianga Harbour. Trying to make sense of what had happened as the parachute ballooned above his head, he remembered a group of blips on his radar for a couple of seconds. Then they just vanished. No noise, not a sound heard. He was dead in the air.

Did those contacts on my radar have something to do with my going down? he thought, focusing on the rest of his flight.

Every aircraft from his flight was in trouble as he watched them heading quickly towards the sea, out of control. He counted twenty-four chutes. He prayed that all his squadrons would survive as he maneuvered his chute towards the beach. As he got closer, he noticed troops with their unusual rifles pointed at him, thinking, How the hell did they know what we were doing? They took most of the airman into custody. A couple of pilots, caught up in the swirling waters of the Hokianga harbour, which was renowned for its tidal rips, drowned. They rounded up the rest of the flight group and marched them into captivity. The aircrew did not know who or what shot them down.

By now, Melbourne Captain Samuel Till was trying to open communication with his aircraft, as the operation was in full swing. He could not understand why they could not get a bleep out of his first squadron of aircraft. There was no contact at all with the war office in Canberra. This was comms silence operation until they had executed the first bomb run. The captain was in communication with his second wave as it ascended in squadron formation from the flight deck and turned south. This flight was to hit the Auckland infrastructure, the navy base at Great Barrier, roads and bridges, and the tunnels of New Zealand's largest city.

Second flight 14 D Blue Squadron was waiting for them over Kaipara Harbour, sitting at ten thousand metres above Mosquito Beach. They sat hovering patiently like eagles, watching their prey. As the Aussies flew over the Pouto Lighthouse, the drones uncloaked and fired a three-second burst of white laser light, then re-cloaked. They observed as, one by one, the aircraft ditched into the harbour as previously, on the first flight the nanos had done their work disarming all munitions. Only the sound of an aircraft breaking up as it hit the water or land, as the case maybe. There were boats to ferry the downed pilots to safety from where they splashed down. In this case, not an airman lost his or her life. They marched another group of bewildered Australian fliers into custody without knowing what the hell had happened to them. One minute they were in a good formation, and the next, their aircraft had died. The surprising thing was the New Zealand Army knew exactly when and where to pick them up. It was quite disconcerting.

Fourteen D squadron then turned their attention to the Alpha Battle group. Melbourne, the aircraft carrier with its three frigates, Newcastle, Canberra, and Wagga Wagga, including their supply ship sitting twenty nautical miles northwest of Ahipara, was not to be left out. The Melbourne was trying desperately to communicate with their aircraft.

Reuben J Webb, the commodore, was quite perplexed. He turned to his captain. 'What in God's name is going on?' he roared. 'Who relayed the question to the officer of the watch who was in charge of communication?'

'Not a bloody peep out of fifty aircraft, no nothing from the war office in Canberra. Someone explain in simple terms what is going on?'

The radar operator, at that minute, announced, 'Twenty bogies just appeared, sir, range twenty-five klicks at three one zero degrees.' Then in a confused voice, he added, 'Bogies just disappeared, sir.'

'Message to battle group Flank speed,' ordered the captain. 'Bring their ships around to steer three one zero. Pass on the coordinates, and engage the enemy once sighted.'

The four ships of the line swung to starboard, leaning into the turn and staying in formation. Their missiles were primed, and all gun crews closed up, weapons ready for action.

From behind them, at twenty-five klicks, and at six thousand metres, twenty drones no bigger than matchboxes uncloaked and gave each ship a three-second burst and vanished. The escorts were just ramping up the knots, climbing up to twenty, when everything went dead. The speed fell off as all ships drifted to a stop, wallowing in the slow Pacific rollers.

'What in the blue blazes just happened?' ordered the commodore to the captain.

'We are dead in the water, sir,' the captain explained. 'The hows and wherefores, I have no idea.'

Information was coming in through runners as all communication was dead.

'Guns are out, radar, nothing electrical is working, sir,' Able Seaman Smith muttered to the captain. 'Nothing is working, sir,' he repeated, 'including the toilets.'

The ships were losing their way and moving dangerously close to each other as the Pacific rollers rolled under the ships' keels. Then, unexpectedly, the comms link came back on. A 3D image of Sir Gary O'Brien materialised.

'Good morning, Commodore Webb, Captain Till. I do hope we haven't spoilt your early morning manoeuvres? It was imperative for New Zealand to let you be the aggressor before we retaliated. Your squadron is now dead in the water and the only way out of this predicament is for you to surrender your fleet. If you agree, we will have you up and running to a maximum of ten knots, enough power to get you back to your home port. It will take a wee bit of time to arrive home. Around nine days. Your aircraft pilots are all in custody. Unfortunately, there are a couple we could not save. Our condolences. We will allow you to communicate with your squadron. There will be no comms to your base headquarters in Australia. We will make sure that all the normal facilities will be back in working order, navigation, et cetera, though no satellite connection as we have knocked them out. Food, hygiene, et cetera, we will restore. Your guns, armament, including all missiles, are now defunct. I'll give you five minutes for you to digest this information. Make sure it is the right decision. Looking at your fleet, you are not that far from colliding into each other. We don't want to sink your fleet, but we will if you don't give me the confirmation I want. Five minutes, gentleman.' The 3D image vanished.

All the officers and sailors on the bridge had watched the communication with open mouths. How could this have happened? They had no clues. How the New Zealanders could get the ships operational was beyond them.

The captain turned to the commodore.

'We have no choice, sir. Nothing is working, and we will ride over the top of the destroyers if we cannot have control back in our hands. I did not know that the Kiwis had this sort of power. If this has happened to us, I don't feel confident about our other squadrons. How the army is getting on, God only knows.'

The communications officer was looking at his watch as everything else was not working, announcing, 'Four minutes, sir.'

'Bugger it,' the captain swore. 'We are between a rock and a hard place. Your call, Commodore,' he said as he passed the buck to the senior naval officer on board. They looked at each other.

'Raise the white flag, Sam. We have done all we can. I don't know what history will say about us. I feel I have let the country down big time.' He swung around and headed out to the docking platform, to just stare at the rollers sliding under the destroyers, which were slowly nudging the ships closer together.

Right on the five-minute mark, Sir Gary O'Brien materialised in 3D. 'Decision time, Captain Till. Can I have your answer, please?'

The commodore came back onto the bridge.

'Ah, Sir Gary, we will capitulate. We don't know how you did it, but our position is now perilous and we need help.'

'Thank you, Commodore. A wise decision. We would like you to take down your flags and run up a white flag on each ship. Once it's done, I will restore your power.'

'Do it!' the commodore ordered his captain in a rough tone of frustration.

Within five minutes, all ships were flying the white flag of surrender. Flashes of white light, each hitting the squadron's five ships, including the supply ship, who was standing alone twenty nautical miles north of the battle fleet. Slowly the power came back to all of the ships, and they pulled away from their collision course with the others. Communication came back as the vessels turned north, heading back to Australia. The last thing the captain heard was, 'We will monitor you all the way home.'

Like a dog who lost the fight, tail between its legs, the Melbourne battle squadron limped home at ten knots. The time was 0645.

CHAPTER TWENTY TWO

Canberra, 0425 Australian Time

Donald Anderson, the Australian PM, was sitting in the main chair at the centre of the war room, looking with delight at the monitor screens, linked to the Emu satellite system, which was following the Australian invasion fleet. He had high anticipation of his plans. The PM ordered complete communication silence until the first of the bombs had hit the ground. He did not know how the SAS were coping or how the army was doing in Wellington. He knew, though, in his own mind, that this part of the operation would be fine. His chief of defence, Andrew Baggs, was not so sure. Even a code contact to let everyone back at headquarters know that the operation was going as planned, a one-second squawk message was likely sufficient. The PM was adamant that, until they dropped the first bombs on an unsuspecting enemy, there was to be no contact with headquarters. All the armed service people were looking at the screens with intense concentration but not too worried, as they knew their forces were superior to New Zealand's. It was the not knowing that made things tense.

At 0428, the screens in the war room went black. Donald Anderson jumped up with a growl, yelling at his staff, 'What the hell is happening? What have you done?'

Air Vice Marshall Paul Jellyman intercepted the PM.

'Just a hiccup; we are going over to Sydney1.'

The pictures on the monitors came back for a couple of seconds, then went blank again. The senior communications technician informed his commanding officer that there was no communication at all. Both satellites Emu and Sydney1 were offline.

'They don't answer anymore, sir. There is not a murmur, no sound at all. It as though they don't exist.'

The PM was livid.

'What do we pay you bastards for? Get the communication back up, now,' he chastised.

He turned to his armed service people.

'Find out what's happened, and report back to me, ASAP. We cannot run an operation like this, blind.'

The SCT informed him. 'We could ask permission to use the other satellites up there. The British and

Americans, plus a host of other countries might give us permission to use their communications, to link with our fleets.'

'Good thought. Carry on, Senior Tech,' voiced the COD. 'Keep us informed.'

All you could hear in the room was the clicking of keyboards and the PM muttering under his breath about what he would do with his men if they could not get their comms back on. There were a few worried looks on the faces of the heads of the three services. They were in a complete bind, not understanding what happened to their satellites.

Every few minutes the COD would ask the senior tech how he was doing.

'It's a real puzzle, sir. I'm not even getting a peep from the space station. There's twenty-four people on board, and they are in contact twenty-four seven. So far no response at all to any of the countries with satellites over on our side of the world, and that never happens. It appears, at the moment, that all comms are down. Could the PM ring his counterpart in the UK, et cetera, and ask if there is a problem with their satellites? It might be the confirmation we need.'

Harold Wade, the deputy PM responded, 'I'll get on to it right away, Prime Minister,' striding off quickly to the nearest 3D link.

Twenty minutes slipped by and the DPM came back into the room, looking like a ghost.

'What wrong, Harold?' the PM spat. 'Out with it.'

'All the countries I rang—the UK, US, France, Japan, Korea, China, Canada, and Singapore all said the same thing. They have all lost contact with their satellites, about the same time as ours. The only difference, the other countries can still trace their satellites, whereas ours have disappeared completely. All our phones on the old cable system are slow as a wet week; they're also down. I tried ringing our embassy in New Zealand. We have no connections at all. The countries are in the same position as us, with no communication whatsoever, to and from their satellites. They are working like hell to bring them back online. When they do, they have given us permission to piggyback to communicate with our fleet. They still think we are running an exercise down south of Tasmania.'

'Well, that's a positive, then, replied the PM, but what would have caused all the satellites to go out together, including the landline? Do you think it has anything to do with the Kiwis? We know they have not got this sort of technology.'

'It could be anything from gamma rays to excess sunspot activity. There is no way the Kiwis can render all satellites useless. No way at all,' voiced the minister of defence, Simon Wills.

'Okay, let's do something positive while we can. I'll order a comms aircraft to fly over to New Zealand and address each squadron. Let's see if it can contact our SAS people on the ground as well,' the COD ordered while looking at the PM for conformation.

'Yes, do that, Andrew. Let's get some positivity into this room.'

Taranaki Coast, 0628 New Zealand Time

The Sydney aircraft carrier and Bravo Battle Group, swung into the wind as the squadron went to battle formation. The frigates, Brisbane, Cairns, and Mackay started their protection manoeuvres around the carrier. Forty Tornadoes—fighter aircraft— waited for the green light. At 0630, they took off to hit Waiouru and Linton Military Camp. A warm, cloudless morning, you could see for kilometres, as the two flights of twenty aircraft each, climbed to ten thousand metres and headed for their destinations. There was no chatter as the flight commanders ordered no comms unless urgent. They did not want any Kiwi comms operator picking up chatter.

Chatter was the least of their problems. With fifty kilometres to go, before crossing over the coast of Taranaki, they noticed two Kiwi navy ships heading towards them. The squadron leader had a smirk on his face, wondering what the hell they could do, when on his radar at fifteen thousand metres, twenty blips became visible, then disappeared. Simultaneously, a flash of light hit his aircraft. Everything stopped working. He tried to communicate with the rest of his flight. They were in the same boat, with no comms, no engines. Their aircraft were dropping like flies out of the sky.

Gliding to an acceptable bail-out point, the squadron leader ejected. It was the only instrument that worked on the aircraft. Thank God, he thought as he bailed out. The flight leader had a little time to think about what had happened as he floated down towards the Tasman Sea. He counted the aircraft. All of them were heading into the drink, the whole forty of them. He could not understand how it was possible, but it was happening now. Everyone had bailed out, which was a godsend. It was then he saw they were going to splash down at the exact spot where the two NZ navy ships positioned themselves, or very close to them. How in the world did they know we would be here at this spot?

Just before dropping into the sea, he smacked the chute release button and plunged into the water as the chute drifted away from him. He had an unobstructed view of where he was in conjunction to the navy ships. It wasn't long before the RNZN pulled him aboard. A rubber away boat scooped him up with ten men from his flight, soggy airmen all asking the same question: How did this happen?

Within the hour, the forty airmen were aboard both boats and were heading for Port New Plymouth Locks. They got no technical information out of the Kiwis. Sure, they were well looked after, wrapping them In blankets, feeding them hot food and drinks, but not a thing about how they came to be at that exact spot or exact time when they went down.

The Sydney's captain, Keith Ash, was in a quandary. There was no explanation for what happened to his aircraft. He was of two minds to send out his choppers to see if he could find them, as he had lost contact with the entire squadron. Then a peculiar thing happened, just before his decision to send out the choppers. Out of nowhere, there were flashes of light hardly seen by the naked eye. The radar had picked up bogies. The contact was only seconds. Then light flashed, and all the ships came to a drifting halt. They were lucky the day was superb and the sea calm as the ships just leisurely drifted apart from each other. With no communication between the fleet, and even though they were under strict instructions not to communicate with Canberra, the captain tried to open a channel, to no avail. The same scenario that happened on the Melbourne, the Sydney got a ping. The comms tech turned to the captain.

'I don't know how they are doing it, sir. We have a 3D call coming through.'

'Kia ora, Captain Ash. I'm Sir Gary O'Brien, chief of defence, New Zealand. I'm sorry to tell you that your squadron is at our mercy. Like your counterpart on the Melbourne, we will give you the opportunity to raise the white flag on all ships. Once you adhere to my orders, we will restore power to you but only enough power to get you home safely. Your weapons are unworkable. We will restore them when you are back in Aussie waters. We gave the Alpha Battle Group ten knots, and we'll do the same for you. All you have to do is run up the white flag on all ships. We shot all your aircraft down before they reached the mainland. Don't worry about your pilots; they are all accounted for and are in custody until this wee skirmish is over. I'll give you five minutes to decide, Captain. You have the option to surrender, or I'll sink your ships.'

'But, sir...' the captain spluttered, 'how did you do this? It's not conceivable.'

'I can understand your frustration, Captain. I really can. I cannot give out our secrets, as you cannot. Please be aware, I will use what we have designed. Please make the right decision. E noho ra.' (See you later.)

'What do you think, Number One? They have just proved they are more than a match for us, and we have not fired a shot. We lost forty aircraft and are wallowing around the Tasman Sea like stranded hippos.'

'If it were my decision, sir, I would run the white flag up. I loathe the idea. Heck, you have to be practical. We have no firepower, and we cannot even use the dunny. I might have a bit of a smile on my face after saying that, sir. I'm pissed off like most men and women on this bridge, and no doubt the crews of the destroyers are the same. We have gone back to bloody semaphore to communicate.'

'I agree, Number One. Message all ships, pull out a white flag and run it up the pole.'

Looking at his watch, he thought, the chief of defence New Zealand should be back with us in a minute. He watched as the white flags raised, hanging limply in the calm conditions. He felt sorry for the men and women he commanded. You could not fight with a dead ship, or ships, and his were dead as dodos.

Right on the dot, after five minutes, the CODNZ was back. No mucking about, straight to the point.

'I see you have raised the white flags as a sensible solution to your predicament. We will give you enough power to take you home. Maximum ten knots. We will monitor you all the way. Once this is over and you have licked your wounds, we will get together for a beer. We will even pay. He smiled. Safe voyage home, Captain. The result is, you did the right thing. We just had a bit more in our arsenal than the Australian government thought. Take care.' His image faded away.

There was a flash of white light hitting all the ships simultaneously. Within minutes, they were all back online, although guns, missiles, or anything to do with armament were dead. They could only communicate with one other, not home base.

The captain turned to his number one. 'Signal to the squadron, max speed ten knots. We are going home.'

It would be nine days before they reached home port, and the political climate in Australia had transformed from the day they left.

CHAPTER TWENTY THREE

0450, Canberra

The Australian PM was losing his temper—banging his fist on the table, glaring daggers at all his cronies, and threatening everyone who was sitting around the conference table in a sweat. All caucus members, including the defence staff, wore worried frowns. The PM was in a dangerous mood, and when he was like that, he was unpredictable. It didn't matter what the experts were saying. All the PM could think of was sending more aircraft. Find out what was happening over in New Zealand, and fix the blackout of communication to all his task forces.

They recorded, back in New Zealand, all his ravings. The laser-spotting that New Zealand was firing at him as he entered Parliament that morning, the Kiwis knew what was going on in his neck of the woods. Every time they had another aircraft ready for takeoff, a Kiwi satellite would fire a laser, killing their batteries. It would take at least six hours to replace them all.

It was frustrating the hell out of the Australian PM. Three aircraft had battery failures and they did not know the cause. Each time they reported it to the war room, the PM's temper was worse.

It was coming up to 0455 Canberra time, 0655 NZ time, with the Australian PM having no clue what was going on. He thought his SAS in Waitangi would now have the New Zealand PM and his cabinet under arrest. By his thinking, they should be on their way back to the aircraft carrier Melbourne. Wellington, the capital, should be in Australian hands, as should Auckland, including army and air force bases, wiped out.

Though, in reality, the New Zealand PM and his cabinet had flown back from Waitangi to Wellington and were, at this moment, in the NCM Centre under the parliament building.

The chief of defence New Zealand was explaining to the cabinet that the New Zealand armed services were certainly on top of the crisis. They had only the Zulu Battle Group to sort out and the blockade ships.

'A piece of bad news,' he ventured. 'We lost a sailor from RNZNS Pukeko in a clash with the RANS Geelong off the coast of the Chatham Islands. They hit Pukeko in the rear gunnery compartment, killing a female sailor. Our ship sank the Geelong and stood by to rescue the crew. Aussies lost twenty sailors. The rest of the crew are now on their way to the Chatham Islands. To be incarcerated there until we repatriate them back to Aussie. We will put the dead sailors that were found around the sinking site into a fish cooler on the Island. We'll sort it out later on about how to get them home. Pukeko will head down to Dunedin for repairs. We have programmed the nanos for the repairs. It should not take too long for her to be back on duty. I believe, sir, that all the loose ends can wait until we have this completely under control, then we can go over everything with cabinet from woe to go.'

'Thank you, Sir Gary, I never doubted your ability, one iota,' replied the PM. 'Please keep us up to date as the day unfolds.'

O655 Inside New Zealand, Territorial Waters, South Island

Zulu Battle Group turned towards Christchurch. This group comprising the aircraft carrier Adelaide and the frigates Perth, Darwin, and Nullarbor were twenty-five minutes late from kick-off. An aircraft had an undercarriage malfunction on take-off and spread itself all over the deck runway, blocking it for nearly half an hour. Captain Mike Holden was trying to keep his cool. Not only was this problem still ongoing, but by now, the first bombs would have dropped on the airfield in Kaikohe, Auckland,

Waiouru, and Linton. SAS troops would have everyone in the bag in Waitangi and Wellington while his group were mucking around like possums in the headlights.

'Runway finally clear,' called out Number One, running up the stairs two at a time.

'What a time to be caught out. I'm surprised, sir, that the powers that be have not contacted you. Wouldn't you think it prudent to break the silence and let them know our position?'

'No, not yet, Number One. There must be a good reason while they are still maintaining comms silence. Right; let's, at last, get this show on the road. Bring her around into the wind, two points, Helmsman.'

'Aye-aye, sir. Two points.'

Slowly, the carrier's head swung into the wind.

The Mirage X100's fixed-wing aircraft were waiting to fly off. These were the last of the old breed of fighter planes. A combination of electric and fuel turbo. They could still do the job they were made for. The large, green light at the end of the runway flashed green as the pilot ramped up the revs. Full brake, then max revs, brake released, and he was tearing down the deck under full power. Within ten minutes, all the fixed-wing aircraft grouped in tight formation and were ready to fly to their targets. The Tornadoes swing-wing aircraft were lifting off to congregate at three thousand metres above the carrier. Once in flight formation, they would make their way to bomb the roads and bridges from Kaikoura to the Southern Alp passes, and the army base at Burnham, while the Mirage group would bomb bridges, roads, and naval bases in Dunedin and Bluff.

Sitting high above both flights, 75 D blue squadron were watching with interest. Their wing commander, a young bloke of twenty-eight, opened comms and uttered, 'I didn't think they would ever move. It's time to get amongst them.'

Splitting formation, the drones dropped ten thousand metres. First flight took the Mirages as they were closer to the coastline. A three-second burst of laser hit the Mirages, killing their batteries. These older-model aircraft, still having the turbo fuel engine, automatically flicked over when the electric power failed. They had to be fired on again. A lesson learnt, the wing commander thought, sending his thoughts which converted to the spoken word through to base headquarters. Make sure when firing on older aircraft that the nanos understand it's not just battery, but fuel as well.

The Mirages hiccuped with the first hit from the laser, then they flicked over to fuel turbo. The second hit, they dropped nose down until the pilots got control. They could glide, though not well, and headed for the coastline. Ejecting close to the Hurunui River mouth, some aircraft were ending up in the sea opposite Gore Bay, others near the Waiau River mouth.

The New Zealand Navy had stationed a couple of their ships between Motunau Beach and the Waiau mouth. New Zealand ships could move quickly to pick up survivors and that is just what they did. Not a pilot lost, but another twenty aircraft were polluting the coastline of New Zealand.

The second wave of bombers headed south. They were going to hit the naval base at Port Chambers. The flight plan was to turn left over Karitane, keeping Seacliff on their port side, over Mt Cargill, then drop into Port Chambers and bomb the hell out of it. The best-laid plans. All went well until, as the flight turned at Karitane, the sky filled with white laser light. All the aircraft controls went soft, losing control, and the pilots only had time to send out a mayday. Unfortunately, no comms were online; nothing worked except the ejection levers and canopy release. By this time, the aircraft were nose down, heading for the drink. Twenty ejected as the two Kiwi ships sitting outside the Aramoana Lock headed to meet the downed pilots. Once again, the pilots could not understand what the hell happened.

The NZ Navy scooped them up with no loss of life. They were taken to the naval base, which they were going to bomb, and held them as prisoners of war until NZ repatriated them back to Aussie.

The Adelaide's captain had a worried frown on his face. Everything was too quiet; the crew were on standby too. He ordered that if anything at all popped up, then shoot it. So all tech comms and gunnery techs were on maximum alert when the radar operator announced, 'Bogies, height six thousand metres; distance, twenty-five klicks, twenty degrees starboard.' In the time he gave the information, the bogies had disappeared. The ship's guns trained on to the coordinates, firing at anything that looked like a target, hoping they were hitting something in the general direction of the radar operator's information.

The flack all around the NZ Air Force drone squadron was a surprise. It gave the fliers a shock as one drone disintegrated. Even though the pilots were many kilometres away in a comfortable seat in the Bat Cave. No one wanted to lose a drone, and the young pilot was pissed, to be sure. In retaliation, the squadron did a left climb to twenty thousand metres, turned, and gave the Aussie fleet a full thirty-second laser strike, out of anger for losing a drone.

The frigate Perth buried her nose into the sea as the front of her bower disintegrated. She became dead in the water, all power lost. Wallowing nose down at twenty degrees, she was relying on the bulkhead doors to keep her afloat.

The Darwin had lost its rudder, and a portion of its stern was shot off. It would go nowhere in the foreseeable future. With no power, the ship was caught in a lazy spinning motion. Last, the Nullarbor lost her bridge. The strike blew out all windows and walls, leaving it exposed to the elements. Everyone on the bridge had cuts and scratches, but no life-threatening wounds. Like the rest of the fleet, she wallowed in the long swells of the Pacific Ocean. It came as a hell of a shock to the Adelaide, who lost all power, as she watched the battle fleet around her become obsolete. There was no loss of life, a few wounded on the Darwin and Perth, but no fatalities. The captains of each ship, perplexed to say the least, did not know what happened. Some sort of electric field that cut the ships to ribbons hit them. It was then their comm tech turned to the captain of the Adelaide.

'Incoming call on 3D, sir.'

Once again, Sir Gary O'Brien came into view as he had previously on the other two occasions.

'Kia ora, Captain Holden, sorry to be the one to bring you bad tidings, but I'm afraid you are all in a spot of bother. If you need anything at all for your wounded, just say the word, and we will send them out to Christchurch Hospital. We did not mean to be so ruthless, but I think the shells got close to our aircraft and losing one pissed my people off. They gave you a full burst of fire in anger. Honestly, you are all lucky to be here: any longer and you would have fried. I'm pleased to stand here and see you are all okay.'

'How in hell did you do what you did, Sir Gary? We only saw your aircraft on our radar for seconds.'

'Trade secrets, sorry, Mike. All I ask of you is to run the white flag up your flagstaff. Once you agree to that request, we will return your power, and the incapacitated ships we will be towed to Lyttleton. You can take the Nullarbor home, if the captain is agreeable to stand on an open bridge, or we can tow her into dock. I'll give you five minutes to decide, Captain.' His image faded away.

The captain turned to his number one.

'Can we contact the other ship's number one?'

'No, sir, no communication at all, and to be frank, I do not know how this has happened. Everything is dead, and the Kiwis know it, and now they are saying they can turn our power on at the flick of a switch. I shudder to think what is up their sleeves.'

'Very well. We are all dead in the water. Semaphore the other ships, run up the white flag.'

Within five minutes, Sir Gary was back on the 3D.

'Thank you, Captain. We see your flags. As we speak, the RNZN tugs Tui and Titipounamu are on their way to you. It is auspicious to have a skeleton crew with those two ships. Of course, it is your decision, whatever you think. Your power will be on in a few minutes. The tugs have been on standby and will be in position for the tows in thirty minutes. Once your power is back online, your radar will pick them up. Have a pleasant trip home, Captain Holden. I'm so sorry it had to end like this for you. Oh, and just as a precaution, we will monitor you all the way back to Australia. One last thing, as I mentioned to Captains Till and Bird on your other battle groups, once this is all over and we are friends again, we will have a beer together and a yarn, my shout. Tēnā koe mō tēnei wā,' (goodbye for now) said he as he faded out.

Within minutes, a white light hit each of the four ships. Sir Gary could have sent the nanos to fix the damaged Aussie ships right away. He was not in the mood to share this technology with the Australians. Just enough power to make life comfortable for the crews being towed back to mainland NZ. Towing the two RANS, Perth and Darwin to Lyttleton for repairs under NZ supervision, out of watchful eyes of Australia. The Nullarbor would go home with the aircraft carrier. They would intern the Aussie skeleton crews until the skirmish was over.

'I don't know how they did it, Number One.'

The engineer swung around in his chair and commented to the captain: 'I have this feeling, sir, they are using nanotechnology. If that's the case, this is pretty sophisticated technology, that's for sure. We have been dabbling, but we have nothing like this.'

'Do you think that's possible, Chief Engineer?' the captain questioned.

'Well, sir, it does point to it. There is nothing I can think of that would cause this sort of damage. It's pinpoint. The way the Kiwi COD talked, all our battle fleets are dead and buried. What they used as an application to knock us out is a big mystery to me as well, sir. I would not like to be in our boss's position when we get home.'

The power came back on, and the captain then spoke to the captains of the stricken ships to explain about the tugs and to ask for volunteers to stay with the tow back to New Zealand. The Adelaide and Nullarbor waited until the tugs arrived. Noticing that they trained their guns very much in line with the battle fleet, it seemed strange to see armament on tugs.

The senior chief of engineering pointed out, 'Look at those guns, sir. They only have a small hole in the barrel end that's a laser gun. Bloody hell, they are ahead of us big time.'

'We will keep your observation quiet, Chief, until we get home. It might help us in the future, though I have a feeling this adventure with the Kiwis will never happen again.'

Making sure the tow was under way, the captain ordered his helmsman, 'Make her go as fast as you can. Let's go home.'

The Adelaide and the frigate Nullarbor turned south, cranked up to the maximum ten knots. Then started the slow journey back to their home base in Australia, leaving behind forty aircraft lying at the bottom of the Pacific Ocean.

CHAPTER TWENTY FOUR

0730, New Zealand Parliament, National
Crisis Management Centre.

The chiefs of staff of the New Zealand Defence Force
were starting to relax, though a few of the politicians
were still not convinced that it might be over, and
the COD had to convince them to stay calm.

Sir Gary O'Brien glanced at the people around
the oval table.

'We now only have to mop up the blockade
ships. At this moment, we have Seventy-five D and
Fourteen D squadrons' eyes on them all. I will get in
touch with each ship through our 3D communication
simultaneously, letting them know the situation.
They'll have a choice: believe what I say is fact and
turn around and go home, or take a strike from our
drones.'

Sir Gary turned to the PM. 'Once this part of the
operation is complete, you will need to be in touch

with the Aussie president to let him know it is safe to move. Personally, I still would like to be in the position to help him even though the president does not want our help. As a backup, we can have fifty of our army boys sitting in an aircraft close to Canberra. Just in case he needs us. It's in your ballpark, Prime Minister.'

'He doesn't want our help, Gary,' the PM clarified. 'I can understand what you are saying. Only to be used if he needs them. I'll get in touch with him again, and see if he has a change of mind,' the PM added.

'With all due respect, sir, let me get the men over there first. It won't take long. They will be on the spot, if required. If he needs them, they'll be there. We don't want the president to be disturbed unduly. He is no doubt, working on his plan to move on Parliament.'

The PM turned to his deputy. 'What do you think, Jono?'

'Well…' he answered, 'it is no skin off our nose, really. If our troops are required, they will be there for him to use without time wasting. So yes, I agree with the COD.'

'All right, Gary. Send them over.'

Gary smiled. 'I'm sorry, sir. They are already there.

I thought you would approve. The men are hovering at five thousand metres, cloaked.'

'You are a cunning bugger, Gary, but I must emphasise, do not use the troops unless you've got my go-ahead or the all-clear from the Aussie president. After what has been happening, I do not want another international event on our doorstep.'

'You have my word, sir. I thought it prudent for them to be close, just in case.'

The PM then continued, 'Once the president informs the Australian population that things are going to be different, we will look at the prisoners' situation, including the SAS troops wandering around the Forest Park. We'll repair the troop ship and send it back to Brisbane with their army on board.'

He turned to Lyn Soo, the deputy leader of the Green Party. 'Lyn, we have marked where every aircraft went down. We don't want the pollution of dead aircraft on our coast if you liaise with your science people to resolve this problem to lift them out.' He paused, thinking. 'Kathy Wong's team might have the solution. Can nanos completely dissolve those planes to atoms? I'll leave that with you, Brigadier Hone Paparoa, Group Captain Earl Quigley, and Commodore Fiona Urlich. Would you advise, Kathy, please?'

'We'll set aside a time to meet up with Kathy, once this scrap is over,' Commander Urlich informed him.

'Prime Minister,' the COD asked, 'let me get back to you shortly. I need to have a yarn with those blockade ships. I hope they take our advice and go home.'

The PM stood up and spoke to his parliamentary colleagues. 'We will meet to discuss our plans for the future with the Aussie president, once this skirmish is over. Also, we will work on a timetable to return the president's wife and family home. We have been lucky. We have only lost one service personnel, plus a drone. The service woman needs to be recognised for her effort. Once everything has settled down, we may find that a lot of the Aussies that came over to NZ under duress might want to go back home. If that is possible, we will not make it hard for them. Next meeting in two hours.'

He stood up. Everyone filed out the door once they turned the cloaking off.

There were ten blockade ships heading towards New Zealand. The eleventh, the Geelong, attacked and sank. She was to blockade Lyttleton Harbour. The rest were closing on their allotted harbours. The CODNZ stood with Cyril Takarei in the comms room. Cyril was also senior comms and voice-over tech.

'Do you think this can work simultaneously, Cyril?' the DOC asked.

'We will certainly give it a good bash,' Sir Cyril replied, looking at the frown on the COD's face.

'Sorry, sir, I was flippant. It will work, sir. We have done it many times before with the parliamentary caucus. There is no reason at all that it will not work for the military. There is absolutely no difference whatsoever. Now, sir, if you would stand on the 3D platform, I have the coordinates of each ship and their comms' frequencies loaded into the computer. Once I activate your image, the ships will each receive a laser strike that will disable their comms, until we decide otherwise. Let me know you are ready, and I'll order the 3D to start.'

The COD stood on the platform and nodded to Cyril. There was a light buzz, then a thumbs up.

'You're connected to every ship now, sir. Their comms are now dead.'

Sir Gary looked at a pinpoint of light. He then gave the confirmation to start. 'Okay, Cyril.'

There was a light humming noise that soon vanished, and Sir Gary O'Brien materialised simultaneously on each of the blockade ships.

The shock of having someone override their comms units and take full control of in-house communication, of which they could do nothing about, left all the captains on the ten Aussie frigates annoyed and tense.

'Good morning, captains and crews on all the blockade ships around the New Zealand coastline. I am Sir Gary O'Brien, CODNZ. I'm contacting you simultaneously to advise you that your mission is now a dead duck. We sank the Geelong around thirty minutes ago, off the Chatham Islands, with the loss of ten sailors. The NZ Defence Force does not, by any stretch of the imagination, want to sink any more of your frigates. If you persist in going ahead with the blockade of our ports, we will sink you. Your operation in New Zealand is over. The Australian first brigade are all POWs. Our air force have shot every aircraft down that you threw at us. Your SAS in Waitangi, Auckland, and Wellington are in our hands. Also, bringing you more bad tidings, your three battle fleets are heading back to Australia at ten knots max. We have disabled all propulsion. All armament remain incapacitated, no workable weapons at all. Two ships from the Zulu battle squadron are now, at this moment, in tow back to Lyttleton for repairs with a skeleton crew.

'What I'm saying, ladies and gentlemen, is your operation is over. We have closed down all your comms, leaving only one special band for you to contact the Melbourne. Receive the information from the horse's mouth, so to speak. Once you have this information, we will require you to do a 180 degrees to starboard and head back to your point of origin. If you do not comply with the Melbourne's commodore, we will have no option but to fire on you. So please be sensible and think it through. You have thirty minutes to comply. CODNZ out.' He faded away.

'That went perfect, sir. We have got them all on our " lazer spot," and we are already listening to the crew's chatter.'

Chattering, they were. The look of bewilderment on the captain's face translated to the officers shaking their heads. All the crew now knew the story, and the information was like a hammer blow. Their officers could not explain or palm this news off. Confirmation was required from the horse's mouth.

The aircraft carrier Melbourne's comms overloaded as ten ships tried to contact the commodore together. Eventually, there was a pause, and the commodore contacted each ship individually to explain what had happened to the operation. He emphasised that not one objective was achieved. The Kiwis had rounded up everyone on the ground, and it would be foolish if any of the blockade ships stayed in NZ waters.

'I do not want you to end up like your battle groups, pottering along at ten knots. I want you at maxim speed so you can inform our HQ staff about what has happened. We have no communication with HQ. It will be up to you to explain to the government what has happened out here. Staying seaworthy, you will deliver first-hand the predicament that the battle groups are in. You are all that's left fully serviceable. My orders are to turn around and contact our HQ forthwith.'

The captains were shocked, angry, and bewildered. What had gone wrong? How did it go so wrong? Finger-pointing was alive and well. Once all the ships had the relative information from the commodore, the comms shut down, leaving the Melbourne blacked out again. Thirty minutes later, on the dot, their 3D came on from an outside source, and the image of Sir Gary was with them once again.

'Your answers, please, gentlemen.'

After the explanation from their commodore, he had ordered them home. There was not much they could do but capitulate.

'I'm pleased you see sense. We will monitor each ship on your return journey. You are free to go: go fast. Let the politicians sort this mess out. Good luck, safe voyage,' he said as he faded into a haze.

The captain of the Mildura was furious and a stubborn bugger.

'To heck with what the Commodore has to say. The Kiwis have made us the laughingstock of the Western nations, and that's not happening on my watch. Turning to his number one, be said, 'We are twenty kilometres from the Bluff Locks. I want to pound that dock to rubble.'

'Sir, I protest,' his number one stated. 'They ordered us home.'

You can stand down, Number One. If you are not up to it, get off my bridge.'

He turned and looked at his navigator, Lieutenant Arnold.

'You are now acting number one. I want you to target the navy base, please. Staring at his previous number one, he said, 'Are you still here? Leave the bridge at once. Gunny, these are the coordinates to fire.' He typed them into the computer. Then he pressed the stand-to klaxon. Sailors ran to their appointed positions, and the forward guns swung around to sit at forty degrees. The onboard speakers screamed.

'Now hear this: close up battle stations.'

'We will fire the bow armament; I want at least a minute on the target with the two forward guns,' the captain ordered.

The old Italian Otabreda could fire forty rounds a

minute over twenty-three kilometres. The computer coordinates locked on to the dock and also the naval base.

'Ready, Gunny,' the captain ordered, 'on my mark, shoot. Helmsman, hard to starboard, Gunny, fire off missiles three and four.'

At the National Crisis Management Centre in the New Zealand Parliament, the general staff were watching the satellite coverage live.

'The captain of the Mildura has gone rogue, sir,' voiced the comms operator. We need to stop him before he does some damage.'

Air Commodore Kieran Vause was already in contact with 75 D.

'Not to worry, sir,' the wing commander replied from the Bat Cave. 'We have it in hand.'

'Let me know the results right away, Wing Commander.'

'Good as gold, sir.'

His order of was sent out instantaneous to the 75 D squadron leader.

'Sink that ship, please, Squadron Leader.'

'Roger, sir,' was the reply.

The squadron leader gave his order for one flight to give the ship a strike of ten seconds, front and rear, that would incapacitate the boat completely.

The wing commander spoke on the secure 3D link to RNZNS Tekapo to pick up survivors and instigate a tow. She was outside the bluff lock, nestled up to a dyke wall. The RNZNS Tekapo roared into power and at full knots, touching nearly seventy, headed out to meet up with the Aussie ship.

'Shoot,' yelled the captain of the Mildura.

Simultaneously, as he gave the order, two white lights hit the forward gun turret, and the other two hit the rear. Instantly, there was no power. The ship went dead. The missiles didn't launch. Unfortunately, the shells from the forward guns hit by the laser strike as they were exiting the barrel, blowing up as the laser light hit them, killing six men in the turret and creating a large hole where the turret once sat, also punching a hole in the hull. The second strike hit the stern with killing power, blew off the rudder, taking four metres off the stern. The Mildura, head down, then stern down, sank.

'Can we fix her engineering?' The captain tried desperately to communicate through comms, but there was no reply as all comms were dead.

'Get a runner down to engineering,' he insisted to the acting number one.

With no power, the bulk doors would not shut. He could feel the ship settling under his feet. The original number one came running up to the bridge.

'We are dead in the water, sir. I've been down to amidship, and the water is rising fast. We cannot hold back the sea. The sea doors won't close. You need to order us to abandon ship, sir.' He stood glaring at his captain.

'It's as bad as that, Number One? Shit, okay, get the crew off. It will have to be by word of mouth. Cut the life rafts away and the lifeboats. He spoke loud enough so all the men on the bridge could hear him. 'Now move,' he boomed. 'Get out of here; save as many as you can.'

Sailors were moving out between decks in an orderly fashion. Engineers cut away the life rafts. Once free, they held them close to the side of the ship as the crew flung themselves into the boats and water. The lifeboat engines started, much to the relief of all concerned, then as the ship settled further, they let go. The life rafts hit the water with a slap and drifted away from the sinking ship until the lifeboats came around and towed the rafts away. Once out of the way of the sinking ship, they turned to watch their ship slide under. Then Number One yelled out. He had spotted the captain still on board.

'Captain, for God's sake, get off the ship. She is nearly under.'

'Captain, Captain,' the crew took up the cry.

The captain turned to his crew, saluted, and was standing there as the ship slipped under the waves.

Ten minutes later, the RNZNS Tekapo came into view, high in the water as she skimmed over towards the small flotilla of life rafts and lifeboats. Cutting power and gently nudging towards them, the first officer of the Tekapo called out, 'We will take all the crews from the rafts, and we will take, under tow, both lifeboats. Is your captain around?'

Number One from the Mildura called out, 'He went down with the ship.'

'We are sorry to hear that. How many of the crew survived, Lieutenant?'

'We have, just this minute, done a headcount: ninety-three survived and seven dead, including the captain.'

'Thank you, Lieutenant. I'll send that info off now. Okay, we are coming in close. Stand by to board.'

Zero seven forty-five, NZ time. This was the last official act of the war in NZ.

CHAPTER TWENTY FIVE

0750, New Zealand National Crisis
Management Centre, Parliament

The NZCOD was explaining to his colleagues, including the parliamentary group, that the last of the Aussie ships were heading home, except, of course, the ones that were sunk. All we now had to do was bring in the Aussie SAS wandering around in the Aorangi Forest Park and over the next week send the Aussie POWs home.

'In the meantime, Prime Minister, will you get in touch with the Australian president and tell him the war is over? He can use our men if he wants to, and when his side of the ditch is in order, we can send his family home.'

'Thank you, Sir Gary. I'll get on to that right away. If you would all excuse me.'

He stood up and went to the communications room. Cyril was waiting for him.

'Ping the Australian president, please, Cyril?'

0550 Canberra Time

Even though the president was expecting the call, he jumped when he heard the ping. Hell, he thought as he rose from his chair, I'm seriously nervous. He chastised himself, Get a grip man. Millions of people will want me in a fit state. He spoke into his watch. It was a small comms unit, asking the presidential guard commander, Colonel Trent Jones to step into his office.

'The New Zealand prime minister has contacted me, Colonel. I want you with me when we speak. Follow me.'

He left his office and walked down the hall to the secure room. They both went in.

'Red one, please, Trent.'

Colonel Trent flicked his pass card at the door, and the locks activated. A very pale red light glowed around the door frame. The president pulled from his pocket the cloaking device, pressed the button, and an electric shield like a blue haze surrounded them both.

Trent had seen nothing like this.

'What is this, sir?'

'I'll explain later, Trent.'

Once the shield was up, the figure of the New Zealand prime minister materialised.

'Good morning, Mr President, and Colonel Jones.'

'Let's stick to first names, Jim. We have known each other for years.'

'Good as gold, Brendan. I'm here to give you a heads-up, so you can do what you have to do with your parliament. I'm also sorry to bring bad tidings regarding the invasion. It is hard for me even to talk to you about this conflict, but, my friend... here goes: All of your army personal are now POWs, except the SAS troop who where jumping into Wellington to secure our parliament. They are wandering around our Forest Park, and we will pick them up shortly.'

'How the hell did that happen, sir? They don't make mistakes like that,' said Colonel Jones.

'I'm sorry, Trent. I cannot tell you trade secrets. Needless to say, there are no casualties; they are just a little lost. We are tracking them as we speak and they will be fine.'

He paused as he looked at both men, who now had frowns of thought on their foreheads.

'I'm also sorry to tell you both; two destroyers of yours sank, and the rest of your battle fleet is heading home, though at a very slow pace. They should arrive back in Australia in nine days. Likewise, I have to advise that you have lost one hundred and fourteen personnel.'

He saw the frown go deeper; the president's facial expression was sad, and the NZ PM moved on quickly.

'One hundred and thirty aircraft shot down. I must also inform you we have towed two destroyers into Lyttleton for repairs. When that's completed, we will send them home.'

'The armed service people killed in action, we will send home to you with full military honors. You lost eighty-four men at the Wellington lock alone. Most bodies are recovered, and we will endeavour to find all missing personnel. We are also searching the Hokianga Harbour for a couple of missing pilots. To make matters worse, there are still some sailors missing from the Geelong, and that search will continue until we find them. I'm sorry to say the captain of the Mildura went down with his ship as did six sailors; we are endeavoring to find their bodies as well.'

'I'm deeply sorry, Brendan, and to you also, Trent, for your losses. New Zealand sends its condolences to all of Australia. Now it's left in your hands to do what you must. Whatever you do, we will support you, Though in my way of thinking, the best course now is to get that bugger of a prime minister and bring him and his cabinet to task. Of course, that is my opinion, not a policy of my government. I'll leave that with you. We are here twenty-four seven if you need anything at all. When you have your end sorted, we will send your wife and family home.'

It shocked Brendan Talbert. He never thought in a million years that the Australian services would get a hiding. To lose that many people. How it went so wrong, he could not fathom. Focus, he told himself; you have a job to do. Sort out his parliament and incarcerate all those involved in this illegal operation.

'Thank you, Jim, for being honest and up front with us. By rights, you could really take our country to task. I really don't know how the hell you did it, and once this is over, we can talk in depth. Now you are right; we have a lot of sorting out to do.'

'One other thing, Brendan, my chief of defence has fifty NZ SAS very close to your residence. He thought if you wanted them, you could use them. I know you said you did not need our help, but the offer is there.'

'Can I say something?' Colonel Jones asked.

'Go ahead, Trent,' the president challenged.

'Well, sir, it would be ideal if the Kiwis took the place of our perimeter guards around the presidential residence. That would release thirty extra men to come with us on the operation; it's not a silly idea, sir.'

The president was thoughtful.

'Okay, Trent, we need a code name so we are all in sync, coming in and out of the residence.'

'How about naming the code after that New Zealand SIS officer who was your caddy, sir. Bluey?'

The president grinned. 'A good idea, Trent. Right. We will do it.'

He turned once again to the New Zealand PM. 'Righto, Jim, it is official. We will expect them sooner rather than later. Send them the code word, and we will tee them up with Trent once they drop in. Do we have a time?'

'Five minutes, Brendan. I'm passing on the information as we speak. Drop zone is at the rear of the residence, away from prying eyes. I better let you go. Good luck, Mr President. We are right behind you. Hare Ra' (See you later). He faded away.

Brendan Talbert didn't muck around. This was not the time to think about the deaths of his fellow Australians or about losing their ships. The cost to the nation was in the future. As soon as the Kiwi PM vanished, he pressed the button on his device.

'Uncloaking; blue code, Trent.'

The colonel flicked his security pass at the door,

which went from red to blue and opened soundlessly. Moving out of the room, he pushed a button on his phone and spoke to his second-in-command. He explained about the Kiwis dropping in and to greet them as friends. 'Give them a quick layout of the grounds,' he said. He had a feeling the New Zealanders knew all about the president's home. 'Then brief our extra thirty men. We move out in thirty minutes.'

0630, Canberra

The president climbed into his electric Rolls Royce. With him was his presidential guard commander, Colonel Trent Jones, sitting up front with the driver. They slowly drove out of the president's residence as they came close to the gate. Two armed New Zealand SAS soldiers materialised out of the trees. The car slowed to a stop. The colonel could not see the faces of the soldiers as they had their full helmets down and were completely dressed in black. One soldier came forward and saluted the president as the front of his helmet came up.

'Captain Ian Dagg, sir. I was in charge of the operation to take your wife off Hamilton Island early this morning. She gave me this to give to you if I ever caught up with you. He handed the president an envelope. I have a note also, sir, from our PM,' he said, handing him the second note. 'Rest assured, sir. We will look after your house.'

'Thank you, Captain.'

He watched the captain slip back into the shrubbery and disappear.

He opened the note from his wife and smiled.

Whatever you do, the family is right behind you. When the time is right, you can move mountains and right is on your side. We are all safe, so there is no need to worry. Get the job done, my love. Let's get Australia back to being Australian again, not a dictatorship as we have now. The New Zealanders are looking after us all very well. Be safe. I'll always love you, Colleen xx.

He was still smiling when he opened the note from the NZ PM.

Bernard, as soon as you have everything in order, we will sort out communications for you. We will open our satellite to you and also open comms to all your navy vessels. Use the comms and satellite any way you want. We'll ping the settings to you once you have everything under control. Stay safe, Jim.

CHAPTER TWENTY SIX

06.33, Leaving the President's Residence,

Canberra

'Between you me and the gatepost... Trent, I'm a tad uptight. That's par for the course, the way things are. Are all the team up to speed?' Asked the president.

'Yes, sir, the police have blocked the State Circuit Road at all entrances. Our men have quietly surrounded the Parliament Building. All cameras are down, and there is no communication inside Parliament. It is a black comms area. I sure don't know how the Kiwis have done this, but it's now going to benefit us. We will go in the back way, as you suggested, neutralising the guards as we go. If they see any sense, they'll stand down and go to Nabin Parliament Park. We have a contingent of police waiting for all those who give up the fight, willingly. I hope our fellow Aussies do the right thing.'

The president's car turned into Adelaide Avenue.

'I wasn't sure about the police when I took the commissioner aside,' the president declared.

'Thank God. We need to stop this dictatorship,' the commissioner emphasised.

'Not one of the police personnel turned down this assignment,' continued the president, 'which proved we were on the right course. The Justice Department might be a sticking point though. I'll sack the high-court judges and promote ones that are not corrupt. I have most of the people I want in my list. My biggest worry is, we don't want a firefight in the building. I want no more countrymen and women killed. Enough is enough.'

'We'll talk them around, sir, I'm positive. Most have got no idea the underlying currents that are happening at the moment. I even heard that a few junior officers think this is all a simulation. We will sort it.'

The car came to the first police roadblock. No flashing lights, all very discreet. There were twenty patrol cars blocking the whole intersection. The president's car slid to a stop, and the inspector in charge came forward and saluted the president.

'All quiet, sir. We had a couple of nosey parkers, and we bundled them away till after this is all over. The road is all clear to the rear entrance. Good luck, sir, and on behalf of myself and all my men, we are with you one hundred percent.'

'Thank you, Inspector. Once this is over, I'll be meeting with all police officers for a debriefing and update. We could not do this without your help.'

The president stuck out his arm and shook the inspector's hand.

'Drive on, please, driver,' ordered the president.

The car swung into State Circuit and hung a left into Melbourne Avenue, which brought them directly to the steps at the rear of Parliament. There were twenty men and women of the president's guard waiting for them.

Major Roberts stepped up to the car, saluted, and opened the door for the president to alight.

'We have every entrance covered, sir,' he informed his president as he stepped out of the car.

'Another fifty of our unit, under Captain Flood, will proceed from the main entrance. We will round up all the non-military staff and herd them into the Senate Chamber. All MPs and secretaries that are here in the building, we will hold in the House of Representatives Chamber. Any hostiles, sir, we will place in the dining room. If we have any real trouble, outside is the Health and Recreation Room. We have one hundred police, which we will use to restrain the violent ones.' He smiled. 'I don't believe there will be much trouble, but I've prepared, just in case. We also have a medical team as well as police. All comms are active for us, not just the PM's group. We were going to have runners, as nothing was working. Then, by magic, we had a comms connection, though only to our immediate units. I don't know how or why, but we'll take what we can get.'

The party lead by the colonel walked up the steps to the rear door. Two presidential guards stood at attention and saluted.

'Oh, sorry, sir, I forgot to mention all regular troops around the building are relieved of their duty. Our men have taken their places. We did not have a problem with the regular army personnel; most, I believe, are relieved to be out of it. Even though they did not know what was going on, they felt sure something was wrong. It pleased them to hand their weapons to our men and head off to the congregation area at Nabin Park. As of now, all army personnel on the outside of Parliament are neutralised,' explained Major Roberts.

The president looked at the surrounding men.

'Thank you, Major. You have everything under control. Right, men, this is it—let's see what the sods are up to. We will hold all the caucus members and ranking officers for the moment in the war room, then transfer them to the Canberra detention centre when we have everything settled.'

It's now come to this, thought the president. It never should have happened. I could have been more forthright sooner. What is done is done. Now let's undo the damage.

They walked into the building slowly, looking around—empty. Nothing stirred. It was quiet, like a morgue. The colonel whispered to his boss, 'They are so confident and arrogant to believe they will pull this off. No guards inside so far.'

'Lets hope it stays like this, Trent.'

The men under Captain Flood had come through the main doors and spread out. They were checking offices and suites throughout the building. He caught up with his colonel as they arrived quietly at the ministerial wing.

'We have found only half a dozen people in the building at this hour. Four are secretaries and one labour MP and a newsman, who sure asked questions. As there is such a small number at the moment, we will hold them all together until we clear out the war room, sir, if that suits?'

'Where have you put them, Captain?'

'In the Rep Chamber, sir, with a couple of guards. The corporal in charge has been told to keep the newsman quiet. He's a bit of a mouth, but we won't have any trouble; Corporal Rouse is one point nine eight metres and just as broad. He scares the hell out of me.'

'Okay, that's excellent, Captain. I'll take twenty of your personnel down with mine. The rest will stay here. If we don't need all of our people, I'll send them back up to you. We don't want to be overcrowded down there,' ordered Colonel Jones.

'Right, men; follow me,' ordered the president.' He opened the door and moved into the ministerial wing.

The designers had lavishly furnished the wing with a thick carpet that softened the footsteps of the group. The president walked through the room and turned right at the end. In front of him were two guards guarding the lift door that would take him down to the war room, three floors below the surface. They hadn't seen him as he slipped back behind the wall.

'Two guards,' he whispered to his colonel. 'We brazen this out.'

'Major Roberts, cover us with your best rifleman,' ordered Colonel Jones.

'Okay to go, Trent?'

'Right beside you, sir.'

They both walked around the corner looking as though they had not a care in the world as the guards bought up the rifles.

'Drop those rifles. Don't you know who I am? I'm your president,' he chided, getting close enough to talk, not to yell. 'I understand you are doing your job. I'm your president, so lower your rifles, now.'

'I'm sorry, sir, but General Eaton told us that no one is to use the lift, and that means you, sir, and you also, Colonel.'

'So you won't obey your president's orders, Sergeant?'

'Sorry, sir, no.'

'That's fine, then, Sergeant.'

The colonel turned to the president. 'We will go back, sir.'

As they turned, they stepped sideways, and there were two phiffing sounds as the sharpshooter fired his rifle in silence mode. Both guards dropped to the floor. The major and a warrant officer came running up. They took a quick look at the two soldiers on the floor, then the warrant officer was on the blower.

'Get a medical team up here, now.'

The warrant officer waved up twenty of his men who were going down to the war room with the colonel and the president.

'I didn't want this to happen,' fumed the president. 'Bugger it, Trent. Those buggers down there have a lot to answer for.'

He walked up to the lift door, blocking out the whimpering sounds of the two soldiers on the floor. Knowing the old code for the lift, he hoped like hell it was still relevant as the doors glided quietly open. He sighed in relief. The lift carried twenty-five people as the first group crammed themselves into the space. The second group of twenty would join them in a few minutes when the lift returned.

The time was 0645.

CHAPTER TWENTY SEVEN

0647, War Room, Parliament, Canberra

The lift doors slid quietly open to a volume of noise. Colonel Jones was on the left of the lift door, Major Roberts on the right, with the president a step back from them in the middle. Behind him were the presidential guards.

To the left and right of the outside of the lift entrance were two guards looking uninterested in their surroundings, as it had been a long morning, and they had not had a break. It came as a big surprise to them that the doors of the lift had even opened. There was no one authorised to come down to the war room. So it came as a hell of a shock to sense the door opening, and pistols with silencers stuck into their backs.

'Stand down, soldiers; that's a direct order,' said Colonel Jones.

The guards had no time to think as they were quickly shunted to the back of the lift and handcuffed together. Their legs were kicked from under them, dropping them to the floor of the lift. One of the president's men stayed with them as the doors closed for the return journey.

Only seconds had passed as the door slid open into the war room. Nobody even noticed, as the volume in the room was loud and exceptionally tense. A lot of recrimination was flying around, with the loudest voice being the PM, Donald Anderson. Another few seconds passed until the president stepped out of the elevator in front of his men who were now spreading out. In a booming voice, he yelled for quiet.

The room was large, with an oval table in the middle and seats for sixteen people. The larger seat was at the front, with its back to the lift: the PM's chair. Around the outside of the seats were the secretarial seating. On the walls were eight large screens, all black with static. At the end of the room was another door that led into the comms room with a staff of twenty technicians. They monitored the airwaves through satellite and 3D communication, internet, multimedia, email, telephone, and even the old landlines. Everything was dead, hence the commotion and volume in the room. It was frustrating the hell out of everybody to not have a clue why this was happening.

A booming voice caught everyone's attention, and the noise abated. The group, as one, looked towards the booming voice, and a few jaws dropped. The PM swivelled around in his chair to see where the voice had come from. Once it registered, he jumped to his feet, outraged.

'What the bloody hell are you doing here, and what are your guards doing here? Get out. Do you hear me, get out!' he screamed.

His face looked red and blotchy, his breathing was ragged, and his face dripped sweat. He looked like a heart attack waiting to happen.

With the conversation keeping everyone glued to the president and the PM, the guards had circled the room. Ten had entered the comms room. A couple of shots rang out, then a head popped around the door and a corporal called out, 'All secure, sir.'

The president walked slowly into the room proper as the lift doors opened, and another twenty of the president's guards came into the room, guns at port ready to fire if need be. They also circled the room, keeping a close eye on whoever made the wrong move. You could hear a pin drop.

President Brendan Talbert had not taken his eyes off his PM. It was as though there was no one else in the room.

'You,' he spoke with a quiet but menacing voice. 'Sit down now and shut up. The rest of you—sit!'

The PM screamed at the president.

'Don't tell me what to do. You jumped-up shit. You better back off; otherwise, you might not see your family again.'

A strange look came over the president's face. It was a grimace and a smile rolled in together.

'Ah, yes, Hamilton Island, where you were holding my family prisoner. Well, I must inform you they have not been there since two a.m.'

"You are lying, you useless bugger. There is no way that could have happened.'

The president turned to his colonel. 'Will you activate the message, please, Colonel?'

Colonel Jones pulled from his pocket a small monitor. He placed it on the table in front of the PM and switched it on. The new 5D image came up for all to see, of the president's wife, Colleen, standing on a balcony overlooking Lake Wakatipu in the New Zealand Alps:

'Good morning, my love. Just a quick communication to let you know we arrived safely. Picked up by the New Zealand SAS just after two a.m., Australian time and flown quickly to New Zealand this morning. We are all safe and well. I was also told that they have not harmed any of the men guarding us. All are unconscious and will not awaken for at least twenty-four hours. They're placed in the guards' bedroom. Time to go, my love; we will look forward to seeing you as soon as it is feasible.'

The sun rising over the Alps made the lake a colour of light red. With 5D, you could even smell the pines; the air smelt sweet. Behind her there was a calendar: the sixth of February with the digital imprint on the time of the message, 6.00 a.m. NZ time.

The messaged ended. The room was completely quiet.

'So, Anderson, the president informed him, you and your party from this moment are finished; I am dissolving Parliament. I want everyone in this room to listen and to take notice of what I'm about to say. This is being recorded as I speak and will go out on all communication 3D networks, net, social media.'

'That will not happen. We have no comms whatsoever,' Harold Wade, the deputy, piped up.

'Once again you are wrong there, as you will find out with my next statement. How did I find out? The New Zealanders have been in communication with me from the start of this debacle. They have every word that has transpired here on record. Now, just shut up, and listen to what I have to say. Any interruptions, Sergeant, and you have my permission to belt them. 'I'm revoking the sitting Parliament of Australia under the Constitution Act of 2165, and by the rights that the Constitution allows me to govern the Commonwealth of Australia until fair elections at the date I decide in the future. I will pick a committee to help me run Parliament and all the paraphernalia of the government. This is my right as president and for the good of our country. This government has put our nation in jeopardy of being a democracy and has changed the shape into a dictatorship. I have all the evidence to support my actions. All the perpetrators will be accountable and placed in custody until the courts tries them for treason, murder, theft, kidnapping, extortion, and any other criminal acts that turn up after a full enquiry. Furthermore, there was the illegal attack of a friendly nation, without the declaration of war, causing the deaths of one hundred and fourteen of our armed service personnel and the sinking of two of our destroyers. Two others are, at this moment, in tow to a New Zealand port, damaged, one hundred and thirty aircraft shot down. All the Australian army personnel on the Yokohama are POWs incarcerated on that ship for the duration. Our SAS personnel are POWs. New Zealand incapacitated our battle fleets to the point they can only make ten knots and are on their way home as are the blockade ships. The cost to this country is tremendous, and the blame sits squarely on the shoulders of all of you sitting around this table. Our reputation as an honest country is going to take years to repair. The audacity to think you could slip across the Tasman to one of our trusted friends to invade, kill them while they were sleeping, is a disgrace beyond conception. We will make you all accountable for your actions from top to bottom.'

The PM jumped up. 'No, you don't, you useless prick. You just allow people to ride over you. You're weak, you hear? Weak. This country always wanted a powerful government, and they got that through me. You will not cart me away, mate.'

He reached inside his jacket pocket and pulled out a pencil—a new type of weapon that could kill at over one thousand metres. It sat in the palm of his hand. Before he could fire the weapon, Major Roberts shot him in the chest. The force of the shell threw him backwards over his chair, hitting the table and landing, along with a clatter of pens and documents scattering all over the floor.

Colonel Jones called through to the police to get a medic down straight away. He turned to his major.

'Well done. He would have got the president as sure as eggs.'

'Yes sir, I know, but I'm going down as the first man to shoot a PM, and I regret that.'

'Don't feel bad, Major,' the president advised. 'I

was fearful for my life. The man had lost it altogether. If it had not been for you, I might be lying on the floor instead of him. We will never mention your name under the Secrets Act.'

At that moment, the doors of the lift opened, and in ran a medic with a couple of senior police constables. The medic did a quick check.

'He is still breathing, sir. He needs hospital treatment now.'

'Okay, son,' the president agreed.

'Major, go with the medic. Get him to the nearest hospital, and I want him protected, even if it means the whole ward. No one goes near him except those that need to. Sort it out. Report back as soon as you can.'

With the help of the police and the major, they carried the PM to the lift. There were people waiting for them to rush them off to Calvary Public ten kilometres away.

The room was quiet and in shock, and going into deeper shock as the president turned back to the table. He looked at Harold Wade, the deputy PM.

'We will incarcerate you and your party at Holsworthy Barracks until we reopen Christmas Island Detention Centre later this year. Stand up, Wade, and walk to the wall. Sergeant, handcuff that man.'

'It was all the PM's fault,' Harold wailed. 'We were all threatened by him, and we had to do as he ordered.'

'Tell it to the judge. Next, Elsie Sanders, you join Wade, please.'

'Mr President, we are friends. I have stayed at your residence.'

'You, Elsie, are despicable, a thief and a bully, and now you will pay. Cuff her, please, Sergeant.'

'Colonel Jones, round the rest of these contemptible people up, please, and cuff the lot,' ordered the president. The presidential guard pushed all the MPs to the wall at rifle point.

Staring at this group, the president spat, 'Simon Wills, Minister of Defence; Secretary David Abbot, Rhys William, Donna Wood, Dean Parker, Olivia Frare, Gary MacNicoll, Charles Drew, Julian Devon, Charles Cox, Stephen Powell, and Cory Rich. You all had ministerial portfolios and a finger on the pulse of a corrupt regime. You all disgust me.'

He then focused on the military men still sitting around the table, looking very pale. They could not believe, in such a short period, things had gone from worse to disastrous. No comms to this situation, and they had high hopes of a quick victory and the kudos that would come with it.

'I am ashamed to even be in this room with you lot. You have lost the respect of our armed services, and the cost is going to be incontrovertibly tragic for you all. From today, you rescind your rank. You will no longer be relevant to our armed services. I have all the discharge papers signed and stamped. Your replacements will come from servicemen and women who have had no contact with any of you, and your corruption has not infected them. You will be taken to the special prison out West until your trial. We will try you as war criminals, and you will forfeit everything. I will wipe your names from all defence history. Your pensions will be forfeited, along with your personal items, including bank accounts. You will not see your family harmed unduly and we will make sure they are taken care of, but you will never see the light of day until your trial. Cuff them, Colonel. Get them out of my sight.'

No one made a sound, their arrogance crushed.

By this time, the police commissioner had arrived to take charge of the people in custody. Twenty comms people in the next room came out with their hands in the air. The rifle shots fired were a deterrent; no one was hurt. Aussie courts would exonerate all of the comms personnel even though the police took them into custody. The war was well and truly over.

The time was 0715.

CHAPTER TWENTY EIGHT

0915 National Crisis Management
Centre Parliament.

A message from our communication people, Prime Minister. The Australian president now has control over their parliament.'

'That is good news, Cyril. Will you please open up our satellites to the president and communication to his armed services, including normal service to all civilian networks? Don't turn them on until I speak first to the president. Give me five minutes, then ping him, please.'

'It will take an hour, sir, to restore their comms. It is easier to cut them. I'll get my technicians on it right away. As soon as we have it reset, I'll give you the thumbs up. I'll ping you in five for the conference with the president.' He slipped back into the comms room.

Jim Lofthouse, the NZ PM, and his deputy, Jonathan Martin, walked to the secure room. Once inside, the locks clicked closed, and they waited for the ping from Cyril, which came exactly on the five-minute mark. The PM activated the cloaking device with the word "Cloak." The room turned to a tinge of light blue around the edges, making it impregnable from the outside of the room. A few seconds later, the blue haze of the 3D comms came on, and the Australian president was standing there with a very grave-looking face.

'Is everything okay on your end, Brendan?' inquired the NZ PM.

'Thanks, yes, Jim. It has left an unpleasant taste in my mouth. I'm so wild about what these people have done to our country, and to you, our friends, it is unbelievable. We have it all under control now. I believe you know what has happened here, Jim, and how you're aware is the big unknown question. We'll leave it at that for the moment. There is so much to do before we can get back to normal. All the perpetrators are now in custody. Parliament is in my hands and also the police and armed forces here in Australia. I'm not yet sure about the fleets, though I am hoping they will come around when I talk to them all. I'm pleased that there have been no fatalities when I took Parliament. We shot Anderson, the ex-PM. He was the only casualty. One of my guards shot him when he pulled a gun on me. Whether he pulls through remains to be seen. Honestly, I don't care one way or the other. In the long run, he will not see the light of day again, if I have my way. I'm looking at the options, and I think, to be perfectly frank, I would like to use The Hague for the trial. There has to be a fair trial; everything must be legitimate. We need the world to see clear signs of no cohesion from the Australian Republic. That's all for the future. I need to get our country up and running and undo what this bloody gang of thugs have done.'

'If you need any help at all, Brendan, the New Zealand PM said, please just let us know. Everything pertaining to the invasion that we have, I'll pass on to you. We have so much in our database to get them all life in prison. Once this initial part is over, I'll send my ministers over with everything you need. You can also call on me if you need a witness. We will deny you nothing. In the meantime, all your comms will be up within the next forty-five minutes. You can piggyback off our two satellites, Wha and Rima. They will be at your disposal until you have yours up and running again. Each one has all the capacity you will need, including military comms. Your 3D, all-media comms, and social media, will be up and running at the same time. The coordinates, we will send to your communication centre and they can sort out the whys and wherefores. No doubt you want to contact your family. This is the number, and you can call her anytime.' The NZ PM touched a small console on the table, and the number came up on the president's 3D monitor. 'Whenever you want your family home, say the word, and we will have them there in a jiffy.'

'Thank you Jim, to have the family home now, as it is safe to do so, would be the icing on the cake after a terrible morning. I cannot understand how my government got so far out of hand. I've been walking around with blinkers on. I cannot believe it got to this stage.'

He rubbed his hand through his hair, looking exhausted.

The president continued, 'In such a small period of time too. From around two a.m, and it's now only seven twenty. Just in five and a half hours, you have stopped the invasion, dead. It must be the shortest war in history. One that should never have happened. I'm so sorry, Jim and Jono, and all of New Zealand, for the last few years. To end up like this, today, is humiliating, to say the least. You have our deepest apologies from the entire country. The bright spot, and one thing in our favour, we have cleared out the rubble—the whole corrupt government—and now we can look forward to a brighter future. I have in place, a workable committee. Naturally, I'm unable to do everything myself. We will sort out elections. That won't be for a while. My committee, once formed, will work out the running of the country. I need to bring back confidence in the government to right the wrongs of the last administration. We have a lot of good people missing, and I will need the goodwill of the public service to find them or what happened to them in our prison system. So much to do.'

'Bringing back the ANZAC spirit, which has been lacking over the years now is a must and important. We will get together here or over your way and work on a united front again. I'll be in touch again soon. I have a lot to get on with. Yes, please send my family home. I'll be in touch with Colleen to let her know you are flying them home later today.'

'Lets say pick them up at two p.m., our time, and that would give you a few hours to sort out your day,' Jim suggested.

'As soon as we have finished with this call, I'll get in touch with her.' Brendan responded.

'All right, Brendan. We will sort out your armed service people that we have as POWs in New Zealand. I'll communicate directly with you. Once again, if you need any help at all, just let me know, and we will do all we can. I'll have our air force standing by to bring your family home. Aren't they lucky they brought nothing with them since they haven't been here long enough to crease the sheets? Talk again soon, Mr President, haere ra.' (goodby for now) The 3D faded away.

'Uncloak,' the PM ordered.

'Right, Jono, we will have a briefing in an hour with everyone involved. I want the POWs issue sorted out. Also, I want the two ships heading to Lyttelton to be restored and out of our hair ASAP. Most importantly, I want all the crash sites cleaned up. If we cannot salvage them, let's talk to Kathy Wong and her team. Our defence people will have been in touch with her. Is it possible to use this nanotechnology to demolish, disintegrate, turn to dust, or whatever the hell they can do? I still can't fathom this stuff at all. I want those downed aircraft and ships removed, if at all possible. Ask Kathy and her team to the briefing also, Jono.'

'One thing, Jim, we need to inform our public about what has happened. Many people were up and about around the country early. We are picking up conversations on what people have seen and heard. To my way of thinking, we need to have a public broadcast. You, me, Rachael, and Rangi at the table, releasing the information to our citizens—what happened, how we stopped it. Without going into the whys and wherefores. Also, that it's over and everyone is safe. It's nearly nine thirty, so it should be before midday. It needs to go out on all 3D and 4D holographic services and all communication pods, internet, and all the independent personal networks. That way we hit virtually everyone.'

Jim thought, I cannot do it all, so delegate. In reply, he said, 'I'll take the broadcast. Jono, you, Rangi, and Rachael can run the briefing. I better get on it.' He pushed communication buttons situated every six metres along the wall. 'Can my writers be in my office in ten minutes, please, and also the parliamentary media? Thank you.'

'Right. I'm off, Jono. Good luck with your briefing. Make sure we have the coordinates for all those aircraft and ships for Kathy, and depths of the sea in those areas she might need to do calculations.'

'Just leave it with me, PM. You can rely on me. You are getting like an old mother hen, Jim.'

'Sorry, mate, I'm not doubting you, and you are right, I need to loosen up more. Okay, time to go. You can look at the recording later and pull it to pieces.' He smiled. 'Catch you on the reboot.'

The PM walked at a fast pace out of the National Crisis Management Centre, took the lift to level eight of the executive suite and walked into his office. It surprised him to see his manager already there, and shortly after, a string of writers and media people were knocking on his door.

When everyone settled down, the PM explained what he wanted to do, and he wanted it by 11.00 a.m. or as close to that time as possible, so he could go over the broadcast and get it right.

The media people said they would be ready in an hour or so as long as they could set up now in the PM's office.

'Request granted,' invited the PM.

The speechwriters were thoughtful.

'It won't be as cohesive as we normally write in such a short time. Chuck in a ad lib or two, sir. We will get on with writing the script.'

They weren't kept in the loop throughout the invasion and knew nothing of any significance that had happened that morning. So it was a surprise to them when the PM relayed it to them, and they had the job of writing it up for the New Zealand population.

Jim left them to work in his office and walked down to the media room, where the make-up people would try to make him presentable.

The PM and his team had no sleep for over twenty-four hours, and it showed around the eyes. He always was a hard man to apply make-up to. He did not like it at all. They mainly patted his cheeks with light powder to take the shine off his face and the darkness from around his eyes.

At 10.55 a.m., the writers came in to say they would need another ten minutes.

'Do your best,' he answered.

At eleven fifteen, they rushed in with the speech. The PM took the papers and spent the next thirty minutes going over what they wrote, crossing out this and changing that until he thought it would do. He got up from his chair, thanking his staff, and headed back to his office, where the media had finished their set-up and were now waiting for the PM to settle.

On the stroke of midday, the New Zealand public saw their PM sitting at his table in the Beehive of the New Zealand parliament building. It was unusual, to say the least. A minute before the announcement, a prelude came over the airwaves to say an important announcement would come from the PM on the news at midday.

'Good afternoon, my fellow New Zealanders,' the PM announced. 'I am sorry to pull you away from your day of celebration of our Treaty of Waitangi, but I have grave news.

'The situation is now completely under control, and for that we have to thank our armed services and our science community for keeping these islands of ours safe.

At six thirty this morning, a Special Air Service team from Australia tried to descend onto the treaty grounds of Waitangi to round up all our members of Parliament. This was the start of an attempted invasion of our country. The SAS jumped into the wrong spot, and our army rounded them all up, and they are safely under lock and key.

'Earlier in the morning, a container ship with a battalion of Australian troops had tried to enter Wellington Harbour. We were also lucky enough to hold them inside the lock gate and render them inoperable. Unfortunately, a group of one hundred ran across the locks' top path into a concerted fire from our army. They lost over eighty men, and even though they were the enemy of our country, my condolences go out to the families of those Australians killed.

'Another SAS group tried to drop onto Wellington Airport, but unfortunately their coordinates were wrong, and they are now wandering around Aorangi Forest Park. I would ask you all not to venture into the park. Keep within a fifty-kilometre distance. We know where they are, and we will pick them up today or tomorrow, at the latest.

'The third SAS group dropped on Auckland. Once again, they were off course and drifted onto Browns Island, where the New Zealand Army was waiting for them. All those troops are now under lock and key. 'I'm afraid this SAS operations were the prelude to an all-out attack on our infrastructure. Using their three battle groups, each comprised an aircraft carrier and three destroyers. They were going to attack all armed forces establishments, as well as bridges, roads, and tunnels, throughout the country. They were going to do this with no provocation. Their prime minister was prepared to sacrifice our people for his gains.

Their president had his hands tied. A short time ago, you would have heard the news that his family were incarcerated on Hamilton Island because of an assassination attempt on his family. Well, that was all lies from their PM and his cabinet. They were holding the president's family as hostages, so the president would not make waves.

'Early this morning, six New Zealand Special Air Service dropped onto Hamilton Island and freed the president's family, and they are now in New Zealand out of harm's way.

'New Zealand could not stop their PM from attempting to invade while the president's family were prisoners. Our armed services had to repel them after our men rescued them his family.

'We shot down all their aircraft, sank two destroyers and mauled their battle fleet, who are, at this moment, limping back to Australia. All the Aussie pilots are in custody.

My fellow New Zealanders, as a government, we did not tell you beforehand. We worried there might be panic in the streets, and the fighting was over before you were sitting down to your breakfast. The safety of all our countrymen and women was paramount. It is with relief to let you know this news today.

'Over the next few days, the stories will come out. I must remind you that a majority of Australians did not know what their government was about. As we speak, the Australian president has walked into Parliament in Canberra and dissolved his Parliament and arrested all those who planned and executed this invasion.

There is a lot of fence-building to do with our neighbors across the ditch. In the future, I'm sure we will be friends again. It will take time for the wounds to heal. In the meantime, you and your families are safe.

'I thank you for watching and listening to my broadcast. Ahiahi pai.'

(Good afternoon.)

CHAPTER TWENTY NINE

8.30 a.m., Canberra Parliament Building

'We are ready to run when you are, sir,' the media chief declared to the president.

Within the last hour and a quarter, NZ restored all communications to Australia. How it happened was a complete enigma to the Aussies, but you don't look a gift horse in the mouth.

Aussie president Brendan Talbert 's first action on his agenda was to reach out to the officer in command of the Australian battle groups.

Reuben J Webb, the commodore of Alpha Battle Group, was the officer in charge, overall, of the three battle groups in trying circumstances. They had no comms at all because of the disastrous encounter with the NZ forces. His only contact with the battle groups was the one he was on. So it came as a complete surprise when the comms officer announced to him they had an incoming 3D call from the Australian Parliament war room.

Oh God, he pondered, the PM is going to fly into a frenzy once he perceives what the hell has happened to his navy and aircraft. The way the politicians in Canberra are, they will make my life a misery.

When he walked into the comms room, and the president came through on 3D, he stared at the image in bewilderment.

'Mr President, how is this happening? There are no communications at all with Canberra or our armed services.'

'Yes, well, good morning, Commodore. There's been a few changes since you left on your adventure. I'm here to explain that I dissolved Parliament. Your government is no longer in office. I am taking over the reins until further notice. The prime minister and all his cabinet ministers, including all armed ranking officers, are now in custody. You, Commodore, are now the ranking officer. I want you to give me your full support. Before you answer, I need to tell you that the armed services will require new officers to replace all those from the chief of defence staff: Andrew Baggs, air chief marshall; Barry Eaton, lieutenant general, Australian Army; George Gannon, vice admiral, Australian Navy; and Paul Jellyman, air vice marshall, Australian Air Force.

'If you agree, I want a list on my desk as soon as possible with your recommendations. We all know you're involved with this illegal invasion, but in your case, you were obeying orders, as the rest of the armed service was. Are you prepared to accept that we can put this behind us and move on to a better relationship? If so, I will promote you to COD when you arrive back at your home port. My office wants a complete analysis of our losses, what went wrong with the overall operation as you saw it. No punches pulled. I need a list of those recommendations as speedily as possible. The New Zealand PM has notified us they governed your battle fleets to ten knots, so it will give you time to work on your reports for me.'

'But how do you know about our situation, sir? Even we don't know the full story; I've no communication at all with the other two battle fleets. How the Kiwis did this, I am stumped. You have dissolved Parliament, you say. What is going to happen with our politicians who will run the country? This is unheard of.'

'How we heard about you was, the New Zealand PM told me. Their technology is ahead of ours, I would have to say. You would know yourself since they have rendered your fleet to ten knots and with no armament to speak of. All the battle fleets are the same. They beat us on the sea, air, and land. One hundred and thirty-four aircraft lost, two destroyers sunk, two more damaged, and are being towed, as we speak, to a New Zealand port. All army personnel have been rounded up. Our first battalion never got off the Yokohama, and when they tried, they lost nearly one hundred. It has been a disaster from the word go. I'm afraid that your colleagues will pay for their mistakes. Their biggest mistake was joining forces with the PM and his cabinet to attack a sovereign state. They should have come to me from the beginning, but no, they were up to their neck in the mire.

'So, this is the state of play. The politicians are all incarcerated as are the chiefs of staff, and will be tried in the near future under the Treason Act. All our fleets are coming home slowly. Still, we have no satellite comms. We have taken a few heavy punches to the head, and our country is groggy. We will get over this, though, but it will take time.

'Incidentally, our PM was thinking of murdering my family, then me, if the invasion was a success. It was the NZ SAS who dropped into Hamilton Island and rescued my wife and family. This gave me the opportunity to resolve the dire position that our country was heading into. Once New Zealand rescued my family, the threat over me vanished. I could go to Parliament to confront the PM and do the very necessary job of dissolving Parliament. Does this answer your questions? NZ have also informed me, they will restore your communications to your fleets as soon as I have finished this connection with you. You won't have your armament back, but we will have transmission with everyone once again. I want you in Canberra as soon as you arrive back in the country.' He paused. 'No, I've changed my mind. It would be advisable for you to be back here as soon as possible. I will authorise a chopper for you from the mainland. Well, Commodore, what is your answer, yes or no?'

'This, sir, is all legitimate?'

'Yes, it is. I don't want to run the country, and as soon as it is workable, we will have a new election. We need a new broom and a new party. I have to start somewhere and, Ruben, you are a cog in the bigger picture. To set your mind at rest, I'll send you the relevant clause in our Constitution regarding the dissolving of Parliament. I think a few of the passages will be enough to convince you I'm in the right.'

A couple of minutes later, the relevant pages came up on a screen for the commodore to read. He took a full minute, then looked at the president to confirm his intention.

'I'm with you, Mr President.'

'Good man. I'll have a chopper sorted ASAP. In the meantime, work on people who you believe would be the best for the heads of their respective services. The chopper will bring you to the president's residence.

Remember, comms will now be online. I want you to have a conference call to all of the captains of every ship involved with this invasion. Explain there is a new boy in town. There will be no, and I repeat, no recrimination to any of the armed service people. I am pleased you are with me and Australia. We will talk again soon.' His image faded away.

Ruben kept looking at the space where the president had been standing, rubbing his jowls with both hands.

'Did you hear all that, Captain Till?' he asked.

'I cannot believe it. The Kiwis sure hit us hard. We lost all those aircraft and a couple of destroyers. Then to be told that the president has taken over. It had to happen, sir. The country was heading towards a full dictatorship. Frankly, I did not want any part of it. I was on the verge of resigning my commission. Maybe we can get back to what we were before. A land of opportunity, not a place of grief and bloody misery. I'll get on to comms and see if we can get the old zoom program up. Running it would be quicker to have everyone on the same page. Sir, congratulations on your promotion. Well deserved, even at a time like this.'

'Thanks, Sam, let's get the comms up and see where we stand.'

A couple of hours later another message came through with the list of all personnel who had vowed their allegiance to the president and the country. The president's staff had been busy once they had restored communication. It was a comprehensive list, including all the police throughout the country, the law courts, judges and lawyers, mayors of each shire around Australia, and the rest of the armed services on Australian soil. Government workers, including ambassadors and their staff, worldwide as well. Last in the list were all MPs who were not affiliated with the party in power. Agreed, they would be right behind their president and help as much as they could. That only left the forces still in New Zealand waters, and the POWs. The president was hoping the commodore would have that under control. Debriefing the POWs when they arrived home would take a couple of days, then ask to state their allegiance, toe the line, or a quick discharge.

With the comms up, the commodore opened a channel to all ships' captains of the Republic of Australia. From his flagship, the commodore explained all information relating to the invasion to the captains, who passed on the information to all navy personnel who served on each ship. They told them about the Australian battalion languishing in the Yokohama in Wellington harbour, about all the SAS personnel incarcerated in Auckland, Wellington, the Bay of Islands, as well as the sinking of the two destroyers, one off the coast of the Chatham Islands and the other off the coast of Invercargill. They were also told about all the pilots who were under lock and key from the top of the North Island to the bottom of the South Island, and last, the casualties of this disastrous operation.

'It's been a dark day for us, the worst in our history,' the commodore explained to them. 'We have lost so much besides the equipment, which is replaceable, but it is the human cost and humiliation that hurts our nation. Not for a moment am I blaming New Zealand; they were the non-aggressive participants. We have to look at ourselves.

'We did not prepare, and took the words of our top military and members of caucus as gospel. They let you down, all of you; they let Australia down. This adventure would never had happened if, as a country, we had voted this pack of wolves out years ago. New Zealand has always been our friends, and we need to be humble to get them back onside again. So, Captains, your orders are to head to your ports. Once there, I want all senior officers to arrange transport to Canberra. The president needs and wants your full cooperation to work with him and swear the oath to his office and Australia. Hoping within a year we can have an election, as he does not want to be head of a parliamentary government. I'm also looking for the right men and women to promote to replace the traitors from the three services who were in cahoots with the PM and his caucus. My orders to you are to bring me a list of who you think would be ideal for the job as flag officer. I want good people. I want to promote them on merit, so who else should I ask but the people who work with them? You have things to ponder and explain to your crews, who also will have to renew their allegiance and prepare for change.

'Before the president signed off, he told me he would get in touch with the New Zealand PM and see if we can't get you home quicker. I gather they can do miracles as we have all so sorely learnt at this point in time. So, for now, ladies and gentlemen, a good morning to you all. We will talk on your arrival home.' The commodore faded out.

Around the South Pacific, all the Australian Republic Navy were getting the same message as the piping whistled throughout each ship with the command 'Now hear this: this is the captain speaking.'

They informed crew members of every ship the information passed down from the president, and they now had to undertake another oath of allegiance or leave the navy. They gave them all the story, and it was now up to them to continue their duty and decide on their individual responses back at port. Morale was at a low ebb.

The president, once he had finished his call to the navy, pinged the NZ PM, who came on instantly.

'Kia ora, Bernard, how can I help?'

'Hi, again, Jim. I was hoping you could help me out. I've been in touch with all of our navy ships heading home. We need all senior staff quicker than the nine days you have given the ships to arrive home. I would be happier if they were home sooner than later. Even at full power they won't be here for three days. Can you see your way clear to grant me this favour? I know we don't deserve it, but this request is to bring a bit of normality to our country and for me to sort out the continuity of our flag staff with better people to fill the gaps. I hope you see fit to approve of this request.'

'One moment, Bernard.'

He faded, then turned to his deputy.

'What do you think, Jono?'

'Actually, Jim, I think it is a good idea. He now is in charge. Let's get his navy out of the way, and I'll feel better. It still a sore point for me, and we need time to think. I don't want three battle groups hanging around in our waters. We had enough for one day.'

'Right, then, Jono. Get in touch with operations and ask them to fire a few nanos up their behinds and send them quickly on their merry way.'

He returned to the 3D platform and pinged the president, who came on immediately.

'Your request is granted, Bernard. I don't want to sound pompous, and please don't take it like that; let your navy personnel know they can bring their running speed to normal capacity. Oh, another thought—I have been in communication with our men who have been doing guard duty at your residence. The aircraft that drops your family off this afternoon will bring our blokes home. Good luck and ping anytime.'

'Thanks, Jim, I appreciate your goodwill.' The president faded away.

Seventy-five hundred D Squadron had been monitoring the battle fleets since the COD ordered them home. The call came from headquarters to fire on each ship a nano blast to repair the vessels. They then could reach normal cruising speed. Each flight of four had been in constant view of the three battle fleets. On the order received, they all fired at their respective targets, then waited. A few minutes later, they could detect the wake of the ships moving faster.

'Mission completed, base,' the flight leader informed the Bat Cave. 'All battle fleets are winding up to normal revs.'

CHAPTER THIRTY

February 9, Canberra

The president was sitting at his work desk in his official office with the media from around the world. Over the last three days, his office was in turmoil, getting his committee up to speed.

Once all the armed service came into line, he began organising who would be needed to form a committee to run the country for up to a year. He looked far and wide to bring in the best people from all parties except the old ruling National Party, the genuinely honest people of that party, deemed tarred with the same brush.

Senior members of his formal committee worked out policies bringing all Australians into the fold. His motto was people first, then health, housing, food, and jobs: the necessities for a population of a democratic country.

Next, the committee looked at the prisons. The disappearance of people out West shocked them.

The president's first executive order was to release all political prisoners and others who never toed the line with the National Party. He also announced a complete revamping of the prison sector; anyone who had abused prisoners were in for a bad time.

He had spoken to the people of Australia on the sixth of February and explained why he had dissolved Parliament. The committee was running the county until they formalised a normal election as soon as practicably possible.

He had not mentioned the attack on New Zealand. This was the purpose of this broadcast. He sat looking at the media. He could not keep this under wraps. His fellow Australians needed to know the truth, how easy it had been to go from democracy to dictatorship in such a short time.

He still had not heard from his armed forces in New Zealand, who were in captivity. He was hoping the information would be on his desk before this media frenzy. It had not come to fruition. Oh well, he thought, the Kiwis will eventually be in touch, though he would have to keep up the pressure on them.

One other major thought on his mind was all the deported Australian/New Zealanders. Sitting down with his committee to flesh out a policy, they came up with the idea that if any Australian or Kiwi wanted to come home, they would compensate them for any wrongdoing of the previous government. It would cost millions. The conversation went around the table. How idiotic the previous regime was to have this policy. Australia had lost an enormous number of well-qualified experts. They needed a tremendous amount of work to fill the gaps. The president, by sending out a white feather to the deported Australians, might heal a few wounds. He was hopeful.

His attention was brought back when the floor producer announced, 'We are ready, sir. Three, two, one, you are now live.'

'Good morning, my fellow Australians.' He paused, looking towards the camera to gather his thoughts.

'This morning, with a saddened heart, I would like to explain the main reason I took the path to dissolve the corrupt Australian government. It wasn't just because the government lied to the public about an assassination attack on my family and had hired the shooter themselves or that they were going to do away with my family and myself down the line.

'It wasn't just the fact they sent innocent Australians out West to the prisons without a trial or that they confiscated property and divided their personal finances amongst the cabinet. Or that extortion was flavour of the month, allowing people to pay millions of dollars to the government so they would not send them away to prison. It's not even the fact they deported millions of Australians to other countries without a fair hearing, which in the long run, has been detrimental to our country. Many very talented people from all walks of life are now living around the world, and the previous government forced them out. I could go on as there was so much the last government had done that was unlawful and unconstitutional. We are still finding out what the government had been doing. It will take a while to understand the workings of this dictatorship, and the harm it has done to us as a nation.

'These mentions are just a small part of the equation. The most important information I am going to relate to you is the considerable effort and planning of your ex-prime minister and the chiefs of staff from the armed services, including the inner cabinet, without consultation with the rest of Parliament.'

Pausing and taking a breath, the president continued. 'The ex-prime minister of Australia ordered an illegal attack on our closest neighbour, New Zealand. His aim was to invade the country and take all their water for Australia. Once he had achieved his goals, he and his cronies were going to create four small states, then move the entire population of New Zealand to the bottom of the South Island below Christchurch and settle Australians on the confiscated land. They would move the Maori population out West to Australia, and like our native population... over time, they would just disappear. The prime minister was a completely racist, evil person. This is the background of why I came to the decision to dissolve Parliament.'

He paused again to have a sip of water. He could see the shock, disbelief, anger, and sorrow cross the faces of the reporters in the room. All the reactions of being told a story that was incomprehensible.

Looking at the camera with a stony face, he continued. 'On the sixth of February, the Australian armed forces attempted to invade New Zealand, by land, sea, and air. This was the catalyst, my fellow Australians, for me to act.'

'They tied my hands to start, as my family was under guard on Hamilton Island. Until a New Zealand special task-force team, in the early hours of the sixth of February, jumped onto the island, freeing my family. They flew them to New Zealand. The Kiwis hurt no guards in this operation. I could then, without the fear of reprisal from the ex-PM, get on and do what I had to do.

'Our armed forces attacked New Zealand and were repulsed. In every theatre of operation, we lost the battle—losing one hundred and fourteen personnel from each of the services, army, navy, and air force as well as one hundred and thirty-four aircraft downed and two destroyers sunk. All our battle fleets knocked out of action. They are due to arrive home shortly. The republic's first battalion are prisoners; all of our pilots are in captivity, including navy personnel. We were humbled and still do not know how we were well and truly beaten.

'It was these acts of aggression against a country we have always have been friends with for nearly three hundred years. We were mates; they always had our backs and we theirs. The ANZAC spirit at the moment is nearly dead, now we have to make it right. Our country attacked a sovereign country with no declaration of war on an unsuspecting population. They were ready for us. It means nothing we lost. We were the instigators. Now we have to go, cap in hand, to mend the fences, to apologise, bend over backwards, crawl, if need be, to make this mateship survive another three hundred years.

'As soon as I know the complete names of the deceased service personnel and the outcome of the prisoner situation, I will let you all know. These days have been extraordinarily taxing, and my priority is to bring our service people home. Thank you for watching. I bid you all a good day.'

The Australian flag appeared, and the national anthem played as the president faded.

CHAPTER THIRTY ONE

Wellington, New Zealand

Kathy Wong was the head of the science group. She was adamant that her nanos could repair every aircraft once bought to the surface. They could store them in hangars safely or even tarps on barges, keeping the downed aircraft well out of the public eye. That led to the problem of what to do with the aircraft once repairs had been completed.

Chief of Defence Sir Gary O'Brian, after consultation with his chief of defence staff, suggested to the caucus, 'Why not, as a peace offering, send them back to Australia? After all, Prime Minister, we don't need them, and the kudos would be valuable in the long run. I'm sure the Aussie president would be agreeable.'

The PM nodded. 'How long to achieve pulling those planes out of the drink?' he asked the caucus.

Commodore Fiona Urlich, of the NZ Navy,

replied, 'I believe, Prime Minister, as long as we have cooperation from the civilian salvage companies, about three months.'

The PM turned to Kathy. 'How long to repair them, with your technology, Kathy?'

'Well, sir,' she replied. 'It only took seconds to knock them out, and it will only take a short time to repair. The way the nanos work, we will deliver millions of them into each aircraft, and by the time you have put them on a salvage barge, cover them with a tarp or something similar, they will be serviceable. From our end it's easy. It will be up to the COD to decide where you want them.'

'Okay, is everyone in favour of this? We will leave the technicalities with the air force to sort out.'

Everyone was agreeable.

'We can use our air force bases, Kaikohe, Ohakea, and the major airports of Auckland, Wellington, Christchurch, Dunedin, New Plymouth, and Hamilton. We will work out the transportation and have a paper on your desk, Prime Minister,' the COD advised.

'Oh, another problem, Kathy,' the COD said. 'We had the transport aircraft in Wellington that did a nose dive out in Cook Strait. Can we bring her back from the dead and the other one at Ninety Mile Beach?'

'The beached aircraft will be fine. It will take a bit to get her off the beach, though, and that's your department. The one in the strait won't be too difficult. We will send a small sub down. There is a private sub in Taranaki. We will rig up a firing platform and flotation pontoons. The nanos we will programme to imitate the pontoons. We can build as many as we like. We will also programme them to manoeuvre around the aircraft and latch themselves on to the fuselage and wings, if, of course, the wings are still attached. Once the buoyancy is achieved, we will fire the nanos at the plane. When she reaches the surface, we'll place her on a large barge, and the nanos will go to work. The nanos can copy anything at all. They can also do this to any aircraft that is too deep for conventional salvage.'

'Right. This is progress.' The PM smiled. 'Next on the agenda is the POWs.'

Deputy Leader Lyn Soo stood up and spoke on the subject. 'I have been having a conversation with the COD staff, and I believe that we have come to a consensus that the Aussie POWs should be sent home as quickly as we can. 'To do this'—she paused, looking down at her notes—'Ah, yes, we transfer them all to one place. The most logical place is Wellington. Anchored off Matiu Island is the Yokohama with the majority of POWs incarcerated on her. It's prudent we send them all home on the same ship, and we will be arranging that within a week. We also have agreed to disallow the Australian Navy to sail her home. We will invite the Japanese crew to return her to Aussie. After all, it is their ship. Kathy has already advised us that the ship will be completely serviceable. All their equipment will be returned to them in working order, with no ammunition. This will only happen with the consent of this government. Questions?' she asked, when she sat down.

Everyone agreed. Only Rachael voiced, 'To give them back their armaments, is that wise?'

The PM replied, 'I think, Rachael, we are of one voice. We do not want to pound the Aussies into the dust. They have lost more than us. I believe we need for them to begin building bridges, and this, I think would be a grand gesture, including returning their aircraft. The destroyers that were towed into the port for repairs can go home as well. We will send them home with a New Zealand crew.

'We rounded the Aussie SAS unit that jumped into Aorangi Forest Park and are with the main Australian body on the Yokohama. So now it is time to gather all the POWs together and send them home.'

He looked across the table at the COD. 'How long would that take, Gary?'

'Three days max, Prime Minister. Let's say we can have them on the ship and out of our hair by Friday.'

'Good, is this agreeable with the rest of the cabinet?'

Everyone said aye for it and no one was against.

'Wonderful, then it's settled. Jono, touch base with the Japanese ambassador. Advise him that the Yokohama is free for his countrymen to board her and prepare for a Friday sailing.

'Gary, will you instruct your personnel to inform the POWs' senior officers of the arrangements. All POWs are to be airlifted to Wellington and placed aboard the ship. We should also ask their commanding officer to send off the killed-in-action personnel file so the country can morn their demise.

'I will inform the president of what our plans are for their armed service personnel. We might just leave out telling them of our good nature, regarding the aircraft and ships we will send back to them in the future. We don't want to kill them with kindness. Anything else, people? Good. If there's nothing at the moment, we will meet again in a couple of days for a catch-up.'

They all stood up and headed out the door.

By the weekend, the Yokohama had left Wellington with all Australian services, men and women. NZ informed the Australian president that he had enlightened the people of Australia, and their loved ones were on their way home.

Military funerals were organised for all the service personnel killed in action. They flew their bodies to Canberra and then the bodies were sent to their individual hometowns, with Australia having a week of official mourning.

The first of the downed aircraft now lifted, work was progressing, with luck having them all up and serviceable quicker than everyone thought. The Aussie destroyers were in operation and with a Kiwi crew, headed out of Bluff and Lyttelton to Sydney, returning them to the Australian fold.

The Australian president was completely dumbfounded when the NZ PM told him that the ships were on their way home. Also when he hinted that any serviceable aircraft would return as well, once repaired.

Ten weeks later, one hundred and forty aircraft flew off from Kaikohe and Ohakea for Williamstown to deliver them back to the Australian armed services. NZ had asked for the Aussie air force to pop over with their pilots as NZ didn't have that many pilots for the task. The C180's transport aircraft landed at Sydney International.

The world wondered how these aircraft were salvaged and repaired on such short notice. No information from the NZ government was forthcoming.

Within three months, Australia and New Zealand made a peace treaty to never again go to war against one another. They reinstated all the old accords, began closer economic ties, and NZ was helping to explore, with the Aussies, any underground water source in the dust belt of the country. In the meantime, NZ had the water pipeline pressure turned up, increasing the outflow to more Australians.

In return, Australia offered all those deported to NZ the opportunity to return to the fold. They would be welcomed home and automatically become full Australian citizens as compensation for the embarrassment of deportation. Thousands went home, but more stayed now that they were settled into a job in NZ. The Australian president was also saying that a New Zealand passport meant you would be an Australian citizen any time you were over in their country. That meant any Kiwi or Aussie had dual citizenship.

The one important event on everyone's mind in both countries was the ex-prime minister and his caucus trial.

Donald Anderson, the ex-PM who had survived the gunshot to his chest; Harold Wade, his deputy; Elsie Sanders, ex-minister of child and youth; Simon Wills, ex-minister of defence; David Abbot, secretary to the Minister Of Defence; and nine other cabinet ministers incarcerated on Christmas Island were transported to The Hague. With them went all the armed service high command: Andrew Baggs,air chief marshall/chief of defence; Barry Eaton, lieutenant general of the Australian Army; George Gannon, vice admiral, Australian Navy; Paul Jellyman, air vice marshall, Australian Air Force.

The president wanted to have the trials away from Australian soil, to be seen as unbiased in everyone's eyes.

Charges against these men and women were for treason, war crimes, kidnapping, the murders of tens of thousands of citizens who died in the dust-belt prisons, and extortion. Other charges brought against them were attempting to invade a sovereign country to murder its population, destroy the country's infrastructure, and the planning of these acts, with the approval of cabinet and the chiefs of staff in each of the armed services. The population of Australia had no inkling of what their government had been up to.

The trials went on for over twelve months, until at the beginning of February the following year, they informed the president that they were all found guilty. The court handed down sentences from fifteen years to life. They gave the ex-PM, Donald Anderson, life. He would serve his sentence not in Australia but in a Russian prison as one of the three trial judges was from that country, though Australia would compensate the Russian Federation. The deputy leader, Harold Wade and the ex-minister of defence received the same sentence at different prisons in Russia. Elsie Sanders received twenty years in a Chinese prison, and all the rest, fifteen years scattered between Asia, Europe, and a few would end up on Christmas Island.

All personal effects, bank accounts, and dwellings of the defendants were confiscated. Those monies would pay for their prison sentences. All armed services personnel were dishonorably discharged and forced to forfeit all gratuities that they would have received. Like their parliamentary cohorts, they lost all their belongings and would spend up to ten years languishing on Christmas Island.

Australia had its revenge for a shady part of its history and looked forward to a better life. New environmental parties were popping up, and Australia's future looked bright.

The first Anzac Day the following year, New Zealand and Australia stood side by side, remembering how they started and the mateship that it had created between both countries. Both were still uneasy friends, though things were getting back to the old days of friendship. Down the line, Australia would not look back, as science was about to change the Australian landscape forever.

CHAPTER THIRTY TWO

Australia

They now employed two satellites from New Zealand with the Australian Department of Science and Technology. For nearly a year they had been doing grid searches for water in Western Australia, the Northern Territory, Queensland, and New South Wales.

The satellites were the same ones New Zealand had used to knock out the Aussies at the beginning of the invasion.

They had scoured the terrain high above the continent and had found some interesting information.

When both countries got together with the information, the Aussies scratched their heads, saying it was so deep they would never get to it.

The Kiwis went on to say there was nothing to lose.

The head Australian scientist, John Underwood, explained, 'The pressure is too great at that depth, and it would take weeks to get under control. Though,' he continued, 'even if we could do it, the place is empty and what damage would it do? It would fill all the river courses and slowly head out to sea.' He gazed into the distance. 'The Murray filled with water would be a sight; the dust storms would die instantly. It's wishful thinking as we have not got the drilling capabilities to do it. We are talking over one hundred kilometres. As you know, the farthest anyone has drilled is twelve kilometres. A nice thought though.'

The Kiwi scientist had been told by his superiors that eventually he would have to explain about the lasers. 'You are working closely with the Aussie scientists, and if we utilise the lasers, they will see the results. It's going to come out eventually. We cannot hide this technology forever.'

The Kiwi scientist, Len White, turned to his Aussie counterpart. Time to talk. 'John, would you mind if we give it a go? Nothing ventured, nothing gained. As you know, we have three points of interest; even if we hit one, that is one hell of a pond under all those three. The biggest is west of the Snowy Mountains. If we can crack that, she will flow back into the Murray-Darling catchments, including the old watercourse of the Murrumbidgee.

'You can give it a go, mate, but how, Len?'

'We are going to use our laser, mate. As long as the place is empty, no damage will happen. There's nothing out there, so we will crack it open, I'm sure. With the pressure, the water coming out will reach a kilometre high, and it should take about three hours to subside. Would that be a fair estimate, John?'

'No infrastructure, just a hole—and wham. Is that your train of thought? Hell, there is enough water down there to flood the Tasman Sea, and with no control, it would only take thirty hours to find its way to the sea. God, that would be something to see. Lasers, do you have them at full power?'

'We won't know until we try.'

'Okay, Len, let's do it. I'll send the coordinates for you to check. When would you like to proceed?'

'Tomorrow morning. We will hover close to the site to film and record everything that happens. Fingers crossed all goes well, and Australia will have water forever.'

The next morning, the satellite Rima sat motionless in orbit after they had sent the coordinates. They waited for a minute and fired off a two-minute burst. To the right of the site, a helicopter sat at least ten kilometres, one thousand metres up, filming and watching intently. They could see the smoke coming out of the ground and then checked their ground monitors. Nothing, not even rock-breaking sound.

'Early days yet, John. It's only warming up, mate.'

Fifteen minutes later, cracking could be heard as the laser switched off. More smoke, then a gurgling sound. The satellite sent a message to Len via his computer to say it had broken through, although just a pinhole, but it would crack open in its own time.

After half an hour, there was a rumble and a small trickle of water, a gush, then a mighty fountain roared out of the ground like a venting geyser . The fountain of water topped at 1.6 kilometres. The water was falling in all directions. Three hours later, it had slowed to one hundred metres. The water was on the move, travelling at just over one hundred kilometres an hour and would take under thirty hours to reach the sea.

The chopper followed the water head. Like a tsunami filling up dried creek beds and old river courses until it reached the Murray riverbed, it took off like a rocket.

From that instant, Australia found more water, one hundred kilometres from Karlemilyi National Park in Western Australia, and west of Daly Waters in the Northern Territory, and also in the Selwyn Range in Queensland.

Australia had now water to resettle its population into all the old states. Millions of trees and bush were in the process of being planted. The lucky country became a green country. It still had its deserts, like the old days, though now with water and tree plantings, the climate changed, bringing more rain to the driest of places.

Australia invited the New Zealand PM to the president's residence for the unveiling of a plaque of friendship and to drink the water that was pouring down from the Snowy Mountains.

'Our country has not enough words to show our gratitude and friendship to you, Prime Minister. It is your people that have helped Australia to get back on its feet. We will hold elections in a few months. The old states are opening; people are swarming back, and each state will soon have their own elections. All we can say, sir, is thank you and we drink to your country's health.' He poured a glass of water from a crystal jug. He raised his glass.

'To friendship and our own liquid gold,' he announced, raising his glass. 'The Murray.'

OTHER BOOKS & CONTACTS

www.owencloughbooks.com

WHISPERS SERIES

Whispers of the Past

Shadows of the Mind

Clearing of the Mist

UPCOMING BOOKS

Bernie The Tram

A children's story

GET IN CONTACT WITH OWEN

owen.cloughbooks@gmail.com

NZ +64 276 496 687

SOCIAL MEDIA

Facebook

facebook.com/owencloughbooks

www.ingramcontent.com/pod-product-compliance
Lightning Source LLC
Chambersburg PA
CBHW071206210726
48293CB00002B/311